Love is
a time of enchantment:
in it all days are fair and all fields
green. Youth is blest by it,
old age made benign:
the eyes of love see
roses blooming in December,
and sunshine through rain. Verily
is the time of true-love
a time of enchantment — and
Oh! how eager is woman
to be bewitched!

# BACHELORS GALORE

Marty made a thoughtless little joke about going to New Zealand to look for a susceptible bachelor with a seven-thousand-a-year wool clip, and unfortunately Philip Griffiths overheard and took her seriously. So when she found that she was to settle in his part of the country, she had to work very hard to show him that she was not specially interested in men and least of all in him.

ESSIE SUMMERS

# BACHELORS GALORE

*Complete and Unabridged*

# ULVERSCROFT
*Leicester*

First published in Great Britain in 1958 by
Mills & Boon Limited
London

First Large Print Edition
published July 1993
by arrangement with
Mills & Boon Limited
London

British Library CIP Data

Summers, Essie
    Bachelors galore.—Large print ed.—
Ulverscroft large print series: romance
I. Title
823 [F]


ISBN 0–7089–2904–4

Published by
F. A. Thorpe (Publishing) Ltd.
Anstey, Leicestershire
Set by Words & Graphics Ltd.
Anstey, Leicestershire
Printed and bound in Great Britain by
T. J. Press (Padstow) Ltd., Padstow, Cornwall

This book is printed on acid-free paper

To my mother, and to the memory
of my father,
ETHEL AND EDWIN SUMMERS
and to my husband,
THE REV. WILLIAM NUGENT FLETT,
All from the north of England who
became New Zealanders

# 1

THE headline had amused Marty . . . talk about a Promised Land flowing with milk and honey! It was probably not true, this report, or at the most grossly exaggerated, but certainly it added a touch of lightheartedness to this venture of theirs, which, to the other two girls, was now tinged with apprehension.

That was why they were here in New Zealand House, something that provided a link between all that was known and dear to them, and the uncharted future in which they would soon plunge.

So they had come up from Tragalgar Square, along "Commonwealth Mile," passing Australia House and the offices of Canada, Rhodesia, and South Africa. It was their office lunch-hour, so they hadn't much time, but they had paused to look in the window before entering the tall, narrow building, because these displays meant more to them than reading

1

about New Zealand.

The last time they had come, the window had been full of apples from somewhere called Sunny Nelson, and butter, but that hadn't meant much. Other times it had been Rugby, which was the national football game, not soccer; and the housing plan had interested them more than anything, because these were the kind of homes they would live in, inhabited by the people who were to become their people.

Today the right-hand window had been delightful . . . full of native ferns and plants, growing in moss, cool and green, and with a stuffed kiwi browsing amongst them, an odd sort of bird, non-flying, with no tail or wings, and with a long beak with whiskers sticking out each side. It made Marty chuckle.

They had spent some time in the large, pillared hall, in the side that was furnished as a lounge, where the racks of New Zealand papers were. They had just been going to leave, when Marty, returning to one of the papers to look up something, had spied the headline.

She laughed. The other girls turned

back as they heard her. She said, in answer to their raised eyebrows:

"I say, listen to this. This really is news . . . much more exciting than kiwis and kookaburras . . . '*An astounding surplus of eligible bachelors in New Zealand!*' Eligible, mark you, girls, not just the misfits and left-overs. Not just the jilted ones! Let's make for New Zealand as fast as we can. Take a job in some wealthy country district, proclaim what wonderful housekeepers we would make, plus lashings of glamor and charm, and marry a sheep-farmer with a seven-thousand-a-year wool clip!"

The next moment a heavy hand came down on her shoulder, spun her about. She found herself facing a tall, bronzed Colonial, evidently angry.

"New Zealand may have a surplus of bachelors, eligible and otherwise, but maybe they are single because they want to be single . . . and in any case they aren't dumb, even if they *are* sheep-farmers or cow-cockies!"

"*Cockies?*" The word was jerked out of Marty.

"Dairy farmers," said the furious

3

stranger. "I repeat — they aren't dumb
. . . at least not dumb enough to be taken
in by girls like you. You might find it hard
to land even one of them. And in the
main we prefer New Zealand girls. Girls
who *are* good housekeepers, and know
all there is to be known about sheep,
and have every bit as much glamor and
charm as English girls. And kookaburras
aren't found in New Zealand — they're
Australian!"

He released her shoulder abruptly,
turned on his heel, and made off
towards the counter as if he was going
to collect his mail, changed his mind,
veered to the right, and charged up the
stairs.

"Phew!" said Marty, recovering herself.
"We can add that to our knowledge of the
New Zealand male. They are not dumb
. . . he meant stupid, I suppose, and they
are certainly not the strong and *silent*
type, and they lack a sense of humor. I
feel shattered. My innocent little remark,
occasioned by that ridiculous headline.
It's probably not even true, and will be
hotly denied tomorrow. But an encounter
like that is almost enough to make us

4

change our minds about going to New Zealand."

Pauline said hurriedly, aware of laughter in a group at the counter:

"I think we'd better get Marty out of here as fast as we can. If she drops any more bricks around here we'll get our passports cancelled, or some such thing. Besides, look at the time: we'll have to fly. I only hope we never meet that man again!"

Marty laughed. "Hardly likely. I might have thought that once, but since I've read about a thousand leaflets on N.Z. I do realize there is a large enough population, thank goodness, to swallow up one completely impossible man."

★ ★ ★

It was early one June afternoon in Glasgow, and on the Springfield Wharf there was the usual activity of near-sailing time. It was a smaller ship than some, the *Captain Banks*, but it carried a lot of hopes and fears, this bright blue golden day, panic and foreboding, excitement, tears and laughter.

5

The girls had no one to see them off, having said most of their farewells in London, and Marty had no one to whom it meant real heartache that she was leaving Britain. That was exactly why she was going. New places and new people could mean healing and comfort. They were sailing at nine-thirty that night. This would be their last glimpse of Home, and tomorrow morning when they awoke, they would be in the Atlantic, out of sight of land.

Why, here on board this very ship, I may find friends for a life-time, kindred spirits, she thought. She turned to survey the crowd, and was aware of a stir, a turning of heads, and some men threading their way through, the first in uniform, the purser, Marty thought, and the last wearing a clerical collar.

"Officials from the Emigration Department," someone near Marty said.

Two of them were, at any rate, but the other man wasn't. He was introduced to them all as the Liaison Officer, the man appointed by the Government of New Zealand to help the emigrants on their trip out, to condition them to

6

what lay ahead, to be a go-between, the official said.

Marty only vaguely heard this. Her eyes were riveted on the man's face. It couldn't be, it simply couldn't be . . . it was . . . the man who had been so rude to her in the lounge of New Zealand House! She was conscious only of a desire to escape, of the giggles of Pauline and Laura beside her, the restlessness of the crowd, who, though loth to leave the shores of Britain still longed for movement in the ship, to be actually away, to know that the new adventure had begun.

Streamers were fluttering from the ship's rails, fragments of sentimental songs floating up from the quayside, excited children getting bored with standing at the rail so long to say what seemed to them endless good-byes to grannies and uncles and aunts they did not realize they might never see again. It wouldn't be distance or time that would keep them apart, but largely the matter of finance, though few of them would have the hope of return in their hearts.

Drawn by some instinct, Marty turned to look into the crowd behind her, and immediately encountered the antagonistic gaze of the Liaison Officer.

"How do you do," he said. "We meet again. May I wish you every success in your venture?"

Outwardly correct, the innuendo in the words flicked Marty's raw spirit like a whiplash. Before she could reply a steward tapped him on the shoulder.

"The padre would like to see you in his cabin for a few moments, Mr. Griffiths," he said.

Marty turned back to the other girls, who had swung round.

Laura said: "What foul luck . . . imagine! Of all the people we didn't want on board, he has to be here!"

★ ★ ★

It was two days later before Marty came face to face with Mr. Griffiths again. He was with the padre. She acknowledged him faintly, and would have passed on, but he stopped and said to his companion.

8

"Here is someone I have met before, though we were not introduced. We met in New Zealand House." He turned to Marty, and said, "This is our chaplain, the Reverend Fergus MacNeill. What is your name?"

"I'm Marty Reddington," she said.

Mr. Griffiths added: "Mr. MacNeill is the minister of my own parish in Mid-Canterbury, in the South Island."

Marty nodded. "I know Canterbury is in the South Island," she couldn't resist saying.

"I thought you would," returned Mr. Griffiths. He turned to the chaplain. "Miss Reddington has read quite a lot about New Zealand. Very wise of her, really, because she intends to stay. You have very definitely decided that, haven't you, Miss Reddington?"

In Marty's clear skin the color rose easily, but she kept it down with a terrific effort.

She smiled at the chaplain, ignoring the meaning behind Mr. Griffiths' words.

"Yes. I feel that's the only right basis of emigration . . . to feel one is going to belong permanently to the country."

The chaplain's tone was warm, his glance admiring.

"That's exactly the right spirit, the one the liaison officers are always hoping to meet. Isn't that right, Philip?"

Marty felt she had answered Philip's taunt rather well. She lifted her eyes to his, and there was no twinkle in them to give her away.

"Odd, but I thought at our first meeting you were a sheep-farmer."

"I am," he said. "This other position was thrust upon me."

Fergus MacNeill said: "The regular Liaison Officer was taken ill two days ago, and had to have an emergency operation, so we were left high and dry. I knew Philip was almost due to come home, and where he could be found, so I recommended him to the department. They were terribly handicapped by the time element, so here he is. The department regarded him as a godsend."

Marty looked amused at this last item. She lifted guileless eyes to Phillip's. "How fortunate," she said.

She turned to the chaplain. "I imagine

Mr. Griffiths is just the man for the job. I'm quite sure that in his lectures on New Zealand he will give us a very true picture of conditions there."

The chaplain's heavy eyebrows rose. These two hadn't even known each other by name, yet this girl sounded as if she knew Philip well.

Marty read his thoughts. "You see, Mr. MacNeill," she said gently, "I met Mr. Griffiths in New Zealand House. I had some odd ideas about New Zealand . . . almost fairy-tale ideas . . . Mr. Griffiths didn't let me labor under such illusions for very long. He quite de-glamorized my quaint ideas. He couldn't have been . . . kinder."

She was disconcerted when Philip laughed, but had the wit to join in. The chaplain chuckled with them. They chatted for a moment or two longer, then Marty excused herself and moved to the rail. She stood there, leaning over, watching the water creaming back, but conscious that her pulses were fluttering.

Suddenly an elbow joined hers on the rail, and a voice she had come to dread said:

"*Very* funny."

She looked up and regarded him steadily.

She said, "Did you think I would let *you* have the monopoly of saying one thing and meaning another?"

"No, I didn't," he said unexpectedly. "Not with that color hair." He smiled, his teeth white in his bronzed face. "You've really gone down very well with the padre. He thinks you're charming and will be quite an asset to the country . . . and the ship's company. He's going to rope you in to help him. Isn't it a pity he's a married man?"

Marty's voice was crisp, cool. "Oh, hardly a pity. I mean, even if he had been a bachelor, no one would call a minister eligible!"

The mobile eyebrows over his steel-grey eyes flew up.

"Meaning?"

Marty gave an impatient laugh.

"Well, would any girl consider a minister's salary against these fabulous wool-cheques we hear so much about?"

"Yes." His unexpected replies were most disconcerting. "I know one who

12

did, Fergus MacNeil's wife. But there aren't many like her. More's the pity. She manages on a shoestring, yet she turned down the chance of marrying her chief . . . he owned three businesses and was madly in love with her to boot. She married Fergus in the face of much opposition from her parents."

Marty was at a loss momentarily, then she recovered herself.

"And has she found it worth while?"

Philip's tone was warm as he answered her:

"If ever you should see them together you'd know the answer to that. She even went teaching while Fergus had this trip to England. He thought they couldn't afford it, even though his expenses were paid. The Church pays his salary while he's actually on board . . . not his own church, but the Presbyterian Church of New Zealand, but he had four months in England and Scotland, visiting folk he hadn't seen for over twenty years. That meant no salary for that time. He kept himself by lecturing and preaching. Rachel went teaching, and kept herself and their two youngsters. In her spare time she did the sick and hospital visiting."

"What a paragon," said Marty, turned on her heel, and left him.

She would do all she could to avoid him. It shouldn't be hard; with six hundred emigrants on board, surely one could lose sight of one man. It wasn't to be. Just after lunch, the padre, coming out of his cabin, saw her and called to her.

"Marty, I want your help with something . . . the other girls with you, too . . . Pauline and Laura, is it? Could you come along to my cabin?"

Marty said: "I'll see if I can find them, padre. They went to help look after some of the tiny tots while their mothers have a rest. I think I'll find them easily enough."

The padre said: "Oh, don't bother to find them. If you come in, we'll explain what we are going to try to do, then you can rope in any of your friends you think would be suitable."

She went in with him, to find Philip rising to his feet. In the cabin one was more conscious than ever of his size.

14

His shoulders were really magnificent; perhaps that made him appear even more arrogant than he was. A fine figure of a man . . . pity he had so little heart . . . and so much liver! Marty was horrified to find that even her thoughts ran on malicious lines these days.

She took the chair Philip offered her, and Fergus began to outline his plan.

"We've got our committees going now, and in another day or so most of the seasick ones will be on deck, so we must get things fully organized. This trip through Panama is the fastest route, of course, but it's the most boring, you see land so seldom. Usually the Liaison Officer has his wife with him, and, of course, she is of boundless help organizing the women's side of affairs." He paused, and Marty threw Philip a look, wide-eyed and innocent.

"Oh, but I'm sure Mr. Griffiths doesn't feel the lack of a wife," she said sweetly. "I'm more than certain he'll be able to handle it, even if he is running in single harness."

She saw the padre's brows twitch together. He would be a hard man to deceive. He had a particularly penetrating eye, and would easily see through synthetic sweetness and innocence. She must watch her step, particularly as he and Philip Griffiths were friends of long standing!

Philip said, rather lazily, as if he didn't care much, but must answer her comment somehow: "Oh, I'm quite willing to concede women have their uses . . . it's their motives that baffle me. But the padre has the floor, not me. He's more used to organizing things."

Marty turned to the padre. "Go ahead, Mr. MacNeill," she said.

"First and foremost," he said, "we must get something jacked up for the children. We have for the older ones. The committee is handling that. There are several schoolteachers on board, men and girls, and they are willing to run a school, purely voluntary, of course, for a couple of hours each morning.

"Not on strictly orthodox lines, but something that will accustom them to school life in New Zealand, and any difference they may find. We'll include information about N.Z., and they'll pass

16

that on to their parents, and become more quickly absorbed in the life of the Dominion.

"We're having the school in the forward lounge. No other children, except school-age, will be allowed in there for that period. This would be a good time for the mothers to relax, but, of course, many of them will have toddlers and pre-school age children. We haven't got a single kindergarten teacher amongst the lot, so we wondered if some of you girls could organize activities amongst yourselves. One of the infant teachers could probably give you a few hints. It's mainly to keep them interested and amused.

"There'll be a women's hour, one of the older women is going to oversee that. The Liaison Officer and I have checked all lists now, and there are one hundred and twenty children under twelve! We'll start a Sunday School this Sunday, too. I'll have a meeting called in the lounge, and ask for volunteers for teachers."

"I'll help you there," offered Marty quickly. She took a sidelong glance at Philip, and added: "That is, if the Liaison

Officer thinks I'm a fit and proper person to teach Scripture to the young."

Fergus MacNeill's voice was sharp. "I'm the one to say that, and I haven't any doubts."

Marty smiled at him, a sincere smile. She was wearing a yellow linen frock, and had blue sandals on her bare feet, and above, a chunky blue necklace about her slim throat, her eyes were as sapphire as the sea that could be glimpsed now and then through the porthole.

"I've been well grounded," she said. "My father was a vicar."

"Good," said Fergus. "I've jotted down a few things you may find helpful and some names. Here they are on my desk. I've got to see the purser. How about you and Philip getting on to it while I'm gone? Shan't be long." He paused at the door and grinned. "You'll notice I've got down to Christian names very quickly . . . typically New Zealand. You two had better do the same." He disappeared.

Philip and Marty were left regarding each other. He said, a smile lifting the corner of his mouth:

"Good tactics on his part, if a trifle

obvious. He realizes there is friction between us, so leaves us alone together."

Marty said, not smiling, "Perhaps he took psychology as one of his degree subjects. Do we prove him right or wrong?"

"For the sake of the work I suppose we must prove him right," said Philip, laughter in his voice.

Marty said philosophically, "Well, we are neither of us teen-agers, I suppose we can discipline ourselves. I've often had to work with people I disliked, and I don't think the work suffered."

"But did it prosper?" asked Philip.

"Possibly not . . . it's quite a point." She rose. "You had better tell the padre he would be wise to enlist someone else's aid."

Philip's hand caught her arm in a grip that hurt.

"Don't be so damned silly!" he said. "You redheads are all the same . . . temperamental as they come."

The color Marty hated ran up into her cheeks.

"I suppose you think *you* are even-tempered! And it's a lot of nonsense about people with red hair being hot-tempered. That's one of these stupid, preconceived ideas. As a matter of fact, it has been proved by statistics that redheaded people are *not* more temperamental than others. I read it in an article just a week ago."

"Probably written by a redheaded journalist," said Philip, laughingly. His laughter maddened Marty more than if he had been serious. Philip added: "Besides, statistics can prove anything. Ever hear about the regiment that put out a statement that there was a much higher death-rate among its non-drinkers than its drinkers? The death-rate was fifty per cent, among the T.T.'s. Some temperance worker decided to investigate . . . he found that only two men in the regiment didn't drink, and one had been killed by a truck!"

Marty tried to look unimpressed, but failed. She laughed.

"Good!" said Philip, patting her shoulder. "It's got a sense of humor!" This, from Philip, was almost too much for her. She opened her mouth to tell him what she had said about *his* lack of humor in New Zealand House, remembered just in time what he had said about redheads and temper, and said instead:

"Come, let's get on with the padre's notes and let him find us at least outwardly amiable." She paused, wondered if she should say it, but couldn't resist it, and added: "But I'm afraid I don't favor this custom of getting on to Christian name terms immediately."

Philip's voice had the lazy, amused note in it that Marty hated. "Suits me. Carry right on . . . Miss Reddington."

The ship forged on through the Atlantic ocean on calm seas in perfect sunshine, carrying them towards the tropics. Things settled down. The captain and crew were used to emigrants, because this was one of the ships chartered by the N.Z. Government especially for this work, and there was a free and easy atmosphere on board.

Once the children's time became organized, peace, or mostly peace, descended upon the ship. With the school and Sunday School being voluntary, they had expected quite a few not to attend, but in the main the parents were only too glad to know their children were under supervision part of the day.

There were lectures, dealing with life in the Dominion, and illustrated by movies and film strips, and, Marty had to admit, Philip did this part of the work very well, though the position had been thrust upon him at the very last moment and he had had little preparation for it.

It was evident Philip knew and loved New Zealand in all its aspects, but didn't over-paint the picture, stressing the newness of the country, warning them that they would miss the sense of history and tradition. He reminded them, laughingly, that it was little more than a hundred years old . . . "You'll realize that the first time you get on some of our back-country roads," he added.

He would contrast the chances that awaited them with the inevitable drawbacks. They would find truly democratic conditions, excellent social security that had long been part of the country's plan.

"I don't doubt you'll miss the gayer week-ends, especially those of you who will settle in the cities. In the country other things will take the place of amusements, though you may find it deadly at first. Nevertheless, once you have accustomed yourself to it, a quieter week-end has many advantages. After all, someone had to work to provide that gaiety, and it's quite good to be one of the folk who have a complete day off Saturday as well as Sunday! And if you work in a shop, you'll quite enjoy shutting down for the week-end on a Friday night at nine — unless you pick on a greengrocer's or milk-bar.

"You'll probably miss the atmosphere of the village pubs you've been used to, and the games of darts . . . only a very few provide that, and you probably won't like our restricted drinking-hours. Everyone gets turfed out of the hotels at six, you know . . . or should . . . but in the main, I think you'll like it, unless to you these things are essential.

"Of course it all means hard work, but you should all be able to own your own homes in time, if you are prepared to put up with less ideal conditions for a little while. Only, I do ask you not to start off with the idea that the streets are paved with gold, or" — his eye flickered over Marty for a moment — "that the country is teeming with rich sheepfarmers." He laughed. "It isn't even teeming with eligible bachelors as that stupid newspaper report would have us believe. In fact, that report must have surprised some of our own unmarried girls quite a bit."

It was an informal lecture, with the padre sitting beside him, and at this moment Fergus chipped in, lightening the situation.

"It was a ridiculous report," he said, chuckling. "My own parish has a quota of unattached males, but hasn't every place? Actually a report like that is very hard on you single girls who are going out to N.Z. You'll probably be humbugged by reporters wanting your reactions to it, and asking has that influenced your decision to come out. Be careful what you say. I'd advise you to be off-hand. If you show too much indignation they'll think you did have that in view. I know you didn't." His tone was kindly.

Philip turned, caught Marty's eye.

24

Well, she could read his thoughts. He was thinking cynically, she supposed, that the padre's remark might apply to most but not to her.

★ ★ ★

It was a glorious night, sequinned with stars in a velvet sky, a night to dream about, to tuck away in some memory chest, and to bring out again when one was old and tired, and the feet no longer tingled with the wish to dance.

Soon the nights would be too hot for dancing, and they had resolved to make this a more formal affair than the others. Dress was optional, but the three girls, among others, had decided to wear full-length evening dresses.

Marty had hesitated about wearing the lilac nylon, but had managed to overcome her misgivings. How stupid to be superstitious about a frock. Daddy had been so scathing about superstition. "Might as well believe in evil spirits!" he had said, thumping his pulpit.

Laura said, "Marty, you look a dream, those brilliants among the flounces make me think of lilacs in the rain . . . tell me, do they have lilacs in New Zealand?"

"No idea," said Marty absently. "I know they have roses and pansies, so I suppose they'll have lilacs too. You look sweet yourself, Laura, like a yellow rose."

"And me?" asked Pauline, suddenly reappearing. "What flower would you say for me?" She looked down at her bright orange skirts disparagingly, and added gloomily: "A common marigold?"

Marty laughed. They all loved Pauline. She hugged her.

"You aren't like a flower at all, you're the very spirit of the sunset!"

Pauline sighed. "But will any one else think so?"

Marty said, teasingly: "If by anyone you mean Sparks, I should think the answer would be yes. He's so obviously head over heels in love with you that it's a wonder he doesn't get his radio messages addled!"

Pauline was not to be cheered up.

"I came on board with my mind irrevocably made up that I would not fall in love with any of the crew. I don't

26

believe in shipboard romance, I wouldn't for anything marry a seafaring man!"

Marty said, softly: "Methinks the lady doth protest too much," and added: "Do any of us fall in love to order?"

It was later, much later. Marty hadn't missed a dance. She had noticed Philip had been fulfilling his part as Liaison Officer admirably, promoting goodwill and happiness among the passengers, dancing with good, bad, and indifferent dancers.

Marty told herself she was watching his movements far too much, it was simply ridiculous . . . it was merely that the man had got right under her skin. After all, it didn't matter that he hadn't asked her for a single dance . . . she hadn't lacked partners . . . and even if she saw a lot of him as a rule, it was only because she was helping him and the padre.

Suddenly he was there before her, towering above her, demanding, always enigmatical. She couldn't tell if he really wanted a dance with her or not, or if he merely thought it policy, seeing she put in so many hours of work in the kindergarten. Then she lost those thoughts as they began to dance.

He danced well, and their steps matched perfectly. Marty gave herself to the rhythm of the music. She hoped he would not spoil things by talking. Their words by now had a habit of striking sparks from each other . . . spoil what? Marty's heart asked Marty's reason. Why . . . the perfection of the music and movement, of course! It wasn't every day you found someone who danced like this . . . nothing to do with the feel of a man's arm around you, strong, warm, his hand over yours. The fact that you were dancing with Philip Griffiths had nothing to do with the odd feeling that night was even more magical than before. It was only that they were near the tropics, and the air was languorous . . . caressing. You recognized that for what it was . . . just like a red traffic-light . . . and you didn't go against it.

"Let's go on deck," said Philip, "this is getting stifling. The next dance will have to be on deck, though we haven't too much room on this ship."

They leaned over the rail in complete silence, and for a very long time. Silence could have a charm of its own, of course, and a deeper intimacy than words, if hearts and minds were attuned . . . but this silence meant only that they were unused to comradeship without friction, and therefore even small talk had deserted them.

Yes, despite all, there was witchery in the night, in the dark, fathomless waters, the line of the creaming wake. On the far horizon, clouds lay, looking like islands in a dream world, the moon making a shining track on the sable waters, and the radiance of the countless stars winking at their reflections in the brilliants sewn on the billowing skirts of Marty's lilac frock.

The filmy stole she had swathed about her shoulders tossed back in the warm breeze. Philip caught it and replaced it, tucking it into the curve of the elbow furthest from him. She was acutely aware of him, and angry that she should be. She felt her heart thudding against her ribs. She put her other hand across, tucking in the errant fold firmly, quickly. The sooner this moment ended, the better for her peace of mind.

Philip didn't withdraw his hand, it suddenly tightened on her arm. His left hand came up to her chin, the fingers strong and cool, exerting pressure, turning her face up to his. His mouth came down on hers. With every bit of self-control that she could command, Marty willed herself not to respond, but she was powerless to move.

As he lifted his head and looked at her, her eyes blazed. Better that he should think her angry, revolted, than willing and quiescent. Whatever look was in his eyes was replaced immediately by another . . . it looked like contempt, but whether for her, or for himself in a weak moment, she did not know.

"You see?" he said, and his voice was harsh. "Even anyone forewarned and forearmed as I was can be bowled over by a girl in a lilac frock, under a tropical moon. You made a mistake, you know; a setting like this is wasted on not-so-wealthy emigrants. You ought to have gone by passenger liner, my dear. It would have cost you more, but paid handsome dividends. On board some of those liners are bachelors

30

galore . . . they're the ones who can afford trips Home from faraway Maoriland. Still, don't let it dismay you, we have some quite good moons in the Southern Hemisphere. Your frock won't be wasted, I can assure you."

Marty felt the color leave her face and her legs turn to cotton-wool. She turned to face him, one hand on the rail.

"Have you ever found yourself in the wrong, Mr. Griffiths? Because if not, a new experience is facing you right now. I didn't buy this frock as . . . as man-bait. I bought it to celebrate my engagement. Two days before our engagement party my fiancé came to tell me that the girl he had loved long ago had come back into his life. We . . . agreed to part. This hasn't been a very lucky frock for me, has it? First disillusionment, then insult. Maybe I should have got rid of it, but when you haven't got very much money, you can't afford gestures like that."

Silence fell between them, unbearable silence.

Then Philip said stiffly: "I'm sorry."

Marty looked up. "It's the correct thing to say, isn't it? That you're sorry!

You may not have intended to ask me for another dance, but please don't, will you? Because I should hate to openly rebuff you."

She turned and walked swiftly away.

But not back to the lounge. She went downstairs to her cabin, which was blessedly empty. With one swift movement she undid the transparent plastic zip, unclasped the circle of brilliants that had clipped the ends of the fichu at her young rounded bosom. There was a flash of silver as she pulled the dress uncaringly over her head, and another as she rolled it into a ball.

The port-hole was just open far enough. She thrust her arm well out, and flung the crumpled mass far out on the waters. It undid like a parachute, settled in a shining circle, and sank.

Marty felt that she had jettisoned with it all feeling, all tenderness, all trust . . .

# 2

THE next morning Marty took particular pains with her make-up. She was working with Philip right away, she knew, typing lists for him, and she wanted no tell-tale smudges under her eyes to give away the fact that his words of last night had kept her awake for hours.

They were nearing the tropics now, and Marty was in white, a cool button-through frock, sleeveless, with a scooped-out neckline.

"Just to look at you makes me feel cooler," declared Fergus, as she came in and answered their good-mornings. The padre had cool drinks on a table, and a wide-mouthed flask full of ice-cubes. They were going to need them.

There came the inevitable moment when the padre was called away. Marty worked steadily on. She lifted her head in search of fresh carbon, to find Philip's eyes on hers.

"How do you do it?" he asked.

"Do what?" asked Marty stiffly.

"Manage to look as fresh as a daisy," he said.

She shrugged. "Well, after all, it's early yet. My cold shower isn't too far distant. I may wilt a little later, of course."

"I didn't mean the weather." He added, deliberately: "I mean after last night."

Marty smiled, wilfully misunderstanding. "I'm so used to late nights. I get along with a very short ration of sleep ususally . . . don't you think it's the quality of sleep you get more than the quantity?"

"I didn't mean the lateness of the hour either," he persisted. "I meant my blunder on the boat-deck."

Marty's laugh was quite an achievement. It sounded as if real amusement lay behind it.

"My dear Mr. Griffiths," she said, "you're surely not imagining I lost any sleep over that, are you?"

She had the satisfaction of seeing him redden, but it didn't cut off the unwelcome conversation. He was evidently determined to apologize. His look was somewhat appealing. Marty wished it wasn't. She'd rather he'd keep on being aggressive, she found it easier that way to . . . well, what? Easier to be scornful, to be derisive, to pretend she didn't care what he thought.

"I thought," he said gently, "I might have awakened too many memories . . . 'old, unhappy, far-off things' . . . for you."

Marty stared at him coldly over the top of her typewriter.

"You are wasting good sentiment feeling sorry for me," she said. "I had a lucky escape. Much better to find these things out before marriage, you know. And I'm much less of an innocent abroad now, so I'm grateful for the experience. I know more about men than I used to."

Philip got up and came across to her desk, leaning on it with both hands.

"Don't let an experience like that make you cynical. It's not worth it."

Her delicately arched brows flew up, laughter in the sapphire eyes.

"But am I cynical?"

"Isn't that what's behind this venture,

going out in search of . . . " He stopped suddenly, warned by the glint in her eye.

"A handsome husband, and seven thousand a year?" she finished for him. The blue eyes were mocking now, looking into grey ones that stayed serious. "It was sheer bad luck for me that you overheard my plans, wasn't it? It cramps my style . . . still, it won't really matter just now, with only emigrants on board — bar you and the padre . . . and the crew, whose salaries can't compare with wool cheques, in any case. And it won't signify when we get to New Zealand, because only the worst of ill-luck could guide me near your territory. I hear Mr. MacNeill coming — you'd better clear back to your desk."

Philip turned and walked out of the cabin, his jaw set. Marty supposed it wasn't easy to have an apology thrust back at you . . . serve him right!

Apart from the friction that seemed inevitable between the Liaison Officer and herself, Marty found she was enjoying the heat. She loved the burning blue of the sky, the awnings on the decks, the officers in their white tropical kit, the bathing in the pool, the starlit evenings when they had pictures on the after-deck in the coolness. The ones who did not enjoy it were those who disregarded the doctor's orders, who didn't sunbathe gradually, but got hideously burnt in an hour or two.

"We've been exactly a fortnight at sea," said Fergus, his elbow joining Marty's on the teak rail, "and tomorrow we'll see land for the first time. I'm glad it's Curaçao, I've not seen it before. I believe it's very colorful and interesting. Did you hear that lecture on the Netherlands West Indies?"

Marty shook her head. "No, I was reading a bed-time story to the Williams children. It doesn't seem possible, does it, that in this limitless-seeming sea, land will greet us tomorrow morning!"

"Yes, and early too. We berth at five. We're going to re-fuel at Caracas Bay, eight miles from Willemstad. But best of all, we'll get mail. Rachel will have umpteen letters awaiting me, I know, and there'll be some from the youngsters. I've got a wad of letters to go off, I've written

Rachel every day. She'll get 'em all at once." He laughed. "I've loved the trip, but never again without Rachel. Didn't realize how much I'd miss her. A family is so complete in itself. I feel I'm only half here . . . I keep turning around and looking over my shoulder every time we see a lovely sunset, or porpoises, or flying fish, and it's so strange to find she's not there."

"Have you told her just that?" Asked Marty. "I mean that would be a wonderful thing to read in a letter from an absent husband."

"Yes, I told her," said Fergus, his eyes soft. "We've always told each other things as we've felt them. In our line we've seen so much of bereavement, with a man feeling cruel remorse when his life partner has gone, because he had never put into words all she had meant."

Marty nodded. "I remember Daddy talking along those lines. Talking of the sins of omission. I was just a youngster, and it had puzzled me, and Daddy said that words could be very wounding, but that nothing inflicted a deeper wound than the word withheld."

She was suddenly conscious of someone on the other side of her, and knew a moment later by her quickened pulses and breathing that it was Philip. She wondered how long he'd been there. His rubber soles had made no sound on the decking. She was annoyed to think he'd caught her in sentimental mood.

Fergus said: "Well, now you've got company, I'll go down to my cabin and see to a few things."

"You could have gone before," smiled Marty. "I've never minded solitude." She glanced meaningly at Philip, but he was apparently gazing absently at the horizon.

"Willemstad *is* colorful and interesting," he said, turning back to her. So he *had* been there some time.

She said, hastily, "There's something about the padre, isn't there?" A lightly mocking note came into her voice. "He has the power to make even me believe in things."

Philip said evenly, "You need not feel embarrassed over anything you said when you didn't know I was near. I liked the sort of girl you seemed to be when you

39

were talking to the padre . . . much better than some glimpses I've had of you!"

Marty caught her lip between her teeth. Really!

"Am I supposed to be complimented? You feel there's hope for me? Allow me to tell you I don't care a brass farthing what you think of me!"

Suddenly Philip laughed. "We certainly trigger each other off, don't we? A pity, in all this beauty, to quarrel!"

He waved a hand. The sunset was catching the creaming curve of the bow-wave, turning it to bronze and flame where it flung up from the green depths. Clouds like immense twists of candy floss were staining the whole sky blush-pink, and piling up into imitation ranges and mountains . . . and somewhere ahead must be Curaçao, set like a jewel in the Caribbean Sea.

She said, quietly: "Then don't let's quarrel . . . for tonight, anyway."

Philip said: "Let's extend it a little longer. I'd like to show you Willemstad. I'll be a bit later than most in getting away, but I've seen it before, and I'll know what to show you. Some parts of

40

it seem like a bit of Holland, here in the New World. I didn't realize that till I visited the Netherlands three months ago. I've not seen the West Indies for years, since I was in my boyhood, really. I went home via the Cape, you know. But I remember it quite vividly, our day here, it stands out as one of the happiest days of my childhood."

"Oh, you travelled as a youngster, too, then?" asked Marty. But of course, he came of moneyed people, and it was easy to travel if you had the wherewithal.

He nodded. "With Dad. He had a business trip Home, and I went with him. Curaçao has a wonderful climate; from December till March, the temperature is just below eighty, I believe, and it's only slightly higher the rest of the year. You can buy everything you want . . . as good as any oriental bazaar, and a good deal more pleasant. All the perfumes in the world, watches, cameras, Danish porcelain, Dutch tiles, Delft blue, native straw novelties; and there are exotic cactus flowers, native quarters, temples, palms, narrow streets and wide. You'll love it."

Marty knew she would love it . . . especially in Philip's company, if they were not quarrelling, but . . . she thought it was safer to quarrel, otherwise she might be lulled into temporary enchantment, something that wouldn't — couldn't last.

It would last only till he once more taunted her with her quest for an eligible bachelor . . .

She said, with not a trace of regret in her voice:

"Thank you, but I've all arrangements made for tomorrow. It was good of you to think of me, especially when it would be so easy for you to find someone more congenial, someone less argument-prone."

"True enough," agreed Philip, feeling for his pipe and beginning to ram tobacco in. "Still, even the most pleasant company can seem tame after all our sorties. Well, whoever you are going in with, don't forget to make sure he gets you back to the ship in time. We sail again at one."

"You won't find me late," said Marty, leaving him to it.

Caracas Bay itself was disappointing

. . . drab, and mainly flat, with a few stunted trees for shelter, and rows of fuel-tanks and pipe-lines that ran directly from the oil refinery.

The ship emptied itself of passengers very quickly, and the fleet of taxis waiting to convoy them to Willemstad was soon on its way. When most of the bustle had subsided, Marty gathered her group of toddlers together, some holding hands, some attached to Marty by leather reins, and with a huge basket of soft drinks and sandwiches, she made her way down the foreshore towards the thickest clump of trees.

After all, she did know a pang of regret when, through the trees, she saw the padre and Philip, accompanied by a young Yorkshire couple, depart in a car. It would have been exciting to have explored this unknown gem, set in the far west, and she might never be here again. Still, she had saved at least a dozen mothers from a weary morning dragging their offspring around sight-seeing.

A cool breeze sprang up, and the children were so delighted with the novelty of being ashore again that Marty

43

stayed longer than she meant to. Then some of the younger ones grew sleepy, missing their mid-morning nap, so she decided to get them back on board.

She was on her way, carrying the youngest and sleepiest, burdened with the basket, and clutching reins in her other hand, when a car stopped behind her and someone got out, slamming the door. She looked around. Philip. Alone.

She kept on her way. By the set of his jaw, Philip was angry.

His voice was hard.

"Miss Reddington!"

She turned again, easing the child against her.

"Yes?" A tone of polite interest, no more. "I'm a little busy at the moment, Mr. Griffiths, but if you need me I'll be free soon. One of the stewardesses is going to help me get them down for a rest."

"I can see you're busy," he said. "What on earth possessed you to do this? You're entitled to go sight-seeing as well as the mothers, aren't you? The kids are their responsibility, not yours."

"If you look at it that way, yes. But,

you know, the mothers haven't had much of a break since they came on board . . . not the ones with tiny tots. They're missing the aunties and grannies who usually gave them a spell, and it's so nice for them to be away by themselves, or just with the older ones who won't tire so easily, and will remember the beauty and the strangeness of it all."

Philip was still scowling.

"It amounts to spoiling the parents!"

"That's your opinion," said Marty gently, "not mine. If you don't mind we'll move on. We're in the sun here. In any case, what in the world has it to do with you if I choose to give up my sight-seeing?"

He said, somewhat bitterly, taking the child from her arms, "It's all right if they appreciate it. I saw a couple of parents acting in a most irresponsible manner, and already pretty tight . . . you've simply freed them to go on a bender."

Marty picked up a youngster who had fallen in the dust, brushed him down, and walked on, saying over her shoulder:

"How pleased you must have been to

see them ... gave you a chance of putting me in the wrong again. The rest of them are probably having the time of their lives, in a perfectly wholesome way, but you'd never give me credit for that."

They got the children on board, a stewardess relieved Philip of the sleeping child, Marty said sweetly, over her shoulder: "Thanks for the assistance getting them aboard, Mr. Griffiths," and went off with them.

★ ★ ★

Two days later they reached Cristobal, and dropped anchor at 11:30 p.m. Marty could sense the restlessness of the crew next morning. Fergus told her they were never really happy till they were through the Canal and the ship was their very own again. The passengers were restless, too, and excited.

Afterwards she found she had carried away a rather jumbled impression, hard to sort out, from the time their ship entered the queue of ships to go through the Canal, to the time when

46

they sailed into the Pacific. The whole ship seemed to be swarming with burly, good-natured negroes and United States Security Police.

Various passengers, interested in engineering, kept telling the girls how the locks worked, how they filled and lowered and rose, but it still remained a marvel to them, explained or not.

There were the wider expanses of the lakes, the minor wonder of knowing they were once valleys, and that the islands dotted about had been mountain peaks.

"This rather reminds me of Lyttelton Harbor . . . the port of Christchurch," said Philip, as he and the padre joined Marty. "But this is man-made, and Lyttelton Harbor was evidently once a volcano crater. Filled in now with the sea."

Sometimes they were down in a dark trough of slimy green walls, then the ship would rise towards the daylight. Sometimes there were mountain ranges on either side, thick with tropical bush. The heat was intense, and already the doctor was treating people for sunburn and violent headaches, yet no one wanted to miss anything. There was something most engaging about travelling on an emigrant ship, Marty decided. No one was bored, very few had seen Panama before, and no one laughed if one made a stupidly ignorant remark.

Philip said in Marty's ear: "We are due in Balboa at six-thirty. The tinies will be in bed this time, and — we hope — asleep. It's Sunday night, so there'll be little shopping done, but I'd like to take you ashore."

Fergus was right beside Marty, sipping a lime drink.

He grinned. "I got in first, Philip. Marty is coming ashore with me, plus Laura and Pauline. As a married man I believe in safety in numbers. You can join us."

Philip grinned back. "I can't see Rachel being jealous in any case. However, I'll chaperone you, and I can report to her."

Fergus chuckled. "The Yorkshire couple are coming, too, so even if Sparks manages to sneak off with Pauline, I'll still be safe. I'll let you off . . . I guess you'd rather have Marty on your own."

Marty said quickly, her color rising, "It's not like that at all, padre. Mr. Griffiths is simply cross with me because he thinks I did the wrong thing at Caracas Bay, looking after the infants — so, purely to get his own way, he is determined I shall do some sightseeing around Panama way, and thus frustrate me in any ideas I may have of continuing to spoil the parents."

The corner of Philip's mouth lifted.

"She has a wonderful opinion of me, hasn't she?"

"Equalled only by your opinion of me," returned Marty.

The padre heaved a sigh. "You make me feel as if I'm back at my own dinner-table, trying to keep the peace between Jocelyn and Grant. You also make me feel incredibly old . . . and wise. Oh — there's Mrs. Mitchell now. Philip . . . look — do go and give her that message."

He waited till Philip was out of earshot, then the padre turned to Marty. There was a glint in his eye.

"I wish you would go with Philip, Marty. We are here a very short time, and he has a pilgrimage to make. I don't want to sound too sentimental about it, and insist on going with him, but I'd rather he didn't go alone. His father is buried in Panama."

"Buried in *Panama*?"

"Yes, he and his father were returning from a trip when Philip was thirteen. Between Curaçao and here his father took ill. They rushed him to a famous hospital here, but despite all they did to save him, he died. He was buried an hour before the ship sailed, and the boy had to return to New Zealand alone. Naturally he doesn't want to be with a crowd."

"All right, padre," said Marty quietly, "I'll go with him."

★ ★ ★

Philip hired a car and the whole night took on a dream-like quality for Marty. They had a delightful meal in an odd little café that reminded her of a saloon in a cowboy picture. Marty was more natural with Philip, knowing the evening would have its poignancy for him, than she ever had been.

50

The drive lasted two hours and took them around Balboa and through Ancon to Panama.

Marty was fascinated by Panama, the blend of the old and the new, though she held her breath at the narrowness of some of the streets they had to traverse, with buildings hanging over the shops beneath.

Presently they came together up a little hill, and stood shoulder to shoulder by a grave, clearly outlined by bright moonlight. They sat down on the edge of it, and said nothing. Past enmity didn't seem to matter. Marty could only see a small boy of thirteen standing at that graveside, then going back to a cabin with an empty berth . . . she put out a hand and slipped it into his.

He didn't release it till they were back at the car.

"Thank you," he said, as he handed her in.

Back in Balboa they had a banana split, luxurious and large, and an iced drink, then walked back to the ship. It wasn't a luxury liner by any means, but in the moonlight it was a study in silver and black, with a grace all its own. Marty knew a sudden urge of affection for her.

"Back home!" she said. "Isn't it strange how a ship so suddenly becomes home . . . and Empire . . . when you disembark in a foreign port?"

There was still that sense of comradeship between them as they walked up the gangway. Perhaps that visit to Phillip's father's grave had wiped out all that had gone before. You wouldn't take a girl you completely detested on a mission like that, would you? Perhaps now, as they entered the Pacific, they would leave all that behind, perhaps . . . Marty suddenly thought of something.

As clearly as if she had been still looking at it, she saw the plain tombstone. It had said: "Richard George Griffiths, beloved father of Philip Richard Griffiths, aged 45."

As quickly as the thought touched the edge of her mind she said: "Philip . . . have you got a mother? I mean did you have one when . . . " She stopped. This could be mistaken for prying, but surely not, not after all they had shared this night.

They had come to the top of the companionway where Philip would leave her to go to her own cabin.

He said slowly: "Yes. I have a mother. She lives in California. When I was eleven she left us . . . for another man. A man who could give her all the things Father couldn't — then."

There was a silence. Marty was searching her heart for words that wouldn't be clumsy, that wouldn't seem trite, that would be sincere and comforting . . .

Before they reached her tongue, Philip added harshly: "You're extremely like her. She was red-headed, too. Her hair was as beautiful as yours. Do you wonder that it seemed to me red-headed women always have an eye to the main chance?" The grey eyes looked down into the darkly-blue ones. It seemed to Marty that they were demanding something from her, she didn't know what.

But that, of course, was sheer imagination. He distrusted all red-headed women . . . and he had heard her expressing the same values that had led his mother away from his father.

The dice was certainly loaded against any sort of understanding between them. She was foolish to have imagined otherwise, even for that most fleeting moment . . .

She said, quietly and with an air of finality, "Good night," and went down to her cabin.

★ ★ ★

Marty had thought the journey through the Pacific would have dragged, for the *Captain Banks* was not a fast ship, but oddly enough the time seemed to fly. Leaving Panama they ran into a wind squall and heavy rain, then three days out had experienced all the fun of the crossing of the Line ceremony.

The clock went back its half-hour each day, the weather grew cooler, and there was more activity on deck during the day. It was noticeable now that the shop on board did much less business; money was dwindling, or else folk were more cautious, realizing they might need all their money for a fresh start in a young country.

The International Date Line was

reached early in August. Marty marked it in her diary, and wrote baldly: "We miss today," then stared at it unbelievingly. How odd . . . a day disappearing.

That day they saw whales blowing in the afternoon and knew the end of the voyage was very near. By tomorrow the clock would be right by New Zealand time, and by evening they would glimpse land.

Pauline and Laura were down below packing, but Marty was at the rail. There was a long line of cloud on the grey horizon, dim and shapeless. Was it cloud, or was it . . . ?

"Aotearoa!" said Philip's voice at Marty's shoulder. "The-land-of-the-long-white-cloud. The Maoris are very apt and very poetical in their naming. Nothing terse about it. Can't you imagine them sighting it from their canoes in the days when the Morioris inhabited the land?"

There had been a sort of armed neutrality between them these last few weeks. They had been careful not to quarrel, not to be alone very much: Marty's doing mostly, but certainly Philip had not sought her out.

He would be as glad as she was that the voyage was over and they would part. They wouldn't know till the morning the ship berthed at Wellington where they were going, bar the ones who had been brought out for specialized jobs, or who were going direct to relatives.

Marty wondered, with only a tiny touch of apprehension, just where they might go . . . North or South Island, city or country? She had said, when the Liaison Officer was making out his lists, that she preferred the country.

Here, on the skyline, shortly to be translated into the background of everyday living, was New Zealand, where in time, she hoped, she would forget Philip Griffiths. It would be good to make a new start where no one would doubt her motives, no one sneer . . .

Philip's eyes were still on the horizon. "Landfall! Somehow it's always a minor miracle, to me . . . league upon league of ocean, and a small ship bearing towards a goal . . . seems incredible, in spite of all modern aids for navigation, that they should know the way across the sea. You and I and all the rest of us completely dependent upon this ship's crew to bring us across this vastness . . . then suddenly, landfall out of nowhere." He stopped, and added: "Here's the padre. Look at his smile, that means Rachel and the kids to him."

The look Marty gave Fergus was sheer affection. The padre had been homesick and unable to hide it this last week. Marty found it endearing. Philip left them.

"Well, tomorrow will mean journey's end for you, Marty. A very trite remark, but inevitable." He looked about and said, in a low voice: "I wonder how many friendships will survive, how many romances. There are some I'd like to keep in touch with myself."

"Yes, I hope I don't lose touch with some. But others . . . " she stopped.

"Not exactly kindred spirits!" Fergus twinkled.

"And I will be glad to be free of Mr. Griffiths disapproval!" confided Marty in a rash outburst.

The padre's beetling brows flew up.

"I know you've bickered, but I didn't think it was quite like that. In fact, I thought that under it all you had been good pals."

"Hardly. He despises me. I'll be glad to be away from him. I can't work in an atmosphere of disapproval."

"You've worked well, none better. Perhaps his attitude was more stimulating than you knew. Don't be too hard on Philip, Marty. He's taken one or two knocks, and maybe you're suffering because he was jilted some time back. An experience like that leaves an aftermath. He's been cynical about women since."

Marty said evenly: "I was jilted too. I hope I don't take it out of other people."

"Are you sure you don't?" Fergus looked wicked, provoking.

A steward at their elbow made them turn. He handed Fergus a radio-telegram.

Fergus read it, then his eyes met Marty's. He executed an involuntary skip.

"Rachel will be on the wharf, she's meeting me after all. Thought she couldn't get away, she's teaching and end of term's still a fortnight away. But she's made it."

This wasn't the time to probe further into Philip's reactions. Besides, what matter? Tonight they would be in Wellington Harbor, situated at the southern tip of the North Island, they would lie out in the stream all night, and berth early tomorrow . . . tomorrow, oh, may it come quickly, thought Marty.

It did. Marty's suitcases were packed, a tight ball of excitement inside her. Pauline and Laura were on deck, gazing at Wellington, Marty was going up in a moment. There was a knock, and Fergus entered, a paper in his hand, and a broad smile on his face.

"Marty, what do you think? I'd hoped for this, but didn't dare say. You're coming to our parish, to a family at Linden Peaks . . . splendid folk, none better. Pioneer homestead. Owned by Joy and Leonard Logie. They have four children. It's only five miles from the Manse, and right next door to Philip's farm!"

# 3

SOMEHOW Marty managed to make the necessary responses to Fergus, thanking him. She supposed that even before he had left on his trip, these parishioners of his had asked him to look out for someone for them. Fergus had never taken the hostility between Philip and herself seriously, and wouldn't realize the dismay she felt.

When the padre had gone Marty sat down on her bunk and covered her face with her hands. This was something she had not anticipated. She had hoped to make her new home amongst strangers, among people who were not prejudiced about her, where she would make her own impression. She tried to remember if Philip had ever mentioned the Logies. He had said once that the remote places were the spots for real neighborliness, but she didn't know if he meant his own place. She had seen, in with so many others that she couldn't now remember anything distinctive, some movies of the padre's parish. Fergus had borrowed them from a parishioner whose hobby was movie photography.

Marty had a patchy memory of a little church set against a mountain background on wide plains, and very little else. It would be some distance from the sea ... she knew a distinct nostalgia at the thought — the sea was a link with England. She shook herself impatiently at the thought. She must not allow herself to be homesick.

Perhaps she would not see as much of Philip as she feared. The distances were great, she had heard, and the holdings or estates large. She hoped Philip's farm was as far from the Logies' as might be. But even at the best, it was grim, especially when Fergus had once said that, however ridiculous the report might prove to be, it certainly was true of his own district. "We've got umpteen bachelors in the place," he had said, and added: "And Rachel, of course, is a born matchmaker, and does her best to rectify this! Thus far she's only pulled it off once."

They were probably all misfits or

woman-haters, Marty decided recklessly, and uncharitably, and she would certainly steer clear of that paragon, Rachel MacNeill! Well, she would work out her two years with the Logies, and do all she could to dissabuse any ideas Philip might put around about her and the husband-hunting . . . and after that? Anywhere at all, to get away from him, the far north, perhaps.

Meantime, everyone except Pauline and Laura would feel she was very lucky to have friends already in the district to which she had been allotted. Now, she ought to go on deck, and see all she could of Wellington. It was eight-thirty, and they were getting near.

Wellington was beautiful on its green hills, the suburban houses climbing high, yet always leaving the crests untouched. It was a perfect harbor, the tall buildings and waterfront occupying the flatter, more spacious bays at the foot of the high hills, and across the harbor there were endless little bays where homes and shops nestled.

The gulls were screaming and circling, there were trains hooting and sirens going, and smoke rising . . . and down below the official harbor launch was leaving the ship. Now they could see knots of people on the wharf they were making for, indistinct still, but those passengers who were being met were straining every nerve to recognize dear ones who had preceded them to this new country, or to pick out relations they had never yet seen.

The padre and Philip turned up beside the three girls, and suddenly the padre gave a shout.

"She's there! There she is — Rachel. Right on the end of the wharf, Philip. Oh, she's got the youngsters with her — won't they be thrilled! She won't be able to pick us out yet in this crowd . . . by Jove, she has . . . that'll be because of my dog collar."

He turned to the girls. "See . . . just beside that woman in the red hat . . . no, not that one — she's in green . . . see, and the children are on her left. Jocelyn and Grant."

The ship seemed to take an interminable time nosing in to the wharf, and by now the people on it had left the end, and were lined up behind the barricade down the middle of it.

Fergus disappeared. Ten minutes later Marty looked down. "Why . . . there's the padre!"

He was off the ship and striding towards the barricade. They watched him say something as he neared, and put out a hand to each of the children, who leapt the barricade, chattering madly. Fergus put both hands out to his wife, who came over it very neatly. She stood a moment, both hands in his, and before she lifted her face for his kiss, held him off a moment, their eyes locking, seeking to bridge the gap of the months apart.

Marty saw her distinctly frame two words: "Safe, Fergus!" and realized suddenly what these months must have meant to Rachel MacNeill. Perhaps she wasn't self-sufficient and efficient, calmly capable of managing on her own . . .

Sudenly a cheer went up from the ship's rail, a tribute to the popularity of the padre. Rachel and Fergus drew apart, they could see the color run up into Rachel's face, then she laughed.

"He's bringing them on board," cried Philip, delighted. "I think the Captain must have invited them for lunch. I'll take you to meet them."

"No, thanks," said Marty hurriedly. "You go, you are old friends. They won't want me."

"Don't be stupid. Rachel will want to meet her husband's newest parishioner."

Marty said coldly: "I'm an Anglican, not a Presbyterian."

"It wouldn't matter to Fergus if you were a Roman Catholic or a Communist. It's a united community at Linden Peaks township. Everybody visits everyone else. The priest often drops in at Logie's. He comes and fishes on their property."

Marty supposed she had better go to save further argument.

"But, Mr. Griffiths, before we go, there's one thing I must say — I had no idea that Fergus was trying to place me in his parish. Believe me, I'd have turned it down if I'd had the chance."

Philip gave her an odd look, started to say something, changed his mind, and grinned.

"Well, it's just as well for your own

sake you didn't. You'll love the Logies, and Joy can certainly do with some help."

Marty continued, her color high. "I know it's as unwelcome to you as to me, but once I get settled in, we'll not need to see much of each other."

The corner of Philip's mouth lifted. "No, that's one consolation," he agreed. "I'll drop you on the doorstep, mutter 'Now heaven help you!' to Joy, and run!"

"*You'll* drop — ?"

"I'm taking you down. It's only sensible. Fergus thought it best." (Marty realized it would hardly be his own idea.) "I'm only spending one night in Wellington. Fergus has to see his committee, and they can't meet right away. I've only got to see the immigration officials. Most of the South Island immigrants are going down on the ferry tonight, but Fergus thought I could see you delivered safely at the Logies'."

"I'd much rather go down by myself and make my own way to Linden Peaks." Marty's tone was ungracious.

66

"I don't doubt it, but Fergus thinks it's the best way, and I can't think of any real reason to offer him, to act otherwise." The amused note crept into his voice. "Don't worry, I shan't give Mrs. Logie any idea of your real motives in coming to New Zealand."

Marty couldn't trust herself to reply to that. She said, changing the subject: "Well, if you insist I meet Mrs. MacNeill now, let's get it over."

Fergus was introducing his family to the Scots master-at-arms at the head of the gangway. He turned as he saw the pair of them approaching, and introduced Marty.

The youngsters flung themselves on Philip, talking madly.

Marty laughed as she greeted Rachel. She said: "How homesick your husband has been for you . . . it's a great compliment to any wife."

Rachel wasn't at all what she had imagined . . . younger, too. Marty had thought she would be buxom and managing, with an air of over-efficiency and calm.

But Rachel was as excited as the

children, round-faced and merry, and dressed beautifully in hunting green tweeds with a bright splash of scarlet.

"A new suit," said Fergus approvingly.

"Yes," said Grant, "that's the pigs. We've done jolly well out of them. I've got a new bike, too, and Jocelyn's got roller skates."

Fergus looked staggered. "Pigs . . . skates . . . bikes . . . what in the name of fortune?"

Rachel dimpled. "The lease of the manse glebe was up shortly after you left. I decided to run it instead of renting it to someone and just getting free milk. And I've always liked pigs. We've got simply beautiful styes and runs, Fergus. You ought to see them. The church managers built them for me, and the sawmiller provided the wood. They're as clean as can be. They don't smell a bit!"

"I suppose you give them a bath every day!" suggested her husband facetiously.

"No. I hose them down, and rub them dry with wisps of straw." This piece of information silenced Fergus temporarily, and Rachel continued: "And I had the

68

pigs given me . . . the ones we started with. Old Sam's looking after them while we are away. We've done so well with them."

Fergus said helplessly: "What are feeding them on?"

Rachel looked guilty. "Well . . . I had to get a cow. They get skim milk. The cow had twin calves. Both heifers." She added hastily. "It's all right. I learned to milk, so did the children."

Fergus waved his hands. "Pigs! A cow! Calves! What else?"

No one was more surprised than he when Jocelyn answered with a note of supreme delight, "A pony, Dad!"

Rachel sighed. "I warned them to break it gently . . . in fact, gradually. I thought by the time we got to Christchurch you might have learned the extent of our livestock. Poor Fergus!"

"To think I was homesick for you," he said, looking grim. "Is there any more to come?"

"Not to speak of, darling . . . only a few ducks and geese and turkeys."

"I suppose you know," said Fergus, "in case it has not occurred to you, my

69

sweet, that ministers do move on from time to time. We might even go to the city next. It's certainly time I was home to curb you."

He looked at his wife then with something in his eyes that made Marty drop hers. She decided she liked Rachel after all.

Marty turned to the children.

"Now, perhaps your father would like to take your mother down to his cabin. I'll show you over the ship, children."

She was rather put out when Jocelyn slipped a hand into Philip's.

"Yes, that would be goody, come on, Philip," the child said.

★ ★ ★

Marty stood at the rail of the *Hinemoa*, the inter-island ferry steamer, watching the lights of Island Bay, a suburb of Wellington, fade.

Philip waved a hand in the direction they were going.

"Now home," he said.

They would make down the coast all night, as far as Port Lyttleton, berthing

70

about seven, then taking the train through the tunnel cut under the Port Hills, to the city of Christchurch, the capital of Canterbury.

"When we are out of sight of land, I'll take you down to the saloon for supper, then you might feel like turning in early."

It was quite a hint. Marty tightened her lips and said:

"I've already given the stewardess a tip to bring supper to my cabin. My cabin-mate is turning in early, as she has a small boy with her. I just came up on deck to let her get him settled without a stranger around. She said she had travelled from Wanganui, and was tired. The train was late and she hadn't had time for a meal, so I told the stewardess, and she's going to bring some sandwiches and biscuits along at nine o'clock."

Philip said, expressing no regret that he was to be deprived of her company, "While I think of it, go easy with your tipping. It's not done much here. All right in the case of the stewardess bringing you supper — that's an extra service, and if a red-cap on the station handles your luggage, but we don't usually tip taxi-drivers or waitresses or bus-drivers here. They're inclined to be embarrassed if we do. They all get splendid wages, and don't expect extras."

Marty looked at him. "There's one thing, Mr. Griffiths, I'll not go wrong while you're around, will I? I mean, you couldn't resist putting me right, could you?"

Philip's voice sounded impatient. It put her in the wrong, made her feel churlish.

"I'm just putting you wise, Miss Reddington. I thought it might make it easier and quicker for you to absorb New Zealand ways, if I made plain statements about the things in which we differ."

"I'm not at all sure I want to absorb all New Zealand ways . . . for instance, I can't say I admire their manners. Of course, I may meet people who will change my first impressions, but thus far I find them . . . " She broke off, choking a little with the tide of her feelings.

Philip's voice was imperturbable, as it prompted her:

"You find them . . . ?"

"I find them blunt, and overbearing and . . . and deliberately unkind!"

She turned sharply on her heel and walked towards the lighted companion-way, aware as she did that a maddening chuckle followed her.

The little boy was asleep when she entered the cabin, but his mother was sitting on the edge of the bed, reading a magazine.

She looked up as Marty came in, and smiled, white teeth flashing between her full red lips, her cheeks the warm, golden brown of the Maori. Marty thought she was lovely. She was wearing a tailored blue suit, with red shoes, and her curly black hair, beautifully dressed, glinted like rippled satin in the glow of the light.

The Maori girl said simply, "My name is Lancaster. Hine Lancaster — Hinemoa, really, same as this ship. You say Hine as if it was spelt Heeny. Most i's in Maori are pronounced like e's, and every syllable is accented equally."

Marty smiled. "Thank you for telling me that," she said. "It does make it so much easier." She crushed down the thought that Philip had tried just that, and been rebuffed. "I suppose you don't want us to talk to much in case we wake the wee boy?"

The girl laughed. "Not Tiaki . . . once he's off you just can't wake him. His name means Jacky, by the way. My father-in-law was called Jack, not John. John is Hoami, and William is Wiremu, George is Hori. I have a little girl, too. You would probably think we had called her Maria. It is that, really, but it is spelt Maraea. The ae together in Maori is i.

"She's with my mother-in-law in Christchurch. She's not been widowed long, and it's company for her, while I went to visit my mother at the *pa* in Wanganui, Putiki."

"What's a *pa?*" asked Marty.

"A Maori village."

Just then the stewardess arrived with the supper, and shortly both girls turned in.

★ ★ ★

74

Marty came up on deck early, feeling Mrs. Lancaster might be glad to have the cabin to herself while she washed and dressed wee Tiaki.

There was a cool wind blowing and very few passengers on the dim-lit deck. Marty felt she would appreciate a few solitary moments to marshall her thoughts and her courage for all the new adventures the day might bring her, but it was not to be. As she stepped on to the deck, a figure swung around from the rail. Philip.

She hesitated, and would have gone to the port side, but he said: "Nothing to see on that side, Miss Reddington . . . nothing nearer than the South Pole. The land's on this side."

She would still have defied him and walked away, but there were two men with him who had swung around, too, so she came to the rail.

There was a chain of lights like a jewelled necklace fringing the coast line. The men with Philip joined eagerly in to point out faintly discernible landmarks, enjoying, as everyone does, being knowledgeable about their own country.

Marty was glad of their presence, which served to keep things normal, and to keep at bay the inevitable animosity that marked any exchange between Philip and herself.

They came into Lyttleton Harbor between the Winking Buoy and Godley Head lighthouse, and entered the deep volcanic habor, with daylight breaking on bare brown hills, tinged here and there with green.

They turned about to go into Lyttlton itself. A good many passengers were on deck now, and down below some were lining up for the gangways. The two men melted away.

Marty said, "I'd better go down and get my luggage together. Mrs. Lancaster should have got her small boy dressed by now."

Philip said sharply, "Mrs. Lancaster? Is she a Maori?"

Marty looked puzzled. "Yes, she is . . . but how did you tumble to that? I mean — Lancaster isn't a typically Maori name, is it?"

"No. Of course not. But a friend of mine, a chap I went to school with, married a Maori girl. His name was Bill Lancaster. I'll go down with you, she may need a hand with the youngster on to the train."

Hine said her mother-in-law would have brought the car over the hill from Christchurch, and presently, lined up at the rail, they picked her out, a dark-eyed little girl in her arms.

Hine's mother-in-law greeted Philip warmly, and insisted that they come with her across Evan's Pass to the plains.

"In fact," she said, "you can drive, Philip, and it will give me a chance of talking to Hine. You and Miss Reddington can come with us for breakfast."

So they came up over the Pass, and down to the plains, edged on one side by the Pacific, on the other by the Southern Alps, crossed a river, got into a stream of traffic city-bound, before they turned off into a quiet suburb, each little bungalow neat in its quarter-acre of garden, where Mrs. Lancaster lived.

Mary felt she could have enjoyed her breakfast more, the bacon and egg, the excellent coffee, the warm living-room, but for the presence of the man beside her, disapproving and hostile.

The meal over, Hine ran them into the city, where Philip was to pick up a brand-new station-wagon for use on his farm. Marty felt that the worst of her ordeal was over.

She could see Christchurch was a beautiful city, laid out in precise, right-angled fashion between the tree-lined belts that enclosed its square mile, a preciseness only broken by the meanderings of the green-banked Avon, but she had little chance of seeing much.

Hine dropped them on a street corner. There was a paper-stand on the corner where Philip bought a paper, tucking it under his arm and hurrying her off to the garage. He was delighted with his new conveyance, walking around it, admiring its lines, talking over its performance with the sales manager.

They had risen and were on the point of leaving when the sales manager said: "There was a nasty accident up your way yesterday . . . hear about it? Late in the afternoon. One of these freak accidents, with nobody to blame. Happened at a

78

crossroads near Lauriston. A big transport started to pull up to give way on the right, and the driver got stung by a bee right on the eye! He drove clean into the side of the car. He came out of it with a broken arm, but the two passengers, man and wife, in the other car, took the brunt of it. They are both badly injured and in Ashburton Hospital."

"Wonder if I know them," said Philip, concerned. "Who were they?"

The man shook his head. "Couldn't tell you the name. It didn't register."

Marty said, "I'm holding your paper, Mr. Griffiths, would you like to look?"

He unfolded the paper, took a moment or two to find the item, grew very still, looked up at her, the color leaving his face.

"It's — it's Joy and Leonard," he said.

"Oh, no!" cried Marty protestingly.

Philip went back to the paper, going over the details.

"The car is a complete write-off. They both have severe head injuries, possibly other injuries, and Leonard has a broken leg and arm. They've not yet regained consciousness and are on the dangerously ill list." He passed a hand over his forehead.

In silence he helped Marty into the station waggon, and drove out, heading towards the river. Marty kept quiet as they threaded the traffic. Philip pulled into a parking place by the river, got out, put three pennies in the parking meter, got in again.

He leaned his hands on the wheel and his head on his hands. Marty waited in silence, feeling deeply for him, dismayed and uncertain. He lifted his head and looked at her.

"And what on earth am I going to do with *you?*" he demanded.

Marty stared. "What are you going to do with *me?* Well — what *would* you do? Get me there as soon as you can, of course. Surely I can be of help in a situation like this!"

"You'd be nothing but a complication and a responsibility!" he told her bluntly.

Marty reined in her temper. This was shock, she knew. He didn't mean it. For the moment he wasn't seeing things clearly.

She said: "I fail to see that. I'm engaged to help with the children. Isn't this the moment when I can be of most help?"

He shook his head impatiently. "The children will be getting looked after by my manager's wife, I expect. She's young, but very sensible, and isn't a stranger. She knows our way of life and knows the children. Or Logie's married couple may have them. I'm not sure, for the chap was most unsatisfactory, I know. Len told me in a letter. But in any case the whole district would rally round. Someone would take the children."

"They won't have had much time to organize that yet," said Marty, "and it's a large house that can put up four children at a moment's notice. Besides, people soon get weary of well-doing, and tired of children. It looks as if the Logies will be weeks in hospital if . . . " She stopped, changed her mind. "I mean, the children would be better in their own home and all together. It's too hard for youngsters, after a shock like that, to have to adjust themselves to different surroundings and people too."

Philip snorted. "You haven't any idea what it's like — you'd be terrified out of your wits if you had to stay in that huge house all on your own."

"I've not always lived in the heart of London. Actually, you know nothing about me. I kept house for my father in a Suffolk vicarage. I spent many a night alone in that twelve-roomed house when he went to meetings in London. It might have been stuck out on the vast Canterbury Plains I've heard so much about, but it was surrounded by an old and ghostly graveyard. I'm not the type to get the vapors if a door bangs suddenly or a tree creaks outside."

"All right," said Philip wearily, "but it's on your own head." Marty was silent a moment from sheer relief. Then she added, "So let's get going. We may be needed."

She had a sudden impulse to put a hand over his as it lay on the wheel, and tell him how sorry she was that this had happened. That she knew how he felt. But she dared not. Her sympathies had been stirred the night they had paid the pilgrimage to his father's grave, and he had rebuffed her. If she made a genuine gesture like that now, he would only think it one of the shallow impulsive gestures common to redheads.

The moment passed as Philip said. "Right. We'll go and pick up our luggage from the station. One thing, we've plenty of room for it in this. That's what I got it for. The cab of my truck is too small for comfort."

Marty knew a faint surprise. From the talk she had heard she would have thought that sheep station owners would have had a car as well as a truck.

They headed south past the hospital and along the road cut through the oaks that homesick pioneers of a hundred years ago had planted in Hagley Park, and on through the prosperous suburb of Riccarton.

As they came out on to the less settled stretches of the Main South Road, a gust of wind hit them, making a definite impact on the driving side of the car.

"Good Lord!" Philip sounded disgusted. "A nor-wester! Wouldn't it! We hardly ever get them so early in the season! They're the curse and blessing of the

Canterbury plains."

He said, in answer to her puzzled look: "They're the most trying winds there are. They sweep across the Tasman as moisture-laden winds, drop their rain on the watershed of the Alps, and tear across the plains as hot, dry winds, scorching everything up, swirling dust and grit into the houses, lifting top-soil and top-dressing and whisking it miles away. Yet the nor'westers make the plains wonderful sheep country — no foot-rot. Too dry."

Already clouds of dust were lifting, and at every gap of trees the wind caught the car and buffeted it.

"It's going to be a bad one. It'll reach a high speed later, perhaps sixty or seventy miles an hour — gale force," predicted Philip. "Oh well, you might as well get used to them soon as late."

Marty said, quietly but firmly: "Take more than a nor'wester to put me off something I've set my mind to."

"Think so?" again the mocking tone. "Well, time will tell."

Time would tell, thought Marty. Time to come when I've proved myself. I shan't do any protesting now.

Harmony did not grow between them as the miles passed by. In fact, even the simplest remark seemed charged with antagonism.

Philip was looking about him as he drove. "They've certainly had a record rainfall this winter, the place is very green."

He caught the look on Marty's face, and said: "Not green as England is green, Miss Reddington. I've got to hand it to you there, I've seen nothing as beautiful . . . but lord, what a climate . . . you certainly pay the price. But when I say this is green for here, you can hardly understand — yet. When you've experienced a summer on these plains you'll understand. Everything is scorched and brown. An artist, visiting here, said you'd use more yellow ochre painting New Zealand than any other color."

Marty wished she could exclaim with delight over the scenery, but she couldn't do it sincerely. If only she could have, perhaps it might have pleased Philip, though why she should bother to please him she did not know. She hoped desperately that it only seemed so barren because this was a bad day, with the countryside wrapped in a pall of grey.

Suddenly they came to the Rakaia bridge, spanning the great river a mile and a tenth wide, a river that did not run sweetly bank to bank, but gouged its way through a mighty river-bed of shingle, running swiftly, treacherously. "Its Maori name means Treacherous One," said Philip "It was a terrific barrier to colonization further south when they had to ford the river."

Marty was wide-eyed. "You don't mean people crossed it, . . . *this* . . . when there was no bridge."

"Just that," said Philip, a hint of contempt in his voice. "The bridge wasn't built till sometime in the 1870's. Sometimes the men — and women — were camped there three weeks when it was in flood, waiting for the river to go down to reasonable levels, though there were always treacherous streams to negotiate."

"It's a wonder the women didn't persaude the men to stop the north side of the river . . . after all, there's still plenty of land going begging by the look of it."

"They had stout hearts, the women in those days," said Philip. "They didn't look on men merely to provide them with pleasure and luxury. They shared every hardship." His tone bit. Marty fell silent. Better a silence heavy with antagonism than this.

They swung over the railway line at Rakaia and headed due west. As they left the township the full force of the nor'wester struck them in blinding swirls of dust. The Alps were there, no doubt, because Marty had seen them from the Port Hills, sixty miles away, this morning, but they were completely invisible now. Marty felt lost in immensity, the plains seemed to go on for ever, flat and drab in the extreme.

She felt appalled by the grit and the unpleasantness, and the sensation, even in the car, of battling the elements. And God alone knew what lay ahead. She hoped she would be able to rise to whatever the situation at Alpenlinden demanded of her when she arrived.

She took out a handkerchief and wiped

her face, looking ruefully at the grime. "The dust certainly gets everywhere, doesn't it?"

Philip nodded. "Yes. That's the worst of these English cars. They aren't made for these roads. I'll get this one sealed against dust at the local garage."

Marty gave a short laugh. "Oh, well, if you can condition the English cars to take it, I daresay in time I'll get conditioned to it, also. In fact, I might even become useful . . . given time and a square deal."

Philip glanced briefly at her. "You're tired, aren't you?"

"Not really. At least, not physically, just tired to death of conflict. It will be good to find a job to do, and to be free of disapproval."

Philip seemed about to say something, but at that moment they turned a bend, and he had to slow down for a mob of sheep. When they had safely negotiated the huge flock, he seemed disinclined for further conversation.

They came suddenly to an opening in the gorse hedges that lined the road, turned in over cattle-stops that rattled hideously, where white painted bars said, "Ngaio Bend", and an aluminum mailbox said, "P. R. Griffiths."

Philip's house was new, and looked as if it wasn't yet finished, but Marty was past taking any interest in the surroundings, she wanted to find out what had happened to the Logie children, and how soon she could get them over to Alpenlinden, and know some freedom.

As they stopped, the back door flew open and Philip's manager appeared, clutching by a hand each two somewhat dishevelled looking children. The Logie twins, Gaynor and Gregory.

Graham Stewart said, "Thank God you're back, Phil . . . way to greet you . . . didn't expect it to be like this." He held out his hand.

Philip said, in a low voice: "How are they?"

"You've seen the paper? Condition still unchanged." A grim silence descended upon them. Marty broke it. She noticed that Gaynor had tear-stains on her cheeks and her leg was bleeding.

"I'm Marty Reddington, and here to help. What's Gaynor done?"

Graham Stewart's expression lightened. "Thank heaven for a woman."

Philip looked surprised. "Why . . . where's Rhona?"

Graham's look was rueful. "She went into the nursing-home at Rakaia yesterday morning, and we've had no word yet. She's still in labor." He sounded worried.

Philip had no help to give over this. Marty said quickly: "Is it her first baby?" Graham nodded.

Marty said, in a matter-of-fact way, "Then there's nothing to worry about. Not in the least unusual with a first. She probably went in far too early." She smiled at him. "I suppose you rushed her in, in case things happened suddenly."

He grinned. "I'd have had her in still sooner if she'd have gone."

Marty nodded sagely. "Well, no wonder there's no news yet. She's had a long first stage. Her pains may even have stopped for a while. She probably even had a sleep last night, which I suppose is more than you had."

Some of the tension went out of the man's face. Marty supposed that even if he knew all there was to know about

90

lambing, he probably didn't know a thing about babies.

Philip gave her a glance that held respect, and even gratitude, she thought. It was immensely gratifying to realize that even if she was a raw new chum, there were still situations where only a woman could help.

Marty didn't rush the children. She said to Graham: "If you show me the bathroom, and where the bandages are, I'll get this graze bound up."

In the kitchen, Robin Logie, a nine-year-old boy, was reluctantly tackling a huge pile of dishes, and Anne, who looked about eleven, was peeling potatoes.

Marty tossed her hat off. "Oh, good, you've got a start with the dinner. I'm Marty. I'll just get Gaynor's leg fixed and I'll be out to help you." She hoped Anne would not mind her taking over, she was old enough to be resentful and had had a shock.

Philip came with her to the bathroom, which was rather untidy, natural enough under the circumstances, but she could see it was well appointed. He sat down on the edge of the bath with Gaynor on his knee.

Gaynor said apprehensively: "I don't want any of that stingy stuff on it!"

"Iodine? Oh, we don't use that much these days. Let me see what's here. Oh, acriflavine . . . that doesn't sting at all, it's a pretty yellow color, not a horrid brown."

She put a thick towel under the child's leg, found some cottonwool and disinfectant, and bathed it, then bound it up firmly.

"That's almost a professional job," said Philip, sounding surprised.

Marty's lips twitched. "I didn't spend twenty-four hours a day in a London office!"

Gaynor sat perfectly still. Marty washed her face gently, found a brush and comb, and tidied the nut-brown hair. The child had a lovely forehead, sherry-brown eyes, and a pointed chin.

Philip put the child down, told her to run off to Anne, and stood up.

"Things are in the very devil of a mess. Graham tells me this couple Len had went off suddenly last week. Len had been trying to get someone through the stock and station agents, and had been in about it when they had the accident. He's got a good single fellow working for him, a young man, but keen, and good with the tractor, but he's in Burnham doing his three months' military. I may be able to get him out, but will have to apply. It will take time. Just to complicate things, lambing's just starting, and Len has got some stud stuff this year. The nucleus of a stud flock. Paid terrific prices. We'll be flat out for weeks. I think I know someone in the village who would take the twins, and the older two could perhaps stay with you in the big house."

Marty set her chin. "The sooner the children get settled back in their own surroundings the better. I'll take the four of them back as soon as we have rustled up some sort of meal. It's too disrupting for little ones to have to fit into a strange household, bad enough both parents being in hospital, without being separated from brother and sister as well."

Philip gave in; he could see nothing

else for it at the moment, though, as he told her, he could see plenty of rocks ahead.

The phone rang. Philip answered it. He turned to Graham. "Rakaia Cottage Hospital on the line," he said.

They saw immediately by Graham's expression that the news was good. He put the receiver down, and turned to them.

"A boy. Eight pounds eight ounces, and Rhona is very well." Care dropped from him. "They said I could come in any time, but Rhona knows what sort of a pickle we are in, she'll understand. I'll ring later and say I'll be in tonight."

Philip grinned. "You'll never settle to anything. As soon as we've had dinner, you take the truck and go. I can't do anything outside till I get Miss Reddington and the children settled at the homestead."

Marty began to set the table.

They went to Alpenlinden through the paddocks and over a creek.

"You needn't worry about that creek," said Philip. "There are quite a number of fences between it and the house. The children have had it drummed into them. What's the drill, youngsters?"

"No one goes near the creek or the pond without a grownup," said Robin and Anne in unison. It was left to Gaynor, as usual, to finish it. "Or we get our bottoms smacked — *hard*," she said, mournfully.

Philip added, "Lennie has even the water-races fenced off where they come near the house. Too much of a worry for Joy, otherwise."

Nevertheless it made Marty realize what a responsibility it was to take care of other people's children.

"If there are other hazards, ones I mightn't know about, you'd better tell me before you go."

Thus Marty came to Alpenlinden more concerned with these things than with its garden or its architecture. She had just an impression of dust-filled air, unseasonably hot, of trees and shrubs bent over before the force of the dry gale, and dogs barking furiously.

"How lovely, dogs," she said, eyes lighting up.

"The dogs," said Philip, "are not

allowed inside the garden. They must stay in the yard. Robin will see to feeding them — don't forget to see they have plenty of water, Robin. He'll let them off the chain when required. We're waging a war against hydatids . . . we'll win it when all the farmers co-operate and dose the dogs regularly and properly, and stop feeding them on raw offal."

"Oh." Marty sounded disappointed. "I've missed a dog since our old spaniel died. Didn't realize you'd not be able to have them about you here. I rather looked forward to the farm dogs."

Anne got in before Philip. "Oh, we've got house dogs. A Boxer, and a wee reddish spaniel, Rusty."

"And we wash our hands every time we touch them," said Gregory, making his first contribution to the conversation.

By this time they were through the gate into the garden and up the back steps. Marty surprised tears in Anne's eyes. It would be coming afresh to the child that her mother was not there to welcome her.

She said, quickly, "Well, Anne, you're going to have a busy time showing me around. I'll want to know where everything is, and how I should do things. I'll make the most appalling blunders, I suppose, so you'll have to keep me right. We'll get the twins down for their nap in a few minutes when they have had a wash, and Robin and you can show me around. In the meantime, I'm dying for a drink of water. Shipboard water is never nice, I'd like a really cool fresh one."

As she expected, they both dashed to get it. Marty swung around to Philip.

"I think Anne's about all in; she's old enough to realize how serious this is. I'll have to get her occupied. Nothing like work to take your mind off things. I know you'd prefer to show me around yourself, but I think we could manage, and it would help if we got the children settled down into a routine again. Besides, I imagine you'll have plenty to do."

"I certainly have. Graham felt he shouldn't be beyond reach of the phone, in case either of the hospitals rang him this morning, so he's not been around the sheep yet. He saw to the milking and poultry at both places, stationing the kids by the phone, but he rushed it through. I

97

thought I'd go round the sheep here now, then go over home. Graham will come over here for the night's milking, and young Robin can do the rest. After tea tonight I'll go into Ashburton Hospital. If they are still unconscious, of course, I can do nothing, but if they have rallied at all, I'll be able to reassure them the children are all right." He smiled at her.

So it looked as if Philip was glad, after all, that she was here; perhaps in time they might lose sight of the enmity that had almost become a habit.

Philip heard the children returning and said hastily:

"You can get me on the phone around tea-time, if anything crops up, and I'll call in tonight after I've been to hospital. It will get dark about six tonight, and be quite dark when I get back, so don't get a scare when you hear me come, will you?"

* * *

Robin and Anne seized a case each, and Marty two, and they went out into the main hall. Marty hadn't been prepared for so spacious a house; she had envisaged something more on utility lines, but this was lovely, a kauri staircase that curved up to a wide landing, the whole covered luxuriously with soft, beige, flowered carpeting, something that wouldn't show dust, she realized.

Fascinating little passages branched off the landing, and the twins, not to be outdone in showing her around, raced along one, and at the end flung open a door. Marty stepped in, stopped.

"Oh, no. This won't be for me. This is one of the best guest rooms. My room will be smaller, plainer, near yours I should think."

"This is near ours," said Robin, and Anne got in quickly, "Mummy did this up especially for you. She said you were coming a long way, by yourself, and you'd want a room where you could get away from us if you wanted to. So she went flat out." Anne giggled. "Mummy had wall-to-wall carpeting in mushroom pink ordered for here, and she had started curtains to match — then Philip wrote to her, and she said mushroom pink would never do for a girl with red hair, so she rushed into town and got this."

Marty was silent. If Philip had written, it must have been from Panama. The padre would have told him he was trying to get her for the Logies. She could well imagine where the reference to red hair would come in. As clearly as if she had seen the letter, she could see the words: "She's got red hair, and a temper to match!"

Yet evidently none of Philip's warnings had affected the warmheartedness of Mrs. Logie's preparations for her . . . oh, if only Mrs. Logie were here now.

Walls were the palest of green, and floor covered with a carpet that was spring itself . . . a pale grey, sprinkled with a floral design in primrose and lavender. The bedroom suite was in grey ash, a Queen Anne design, and the curtains and covers in primrose, with some in lilac.

"To match the wistaria outside, Mummy said," Anne told her, delighted at Marty's reactions to all her mother had planned.

"You don't mean I have wistaria outside my windows?"

Robin flung open the glass doors at the end of the room and disclosed a small porch with an arched entrance to the room. It was utterly charming, and covered in the same carpeting as the bedroom, it made it seem larger. It held an easy chair, with chintzy cushions that matched the other room, a long padded seat under the windows that were indeed wreathed about with the gnarled bare stems of an ancient wistaria, and they looked out on to a tree-encircled lawn. There was a sturdy-looking writing-desk, complete with blotter, pad and envelopes, and even some stamps for airmails home.

Marty made her voice steady, matter-of-fact. "I can hardly wait till your mother gets home to thank her for all this."

She saw a strange expression flit over Anne's face. It was as if, for a moment, a shadow lifted. That was what Anne needed, some reassurance that her mother would come back.

Marty rummaged in her case for an apron, and slipped it on. That would make her look less of a stranger.

"Tonight, after tea, you can help me unpack. I've got some awfully nice English sweets that I got at the shop on board the ship, and some games and books. But we must get tidied up now. Where's the bathroom, and we'll get the twins ready for their nap."

Naturally, with so much happening, the three-year-olds didn't go down without protest, but almost as soon as they got them tucked down, they fell asleep, and the other three stole quietly downstairs.

The kitchen was a large one, dating back to the early days, when families were large, and a great number of shearers and harvesters had to be fed; but it was modernised, and had an electric stove and a solid fuel one.

Marty loved the house, but was somewhat dismayed at the size of it. The downstairs rooms were already horribly dusty with the wind that seemed to be increasing in strength every minute.

"Now what about food? How do we get it? And where? And do you have to bake your own bread?"

"Granny used to in the old days, but we get it with the mail now, on Mondays,

Wednesdays, Fridays. Sometimes when Granny is here on holiday, she bakes it, 'cos we love it, but it's too much work for all the time. We get mail every day."

Anne interrupted Robin. "And the township is only five miles away. We get groceries once a week, on Thursdays, and in any case there is plenty in the house. Come and look, Marty."

There certainly was. The big refrigerator in the kitchen was plentifully stocked with meat, milk, cream, butter, and Anne led the way to a room off the kitchen.

"Our storeroom," she said, with obvious pride. "They had to have one in the old days, and Mummy likes the idea and keeps it up."

It was like a grocer's shop, lined with shelves, with tinned goods of every description. One side preserved fruit from the orchard, fruit of every description. Marty had never seen so much, or such glowing colors.

"But she can't do all that herself?"

"Oh, we all help, even Robin!"

"I like that! *Even* me! I do a darned

sight more than you do, Anne. I like it better than you."

"Well, that's nothing. I like chopping kindling better than you do, and I do help with this. I pick the fruit as well as you do, and — "

"That's enough," said Marty firmly, but glad to see them normal enough to quarrel. "What's this, in this jar, full of seeds?" She picked up a jar of olive-green pulp, thick with what looked like black apple pips. There were several of them, small jars.

"Passion-fruit. Don't you get them in England? They grow mostly around Nelson in the South Island, it's hot there, or in the North Island. They grow on vines. Mum buys them to preserve. You can grow them in sheltered parts in North Otago, too, but they are mostly banana passion-fruit there, longish yellow things, with the same kind of pulp inside. They have a lovely pink flower."

"But what do you use the pulp for?"

"To flavor fruit-salad; it's beaut. Or to put in with icing. And Mum makes melon and passion-fruit jam. Open a jar and try a bit on a teaspoon."

Marty did; it was delicious, though rich. She looked about her. There was a deep freeze chest in one corner, packed with frozen foods. She thought housekeeping ought to be fairly easy here with all the gadgets. She had noticed a dish-washer, a floor-polisher, a cake-mixer, a liquidizer, a milk-shake mixer, a spin-dry washing machine, and a clothes-dryer.

Robin had explained: "Mum can't often get help in the house, so we got all the conveniences we could."

Now it was night, half-past eight. Marty had discovered that this meal they called tea was really a supper. They had afternoon tea, a hand-round affair, tea and scones and cakes, at three or a little later, and then this meal at about six, though Anne had explained that, as she and Robin were away at school all day, Mondays to Fridays, the family at home had lunch in the middle of the day, instead of the dinner most farmers had, and they had dinner as the evening meal at six.

It had been a long day and an upsetting one, but now Marty felt at peace. She had won her point with Philip. In spite of the calamity of finding her employers were in hospital, she was here, settled in, doing a very necessary job.

Fortunately Robin and Anne had chosen to go to bed quite soon to read, and had both fallen asleep over their books. Marty had tucked them up tenderly, poor lambs, and tiptoed downstairs to tidy up.

She was glad of the company of the dogs. They had accepted her all right, and were now curled up in the baskets in the kitchen. She heard a low growling in Muggin's throat, and thought it would be Philip.

Marty felt a rush of gladness as he came in. That, she told herself sternly, was merely because he was the only person she knew around here, the only link with England.

He dropped into a chair and looked at her. She knew from his eyes that the news wasn't good. He leaned forward, his hands clasped between his knees, and looking at them, he said: "They're still deeply unconscious, no change whatever. They are being well looked after, of

106

course, but — there's nothing we can do. Just wait. To see Joy and Lennie like that! Joy is so full of the sheer gladness of living, and to see her lying so white and still and uncaring . . .

Marty would have given anything to be able to go across to him, to have the right to put her arms about him, to lay her cheek against his in wordless sympathy.

Instead she said: "I've got some hot coffee ready, and some toast."

They drank it in companionable silence. Marty didn't know if their common anxiety had drawn them nearer, or if it was just that for the moment they were both too deadly tired to fight.

"That wind is still strong. I'm beginning to think nor'westers really are as bad as they are painted!"

"Actually, it's veering around to the sou'west now. Thought it would at this time of year. We'll get rain before morning." He added: "I'd better be on my way. If I sit here long, I'll go to sleep. Just imagine — at this time last night we were easing out of Wellington Heads, and all seemed set fair. No idea of what was ahead. You're dead-beat, too, aren't you?"

Marty admitted it.

"Just as well . . . it's a strange place, and you'll be too tired to be nervous."

"You're determined I must be nervous, aren't you?"

She sounded like a petulant child, and knew it. Philip just laughed, his merriment aggravating her further.

"Well, if you hear any odd sounds, like souls in torment, it's just Joy's guinea fowls, and if you're anxious at all, ring me. 34S. The local exchange closes down from midnight till eight in the morning, but we're on the same party line. It's three short rings. I'll show you."

"I don't imagine I'll be ringing you," said Marty shortly.

She had intended just to drop into bed after he left, but she unpacked, finding spacious chest and drawer room in the bedroom Mrs. Logie had prepared so lovingly. It would be easier to do it now, with the children in bed, and leave her free to cope with dust and dirt tomorrow.

She had a bath, exulting in the hot water, relaxing limbs and mind. She would pray, oh, how she would pray that the children's parents might recover. She towelled herself vigorously, feeling a new woman. She would go downstairs and look for a torch, so that she might have a last look at the children. She might disturb them if she switched on the light. The twins would be confused if they saw a stranger, and might call for their mother.

Marty buttoned her blue velvet housecoat about her and descended the stairs. She wasn't quite to the landing where the stairs turned when, without warning, the lights went out. The darkness was utter and unnerving. She hesitated, one foot swinging, and clutched the banister rail.

It must be a general power-failure. No wonder, in a wind like this. Suddenly she heard the oddest sound, like the tattoo of a thousand drums, constant, unceasing. Marty's hair prickled and her palms grew damp. What on earth . . .

She steadied her panicking thoughts. It isn't an eerie sound, so don't be silly, Marty, my girl . . . it's just that it's odd, unfamiliar. Then she heard the rain sweep against the casement window on the landing, and realized that it was heavy rain on the corrugated iron roof. Some of the house, the older part, was roofed with tiles, though most of the houses here had iron roofs, but Philip had said this wing had been altered, and had been done temporarily with iron, during a post-war shortage.

Rather shaken, Marty continued down. She must find a candle or a torch, because if the black-out continued she must have some means of getting to the children should they need her, and she doubted if she could find her way to their rooms in darkness.

She went slowly, from step to step. She remembered Daddy saying once, as they settled into a new vicarage: "A house is never really your own till you can walk confidently anywhere within it, in the dark."

He was certainly right. Marty eventually found herself in the living-room, after blundering into a cupboard in the passage, and almost missing this door altogether. She groped to the mantelpiece and found the box of matches she had used to light the fire which by now was merely grey ashes. The box wasn't very full.

The matches helped her to search the store-room and kitchen for candles, but not one was to be found, or a torch. There were so many drawers and cupboards where they might be, and she daren't use too many matches.

Suddenly she remembered there were pale lemon candles in silver candlesticks in the drawing-room. She felt her way to it, anxious not to use any more matches, and hoping she wouldn't knock anything over, for she had noticed this room was full of good ornaments, stuff that might have been heirlooms in pioneer days.

It was a great relief to put up a hand and grasp a candlestick. As she went upstairs with it, she felt like someone strayed in from another century. She carefully switched off as she went, lest the lights come on when she was asleep.

All the children were sleeping like angels. As she bent over small brown Gregory to tuck him in, he rubbed his nose and said sleepily: "Mummy?"

111

Marty said softly, "Yes, darling," kissed his smooth cheek and swallowed a lump in her throat. She went to bed, and fell asleep before she had time to worry over anything.

# 4

SHE awoke to a blaze of sunlight, and realized she had overslept. But it needn't matter as the children were not going to school. Tonight she would find an alarm clock. It seemed still, after the howling gale of the night before.

She slipped out of bed and went to the east window. It was high, and she could see over the tree-tops past the river-bed towards some faintly indigo hills. Oh, that would be the Cashmeres around Christchurch. It didn't seem so remote when you could see the hills above the city.

She came back and went through the glass-doored archway into the porch. It looked north-west. Marty stood entranced. Nothing in yesterday's dust-blinded landscape had prepared her for this.

Beyond the garden lay emerald fields — she thought they called them paddocks here — that sloped down to the creek where willows were greening. There wasn't a house in sight. She could see a horse in one smaller field, the sun shining on chestnut flanks, and further away some sleek Jerseys.

Past the creek the paddocks were larger, some wirefenced, some gorse-hedged and beyond that they swept right to the mountains. Incredibly tall, lovely mountains, with grey-blue shoulders, and glistening snowy peaks. Some of the lower mountains, foot-hills really, were covered with bush, dark and dense, and the whole alpine range was still lit with the dawn flush . . . it was rose and golden, coral and mother-of-pearl and amethyst, deepening and paling, tinting baby clouds till they looked like soap bubbles, shining and iridescent.

Below her lay the garden, a bed of violets right beneath the house sending up an enchanting fragrance. A bed of primroses and polyanthus was a blaze of color, and over a garden seat, in all the glory of powdered gold, hung a perfectly symmetrical mimosa tree.

She heard a scamper in the passage, and Gregory and Gaynor came tumbling in, literally. They inevitably collided in doorways. Marty was to learn. Well, the day was upon her and she didn't doubt it would be a busy one.

Graham came over as she was cooking breakfast, to milk the cows and go around the sheep. He sniffed appreciatively.

"Coffee!" he said longingly, and was easily persuaded to have some and some toast. He was full of the new baby's charms, and already sure no other baby was quite as wonderful.

Marty had been relieved to find the power on, but dismayed when she found the heat storage stove wasn't hot enough to cook anything on. Robin thought her strangely ignorant, and laughed when she looked for switches.

"It's on all the time," he said. "You lift these lids and put the kettle or the pots on. The oven is always hot, too . . . about three hundred and fifty degrees to four hundred, and if you want it hotter, you switch this booster on . . . see, it shows a red light. That takes some of the heat away from the elements on top, though. But you see when there's a power failure it takes a long time to heat up. It takes thirty-six hours to heat up from dead cold when we are away on holidays. It must have been off most of the night, because it's only luke-warm. We'll cover the lids up with this old eiderdown, that'll conserve the heat."

Anne managed to get in: "We could just have cornflakes with cold milk, and use the electric percolator for the coffee."

Marty gazed wrathfully at the stove. "I can't see the advantage of a stove like that!"

Anne giggled. "Well, you see, Marty, power is expensive away out here . . . Now shut up, Robin, I'm telling this . . . You see, there are miles between the houses. So years ago, in the . . . in the — what did you call it? You know, where wasn't much money, oh yes, the depression, everyone had these sort of stoves, because they just charge you a flat rate for them, about sixteen shillings a month, but now the wool cheques are so good, most of the farmers' wives are getting ordinary electric stoves. Mother has one ordered, but she's going to keep the fuel range, just the same. We'll light that for dinner."

Marty looked at the coal-stove in dismay. It was quite unfamiliar, too, wouldn't Philip crow! She hoped he would stay away all day. But she'd have a go at it. Probably Anne would be able to tell her something about it.

Marty laughed. "I suppose there'll be lots of things you will have to teach me. Now, Robin, you get going feeding the poultry, and Anne can help me. I'd love to explore outside, but I daren't. Too much to do. Mr. Stewart said you'd mix the mashes."

Robin departed, the twins with him, and Marty and Anne tackled the dishes and the beds. Marty thought the dishwasher wasn't much of a convenience. It took so long to stack, she'd just as soon have whisked them through in the sink.

"Now show me the exact technique of lighting this stove."

Anne wasn't very sure herself, but Marty experimented, found it had a good draught, and with some fierce West Coast coal for starting it, and some slow local coal to keep it going, soon had the oven hot. She banked it up and began removing dust from the downstairs rooms, but found the children interrupted her a good deal.

This was probably because she was a stranger, and because they still felt the need of reassurance. However, the main thing was that they should have a good dinner today, and tomorrow the older children would go to school. She found out that the school bus passed the gate and took them the five miles in.

The sunshine still enchanted her, dry and golden, glittering on the mountain snows.

"Is this an extraordinarily good day for this time of year?" she asked Anne. Anne shrugged and looked puzzled.

"I mean, Anne, that this could be a day out of the box — you know, an Indian summer day, for winter, or is it usual?"

Anne said: "Oh, we get days like this right through winter, especially in June. July and August are often our wettest months, right in lambing time. We get a lot of frosts here, especially when the snow stays on the mountains, but the days are mainly fair. Dad says we could do with a heavier rainfall."

The phone rang. Philip.

"I've some better news. Joy has recovered consciousness. Not fully, but improving. The Sister is going to tell her the children are all right, and that you are at the helm. I hope she doesn't ask about Leonard. No change in his condition. How did you get on last night when the power failed? Or were you asleep?"

Marty chuckled. "I was on the bend of the stairs and hadn't a clue where candles or lamps or matches were. I finally remembered the fancy ones in the drawing-room and groped my way to them."

"Good girl." Gracious! Was Philip Griffiths actually approving?

He continued: "We didn't know it was off till one of the motherless lambs we'd brought in kicked up the devil of a shindy during the night. It was two a.m., and I was worried about you. I didn't dare ring you, because it would have meant your trying to find your way to the phone in the dark."

Marty went happily to finish cooking the dinner. Graham appeared with a

119

lamb, slimy and weak, and asked Anne to help.

She knew what he was after, produced a large case lined with blankets and with a sort of lamp attached. This was plugged in on the sunny back verandah. The weakling was put into this and Graham and Anne began preparing a bottle for it. Marty was fascinated as they fed it.

"Wonderful what a difference even one drink makes," said Graham. "It wasn't a very bad night, but the mother had died before the lamb could get a drink. If they get even one drink, they survive. We'll have to bring this one up by hand for a day or two, unless we lose a lamb and give this to a foster mother."

The gentle warmth of the lamp was beginning to dry the wool out. "Sometimes we have five or six on the verandah, and two or three in the kitchen," said Anne.

Marty realized there was more to being a mother's help than she had imagined.

When Graham left, she told Anne to set the table on the terrace that looked towards the mountains.

"I'm not going to waste any of this

glorious sunshine," declared Marty. Anne thought she was decidedly queer, but awfully good fun.

So it was that Philip found them, when he came over at one o'clock. He'd been unable to make them hear at the back door, and came around to the terrace.

She saw him come around the side of the house, and went to the steps to greet him, neat and trim in a grey skirt and emerald green twin set, with a green checked gingham apron tied over it. She looked as much a youngster as any of them.

He glanced scathingly at the table.

"Just having a picnic lunch? Something easy? Don't you think the youngsters should have settled down to plain, wholesome food today?"

Marty looked at him. He thought she was taking the easy way . . . sandwiches and biscuits, buffet fashion, she supposed. She subdued the spark in her eyes, and said gently, much too gently for Marty:

"Would you like to check on what we're having? Just to make quite sure it's nutritious? Please feel free do do so."

At that moment Robin and Anne

appeared in the doorway, wheeling in the kitchen tea-trolley. Marty turned from Philip, lifted the twins, complete with feeders, on to their chairs, picked up the serving-spoons on the trolley and untied the top of a large enamel basin.

The most delectable odor rose to Philip's nostrils. Steak-and-kidney pudding, rich with thick brown gravy, onions and carrots. Marty filled five plates. Took the lid off a vegetable dish, disclosed potatoes, baked in their jackets, then another, with cauliflower in a white sauce, with grated cheese, delicately browned, on top.

She looked across the steam at Philip.

"You wouldn't care for some, I suppose?" Her tone was as cold as the dinner was hot.

A reluctant grin broke his severity. "You know da — jolly well I'd love some. Say, 'I told you so!' and get it out of your system!"

The steak-and kidney was followed by an apple pie with a delicious short crust. Philip did full justice to his two helpings.

"But if the stove was off, how did you

get the oven hot enough for pastry?"

"I used the fuel range."

Philip looked at her with respect. "Had you ever used one before?"

She shook her head. "But Anne helped. Would you like tea or coffee? I made some scones."

"I couldn't resist that. Tea, please."

The children ran out on the lawn to play, the dogs leaping about them. Marty piled the dishes on the trolley, wheeled it out to the kitchen. Philip followed.

She made the tea, buttered the man-sized scones, light as a feather, Philip, leaning against the table, watching her. She was acutely conscious of him. She put the cups on a tray, went to lift it. Philip took it from her, put it down.

He took hold of her by the wrists. She kept her eyes down.

"Look up at me," he said, so perforce she looked.

Her pulses began to race, she felt a tide of warmth along her veins. Fancy feeling like this merely because a man's eyes looked into your . . . *Marty, where's your pride, don't give yourself away.*

"I was wrong about you, wasn't I?

123

Very wrong. You're certainly going to pull your weight, aren't you? Was I wrong about you in other ways too . . . I mean . . . ?"

Marty was never afterwards able to analyze what prompted her to answer as she did, wilfully and deliberately. He was all ready to be forgiving and magnanimous, wasn't he? Whatever her motive had been at first in coming to New Zealand, he was prepared to admit her better nature was triumphing. How dare he be so patronizing! And why was she so weak-willed as to positively yearn to leave her hands in his, to return the pressure of them? She knew him only too well, and the power he had to wound her . . .

Her lip curled. "My dear Mr. G . . . Of course I'm willing to pull my weight. I'm out to make a good impression . . . after all, as you know, there's a lot at stake!"

What he might have said next she was not to know, for at that moment Anne and Robin erupted into the kitchen.

"May we have a scone, too?" they asked.

Marty buttered them one each, and

one each for the twins, too, and by the time she had done it, Philip had drunk his tea, said good-bye, and ridden away.

She didn't see him again till next day, though he made a brief phone call that night to say Leonard was recovering consciousness, and that there was more improvement in Joy's condition. Marty had slept well, and it was an easier day with the two children departing at 8.15 on the school bus.

She managed to get the top floor of the house cleaned as well as the ground floor, and felt that soon she would get into a regular routine. She gave the twins their dinner at twelve, and tucked them down for their nap, happy in the thought that she would have a couple of hours entirely to herself, with no need to look constantly for the twins to make sure they weren't in mischief.

Marty had a light lunch, relaxed with a magazine for twenty minutes, then put a leg of mutton in the oven. She would do the vegetables now, and make a pudding. Perhaps it would be a good idea to make a steamed pudding, as it was colder today, though bright with sunshine, after a frost.

Then she sat down to read the booklet of instructions she had found for the washing-machine. She ought to do the washing tomorrow.

A shadow fell across the open doorway, and she looked up. Philip . . . and decidedly cross.

"Who put the cows in that paddock?" he asked.

Marty stared. What could be wrong with that? She felt that the sooner she started to help with the outside work the better. She'd not been engaged as a land-girl, certainly, but in an emergency like this she would like to feel of some use.

She said now, calmly, "I did."

"What for?" His voice was silky with suppressed anger.

"Well, I thought it a jolly shame to leave them in that barelooking field, so when I saw that one, so green and lush, I got them in. They were no trouble, went in quite docilely."

"Docilely!" said Philip. "It's a wonder they didn't push you over to get in. You've put them in the clover! Clover!

And the whole lot of them has got bloat!"

Marty gazed at him uncomprehendingly.

"Ring up Graham, and tell him to come over here right away — tell him hell-for-leather . . . and if you can't get an answer you'd better . . . oh, I suppose you can't ride either. Can you ride a bicycle? Well, thank the Lord for that — if you can't get an answer, get a bike out of the shed by the garage and go for your life over to my place down the track, and beat the gong at the back door to bring Graham from wherever he is."

"But what's — "

She got no further.

"Look, if I'm going to save the cows I can't stand here lecturing you on what bloat is . . . the cows are down, and I've got to get them up. They may have been down some time and I may not save them. I'll have to improvise a trocar, and if there's one thing that makes me sick, it's using that."

He turned away, janked open a kitchen drawer, scattering the contents.

"Do you know where the steel is . . . the steel for sharpening knives?"

127

Marty did know where that was. She produced it. She swallowed and said: "Do you have to use a sharp knife?"

He said grimly: "I'll have to sharpen the steel with a file pretty quick, and stick them with that. You can use even a pocket-knife if you're stuck. But this makes a bigger hole, more like the trocar."

Marty felt her stomach turn over as she rang three short rings. She got Graham immediately, and his exclamation, which he immediately apologized for, was enough to make her feel worse. She had evidently committed the worst crime in the farming calendar. They couldn't be more horrified if she had fed the cows on arsenic!

Graham said quickly: "Look, I think the vet's at Uplands. See if you can get him. If all the cows are down we'll have to work fast. If he's not at Uplands ring the next farm."

Marty felt miserably that soon the whole district would know that the little English girl had put the cows in the clover. The next hour or two was a nightmare to her.

She crept over to the side of one of the big barns near the clover paddock, and peeped around it at Philip. She saw him tackle the first one, measuring a handspan from the hind leg of the cow; saw him plunge the steel into the distended flank, and spring away. When Marty saw the green fermented mess pouring out, she felt more ill than ever she had when on theatre duty in the hospital. She went back to the house.

The children came in off the school bus, and were almost as appalled as the men. Robin, smugly knowledgeable, said:

"Just as well this isn't a dairy farm in the Kaikato, Marty. You might have killed the whole herd."

Marty told him coldly to go and wash his hands.

"No fear," he said, "I'm off to watch the fun!" Callous little brute, she thought!

Marty felt she couldn't settle to anything until she knew the cows either were on their feet again or had succumbed. She made frequent trips to the corner of the barn in the big stableyard to peep around it. She wasn't sure but she thought things were improving. In between her anxious peerings she managed to get on with the preparations for dinner.

She decided the next trip must be her last; she didn't want to be caught looking, anyway. She heard Philip call out to Graham, "I think we caught them just in time," and drew a breath of heartfelt relief. If the Logies came home to find their herd of milking cows wiped out, it would be an even worse start for her than if Philip had bluntly told them she was on the look-out for a wealthy bachelor.

She straightened up, and at that moment heard hoofbeats in the stable-yard. She hoped it wasn't more reinforcements to witness her folly. It was quite enough to have Philip and Graham and the vet know it, though, in any case, she thought miserably, it would be too good a yarn not to spread — how the little new chum at Alpenlinden had thought she would give the cows a real treat and let them loose on clover!

Marty turned to see a woman rider.

She had longed, during the last day or two, to meet some of the women of the district. They would come in time, she knew, but at the moment were giving her time to find her bearings, and she had thought wistfully of a motherly sort, with an ample bosom and an adequate apron, full of advice and philosophical humor to counteract Marty's fears and problems.

But now, she knew at a glance that this horsewoman wasn't the answer to that wish. She sat her mount superbly, arrogantly, bringing the dapple-grey mare right up to Marty, who moved nervously.

The girl swung down, carelessly, yet with grace of movement. She was taller than Marty, and was strikingly beautiful, with dark, smooth hair, entirely unruffled by her ride, drawn back into a knot at the nape of her neck. Her skin was white, matt-surfaced, and the skilful red of her mouth showed against it to perfection. About the slender column of her throat she wore a silk stock, carelessly fastened, and her riding-habit was the last word in elegance, olive green gabardine, fitting like a glove. Her sherry-colored eyes, fringed with black lashes, surveyed Marty appraisingly. She tapped at her high riding-boot with the silver-mounted end of a riding-crop.

Her voice was cool, patronizing. It brought the color to Marty's cheeks.

"Might I ask who you are?"

Oh, for the friendly greeting she had hoped for from the women of the district.

Marty said: "I'm here to help Mrs. Logie in the house."

"Oh, the maid."

Marty was instantly conscious of her ruffled appearance, sure that the turmoil of the last hour showed in her face.

"Did you want something?" she inquired.

The sherry-colored eyes narrowed.

"English, aren't you? Just recently arrived?"

"Very recently. I came on the ship Mr. Griffiths was Liaison Officer on. I've not met the Logies yet."

There was no spontaneous expression of horror for what had happened to the Logies, merely an abrupt, "What's your name?"

This was to place her very definitely as

the maid, Marty knew . . . so much for democratic New Zealand. Marty looked demure, and said meekly:

"Martha."

The girl looked amused. "But how appropriate."

Marty lifted guileless eyes to her. "But my second name is Mary," she said.

She was met with an uncomprehending smile; the girl had missed the allusion completely. Marty could remember her father saying, "I've always had such a sneaking sympathy with Martha — the world has need of its Marthas. I'd like you to be Martha most of the time, one of the world's workers, but when necessary . . . and listeners are very necessary at times, to be Mary."

The next moment Marty lost her feeling of superiority, fleeting as it had been, when the woman said impatiently: "I came to see Mr. Griffiths. Where is he?"

Marty flushed deeply.

"I — I — I'm afraid he's busy, very busy." She stumbled.

She was surveyed coldly.

"He won't be too busy to see me, I

can assure you," she was told. "What's he busy with?"

"With — with the cows. They've got bloat."

"Good Lord! How did that happen?"

"They . . . ate clover."

"Do you mean they got in accidentally? Was a gate left open? Or a fence broken down?"

Marty said reluctantly: "No — o. I put them in the clover."

The reaction was the same as Philip's and Graham's

"*You put them in the clover?*" Then the odd eyes, topaz bright now, glinted with cruel amusement. "Really, how dim *can* one get, I wonder?"

Marty's chin came up. "I'm new to all this," she said. "No doubt I'll learn by experience. Mr. Griffiths is in the paddock behind the red barn."

Marty walked past the woman, and just as she opened the gate into the houseyard, Philip must have come around the corner of the barn, for quite distinctly she heard him say:

"Why . . . Louise!"

Louise . . . a beautiful name for a

beautiful woman. Not a plain, everyday name like Martha! There was something in the way Philip said it that stirred uneasily at Marty's heart. That was absurd, because the woman had been wearing a platinum wedding-ring and an immense solitaire diamond on her left hand. She was evidently well and truly married. As Marty shut the gate, carefully . . . at least she had had that drummed into her, that you never, never leave gates unfastened . . . she heard Louise laugh. Her voice floated back to Marty.

"Poor Philip . . . having quite a time, aren't you, darling? But really, you ought to have more sense than to let raw English immigrants loose on the homestead."

Marty was glad to reach the sanctuary of the house, and gladder still a little later to hear hoof-beats retreating.

At last the commotion subsided. Philip sent word by Robin that they were nearly through, and did she think she could put on a cup of tea. Marty panicked. That meant they would come into the kitchen for it, and she'd have to face them.

She ran upstairs, powdered her hot face, put on a clean apron. To her surprise the men came in amiably, though she hated their air of smug virtue, as at a hard job well done. By a terrific effort at self-control she greeted them as if nothing had happened, though she refused to meet Philip's eyes. She said, as they washed at the sink on the verandah: "I've got dinner for the children, so if you'd like some there's plenty." Graham looked at Philip, and sniffed the appetising aroma.

"Well, I'm all for it — how about it, boss? Neither Philip or myself are any better in the kitchen than you are in the farmyard!"

The three men laughed heartily, and Marty hated them for the laughter. However, it cleared the atmosphere. Marty hurriedly thickened gravy, made sauce for the pudding, whipped cream. The mutton was delicious, as home-killed mutton should be, there were roast carrots, potatoes delicately browned, and baked pumpkin. The soup was cream of celery.

By the time they had done justice to the pudding, the men had mellowed.

The vet grinned across at her. "I could

forgive you anything for a pudding like that."

She poured coffee, put fresh cheese straws in front of them. Philip leaned back, relaxed, then turned to Robin, who was finishing his glass of milk.

"In all the fuss and commotion, I don't believe you've seen to the poultry, have you?"

"Crumbs, no!" Robin wiped a hand across his mouth and started up.

As he went out of the door Marty said casually: "Don't forget to lock the ducks up, Robin. I mean the ones with the ducklings. You left them shut up, so I opened the gate so they could go down to the pond."

Her words had a strange effect on the children and Graham and Philip.

Robin said: "*What?* That pond's full of eels!"

"Eels!" said Marty. "Do you mean — ?"

Graham finished it for her. "It means there won't be a duckling left. We never let them near till they are big."

Philip looked across at her. "Well, ducklings aren't the price cows are, but I think I'd better insure Len against calamity for the time you're in charge, Miss Reddington!" and he laughed.

It could have been his way of lightening the situation, but his laugh finished Marty. She rose to her feet, shaking, and fled.

She reached the haven of her own room, flung herself down on the bed. She'd never live this down. The ducklings might not have represented much cash, but they had been sweet, black and yellow, and adorable. The black had a purply tinge, and Marty had thought they looked like a cluster of purple and yellow pansies . . . and ugly, slimy heads had come up underneath them as they joyously took to the water, and dragged them down. Marty wept.

By and by she felt a little hand come into hers, and she lifted her head and found Gregory, his brown eyes fixed on her anxiously.

He said, gravely: "I did it too. Let the ducks out. When I was very little. They spanked *me*!"

Marty laughed suddenly, sat up and hugged him. "I daresay they wished I was small enough to spank, darling."

"Don't cry any more, will you, Marty?"

"No, I won't, pet. Gregory, do you know if they've gone? Mr. Griffiths, and Graham, and the vet?"

Gregory nodded. "Anne's clearing the table, Philip said she and Robin had to wash up, and we all had to be good. I are good, aren't I?" Marty assured him he was an angel. He added "Why don't you call him Philip? We do."

Marty said hastily: "I've not known him very long yet."

"But you call Graham, Graham!" She took Gregory's hand and went downstairs, saying gaily: "Do you know I'm just in the mood to make fudge tonight." She wished she'd never snubbed Philip about the Christian names. She'd noticed Graham look curiously at them as they continued to be formal, and he himself had bitten off her first name sharply once or twice, not liking to do it, evidently, when his boss didn't.

There was a note against the vase of mimosa, wattle Philip called it. From Philip.

It said: "Dear Marty, thank you for the dinner. If only you leave the farm to us we'll pull through. Your guardian angel — or the ducks — must have been on duty and muzzled the eels — they were all there. Philip." It was a kind note. Marty felt a glow about her heart . . . and he had begun it "Marty", so she could drop formality now. Then her eye fell on the P.S. Scorpion-like, the note carried its sting in its tail. It ran: "P.S. — The vet. is a bachelor . . . a most eligible one, and the way to a man's heart is through his stomach!" Marty screwed it up savagely and threw it in the fire.

As she tucked Anne in, the child's arms came up around her neck to kiss her. Anne said, sleepily: "Gosh, I'm glad you were looking after us, Marty. You're fun. That was lovely fudge. Hope that Louise doesn't come around here much. But she's not staying long."

Marty said curiously, "Doesn't she live here?"

"No. She lives in Australia now. She flew home to visit her mother at Ranui. She used to live here. She was going to marry Philip, but she married someone else instead, a little fat man. Wasn't that a funny thing to do? But Daddy said that Philip had a lucky escape."

Marty tucked her down and put out the light. So that was the woman who had embittered Philip. She wondered how he felt, meeting Louise again. Marty was suddenly conscious of the fact that she was glad Leonard Logie didn't like Louise. Good gracious, that was positively catty. Marty went downstairs, the unacknowledged wish in her heart that Louise would not stay long.

# 5

TWO days later Philip came to take Marty into the hospital to see Joy. She and Len were off the seriously ill list, but were still badly injured people.

"We'll leave the twins at Sandersons at Lauriston," he said.

Marty was very quiet. She wanted to be undisturbed when she met Mrs. Logie, for the few minutes allowed. Joy had constantly asked to see the girl who was looking after her children.

Philip said suddenly, a note of laughter in his voice:

"You certainly made an impression on the vet the other night." Marty did not reply, so he added: "I'm not taking a rise out of you. You did make an impression — a good one."

"I know I did." Her tone was calm. Philip shot a glance at her. She continued, in an indifferent tone, "He rang me this morning, to see if I would go to a dance with him in Ashburton, on Saturday night."

Philip hesitated, then said: "Are you getting a baby-sitter in? Would you like me to ask someone? Or come myself?"

Marty was roused. "Do you think for a moment I'll go — leave the children who are my responsibility?"

Philip said quietly: "You are entitled to time off, you know."

Her tone was sharp. "I'll take time off when Mrs. Logie gets home. Not before."

She felt that he approved that, but couldn't resist goading her.

"But what a pity to have to pass up an opportunity like that. I told you he was a bachelor, and an eligible one, didn't I?"

Now her tone was dry, controlled. "It depends what you mean by eligible."

"His father is Hervington-Blair of Blair Hills," said Philip. "That won't convey anything to you, but if you were a New Zealander, it would. His great-grandfather came out in the *Charlotte Jane*, one of the First Four Ships. Great landowners, politicians, philanthropists, but Morgan's heart is in veterinary

143

work. Eligible is the word all right; why, a seven-thousand-a-year wool clip is nothing to the Hervington-Blairs. They've got a finger in every pie in the Dominion, and overseas. And Morgan has the name of being hard to please where girls are concerned."

"Of course," said Marty levelly, determined not to lose her temper, "one does look for other things besides money."

"What, for instance?"

She waved a hand. "Oh, kinship of spirit, a sense of humor, kindliness . . . yes, Philip, *especially kindliness*."

"Morgan *is* kind — "

"I imagine he is . . . in contrast to some of the men I've met here. That wouldn't be hard."

He took the point, laughed. "You're a foeman worthy of my steel, Marty." He added, in a different tone: "So . . . you're looking for a kindred spirit, kindness, a sense of humor . . . all this and money too? And what about love, Marty, what about love?"

What about love? She daren't answer that truthfully. She looked at the lean, sinewy hand on the wheel, then averted her eyes. Oh, Philip, Philip, what about love?

"I've tried love," she said, in a tight voice, "and found it wanting. Do you mind if I change the subject? I'm thinking mainly of Mrs. Logie and how we'll find her this afternoon."

They found her swathed in bandages, but able to smile a welcome with her eyes. Philip stooped and kissed her cheek, and murmured something Marty couldn't hear. Marty touched her fingers gently.

"I'm sorry to meet you just like this, Mrs. Logie, but I'm looking forward to seeing you in your own home before long."

Joy's voice was weak. "I'm so grateful that they are in their own home. I knew by all Fergus and Philip told me that the children would be all right." A shadow darkened her eyes for a moment. "Philip, would you see Lennie now, and come back and tell me how he is? Not what I'd like to hear . . . something carefully censored so's not to set me back — but how he really is. I lie here and imagine all sorts of things, but you wouldn't lie to me."

Philip rose instantly. "Right, Joy. They tell me he's doing better, in fact the doctor said he was more pleased with Len than with you."

A light lit the green eyes in the bandage-swathed face for a moment. Philip said:

"I daresay there are lots of things you want to ask Marty about the children."

He was back shortly, calm and confident.

"It's all right, Joy. Len asked exactly the same about you. He's got the broken arm and leg to contend with, of course, but I think his head injuries aren't as bad. They have just told him that in a day or two they might be able to wheel his bed along here . . . or yours to him, forget which."

Joy was as radiant as possible with so small an area of face visible.

"Then things aren't so bad. If we are both still in the one piece, we'll make it yet. When I first struggled back to awareness again, I was horribly afraid that the children might yet be left orphans."

Marty swallowed. Parenthood certainly

brought responsibilities. Joy wasn't concerned for herself, just for the children.

Joy took a breath, smiled, and added "But here we are with the incredible luck of having a trained nurse to look after the children. If you knew what it means . . . I've been lying here letting my imagination run riot, seeing all sorts of things happen that only a mother could foresee, or cope with."

Marty saw Philip glance at her quickly, then look away. He evinced no surprise at this item of news, merely smiled, and said: "Yes, we did the right thing, didn't we, bringing Marty here? Well, we must go, the nurse is hovering anxiously in the corridor. If this visit hasn't excited you too much, we may be allowed longer next time."

Philip waited till they were heading up Alford Forest Road, then he said quietly, reasonably:

"I think you might have told me you were a nurse, Marty. You've made a fool of me. I've not only put my foot in it wholesale, advising you to give the children wholesome food and see they get to bed early, and so on, but have advised you in a very amateurish way from my recollection of what Joy used to do, on handling them and what to do if they hurt themselves in any way. I was most concerned lest some accident might happen to them, at this distance from a doctor, and with an inexperienced girl in charge. But you didn't reassure me; just let me blunder on."

Marty flushed. She knew she was in the wrong, so she said coolly:

"You never asked me if I could do anything but typing and shorthand. You were so sure I was a feather-brain. I thought that nothing but practical demonstration to the contrary would convince you. I was not the one, in New Zealand House, who confessed to being able to attempt nothing more in the cooking line than a fried egg. And I'm quite sure that if I had said to you, on the way from Christchurch, when you were so pessimistic about my being able to cope, that I had kept house for my father longer than I had been a typist, and that I had trained as a nurse, it would only have made you more determined to make me realize that nevertheless an English girl, horribly ignorant of country ways, couldn't compare with a New Zealand one."

"Marty! You don't honestly think that! Some folk, but precious few, may be prejudiced against newcomers, but I've never dreamed you thought that of me. I thought I'd done all I could for the folk on board the *Captain Banks*, to help them settle in as soon as possible, and as painlessly. It wasn't just a job to me, thrust upon me at the last moment, but a mission.

"If you think that, you have no idea how strong the links are that bind us to Home. Most of us are no more than fourth-generation New Zealanders, and plenty are only second. Nearly all of us can say, and are proud to say, 'My parents came from Home' or 'My grandparents came from Home.' We're very much a part of the Commonwealth. We aren't foreigners."

"That may be true enough generally," said Marty bitterly. "I saw what you did and how you did it on board the ship, so I do realize it's just personal antagonism between the two of us. We simply rub each other up the wrong way. We don't meet on common ground at all."

She managed a grin, and added wickedly: "But don't feel too frustrated. I'm not infallible, in fact, I'm not even fully trained, so you might easily find something to cavil at yet!"

She saw Philip's hands tighten on the wheel, and knew her words had found their mark.

He said: "And why didn't you finish your training?"

"I had my reasons — personal ones."

His look was shrewd. "Not enough money in it, perhaps? Or too few opportunities of meeting the right people . . . unattached doctors, for instance."

That bit, but Marty managed a laugh.

"By the way," she said, "it won't help Mrs. Logie if she guesses there is friction between us, so when we visit her again we must be careful. I shall be all sweetness and light, you can be all kindness and chivalry."

Philip changed the subject. "On Sunday morning, it's service here, at St. Ninian's, here in Linden Peaks. Fergus's first one back in N.Z. There'll be a good crowd out."

"What do you mean? Don't they have service every Sunday morning?"

"No. Alternate Sundays the service is at night. Fergus has five preaching-places altogether. That's usual in the country. You don't just serve the village you are in. His parish goes twenty miles in one direction, more than twenty in the other. He takes a service in the afternoon, also. Some places have two services a month, that way, some only one."

"Mr. MacNeill must do a terrific amount of travelling."

"He does. The church recognizes that, and pays him nearly three hundred pounds a year car allowance. It only just covers it. Depreciation on our roads is something to be reckoned with. He does so much country visitation, too. In some parts he spends a night or two away, staying at a homestead, and taking an odd service in people's houses. That's the part he loves about the country work. Much more satisfying, he says, than tea-parties in town.

"We have Sunday school during the

service, because most of the children have to be brought. The two older ones go to Sunday school. I'll come over and pick you up, if you think the twins won't be too much for you during the sermon. Or would you prefer me just to take the older ones? I know you are Anglican."

Marty said: "Is there a Church of England in the village?"

"No. The nearest is Barrhill, an out-station of St. Mark's, Rakaia. When Joy and Len get home, I'll take you there on alternate Sundays if you wish."

This was heaping coals of fire on her head, and it would be churlish to refuse. She had been ungracious enough as it was.

She said: "Thank you, Philip, that's very kind. I shan't bother you as regularly as that, though I'd like to go occasionally. Daddy was very ecumenically-minded. He'd think I could worship just as well in a Presbyterian church. When we lived in Northumberland, where Presbyterianism is strong, and there was a good deal of intermarrying, he and the local minister were very friendly, and they both used to agree that it didn't matter much which church a newly-wed couple joined up with, as long as they both went together."

"I agree with that," said Philip. So it was that, for once, they came home in peace.

★ ★ ★

The days slipped by and August was nearly over. Now the lambs were coming thick and fast, and there was little time for argument, or for fellowship.

Graham's wife came home, and Marty found a new friend.

"Thank goodness you're a nurse," said Rhona. "I'd not realized what a responsibility it was, coming home with a new baby. The first night I was scared stiff to sleep. I kept listening to him breathing in case he suffocated or something. I nearly drove Graham wild. But at least I do know that if I'm at all puzzled, I can ring you. The Plunket nurse will call every week till he's three months old, but I've never felt so helpless in my life. I've never even handled a new baby before, much less become responsible for its very life. I certainly had no idea how much work they entailed . . . but look at him, isn't he adorable?"

Marty looked at the young mother instead, and her look was shrewd. There were shadows under the big brown eyes, and a look of strain about the mouth. Later Marty went in search of Philip. She found him in the milking-shed.

"Philip, I want to talk to you, but I'm a bit diffident."

That was disarming. He smiled down on her, twinkling.

"It's a new experience to see you diffident, Marty."

"It's Rhona. It's a terribly busy time of year to bring a new baby home, and, like all new mothers, she's over-anxious. She doesn't realize she's not perfectly fit yet, and that she needs more rest while she's feeding the baby. Probably neither you nor Graham realize that nursing a babe is as big a drain on the mother's energy as pregnancy."

Marty sounded very matter-of-fact.

"It's not as easy for her, Philip, as if she was in her own home. Then she could let things go, if she wasn't up to it, or if the baby had an off day. She keeps your house perfectly, too perfectly. She ought to be told to take things more easily . . . but it would have to come from you. She'll crack up if she doesn't rest more. As it is, she's on her feet from morning till night. She ought to have an hour's rest after lunch when she's got baby down again. But please don't think I'm interfering or suggesting you work her too hard."

Philip put his hand on her shoulder.

"I don't think you're interfering. Don't worry about that. I know it's not ideal. Young couples should be on their own. Not only that, but as yet my home is small, and I know she worries if the baby cries during the night and disturbs me. I've had plans for a married couple's cottage to be put up, but it's going to take time, and I'm afraid we've let it slip with all this extra work on Alpenlinden. Only last night, I was reading in the paper about some pre-fab houses. Could get one down. Won't be as charming as a cottage, or as roomy, but the main thing would be to resolve the situation. Meanwhile I'll have a yarn with Rhona and tell her not so much spit and polish. Is there anything else you could suggest?"

Marty hesitated. "Ye-s. But I run the risk of — "

"Risk of what?" His glance was keen.

"The risk of — being misunderstood."

The corner of his mouth twitched. "I'll try not to misunderstand. Come on."

"Well, I'd like to be of practical help. It's not much use criticizing. I wondered if it would help Rhona if I offered to give you your dinner at Alpenlinden. You are always across about dinner-time, milking and going round the ewes. But I wouldn't like you to think I . . . " she stopped again, color flaming into her fair skin.

Philip stared, then understood. He chuckled.

"It's all right, Marty." The grey eyes danced. "After all that has happened between us, I'd not suspect you of trying to set your cap at me!"

Marty was weak with relief, and laughed with him.

"Yes. It's pure neighborliness."

"I'll remember that," he assured her solemnly. "Actually, I think you're a brick to offer. It's extra work for you, and goodness knows you work hard enough now."

The unexpected tribute brought the tears to Marty's eyes. She turned away quickly, embarrassed. Philip swung her around.

"What's the matter?"

"Nothing — nothing. I'm — I'm just being silly."

His hands gripped her shoulders. "Tell me what it is? Are you suddenly homesick?"

She shook her head again. "Philip, let me go. I'm just being childish."

She twisted in his hold, then suddenly winced.

He let go of her shoulders then, and caught her wrists.

"I hurt you. Have you strained your shoulder?"

She was glad to get away from the more personal theme, and had blinked away the tears by now.

"No . . . it's always tender."

"What do you mean, always tender?"

She shrugged. "A relic of the blitz. I was only ten and they thought in time it would be as good as new. But it played up again when I took up nursing, and I had to give it up because of it and take to typing. I couldn't lift the patients. Occasionally it gives out. But not often."

"Tell me about it . . . if it doesn't upset you. What happened?"

"A beam fell on me. Right at the end of the war, it was. It was rather a while before they got me out."

"You mean . . . you mean you were buried?"

"Yes."

"How long?"

"Six hours."

He was silent. Suddenly there was kinship between them, one of the rare occasions when Marty knew that if only they had met under different circumstances, they might have found . . . they might have found — well, much in common.

Philip broke the silence by saying: "Are you sure it won't add too much to your own work? School breaks up for the spring vacation next week, and you'll probably find it somewhat hectic. Most mothers feel glad when the children get off to school again."

"Our mother didn't," said Marty. "Mother loved the holidays as much as we did. She was always busy with parish affairs, but every moment she could spare she was out with us gipsying about the countryside, picnicking and bathing."

Philip said curiously: "I thought you were an only one!"

"I was the youngest of four. I had two brothers, and a sister. We all slept in the same wing of the Vicarage. The others were killed when the wall fell."

Philip's hands slid from her wrists to take her hands within his strong warm ones. He drew her nearer him, bent his head, laid his cheek against hers in wordless sympathy.

There was a step outside, and they sprang apart. Philip picked up a bucket, Marty moved swiftly to the door. It was Louise, once more in riding-clothes, perfectly groomed.

She looked from one to the other. "Graham told me you were here, Phil," she drawled, in the curiously harsh voice that was the flaw in her charm. "She

159

didn't say Marty was, too."

Marty felt guilty, for no reason at all. "Oh, I just came over to see Philip about something. I'm going now." She made her escape, aware that her color was heightened.

If only Louise had not come just then! That had been Philip at his best, as he should be, had not first his mother, then Louise, warped and twisted him in his opinion of women.

And yet . . . perhaps after all it was as well they had been interrupted. These softened moods soon passed with Philip. Many more moments like that, and she would betray herself. She was reading too much into it. Any man would react like that in a sympathetic moment.

Philip's step was light as he came along the verandah that evening, whistling, and Marty's heart lifted. He was glad to be coming. He stood in the doorway and smiled.

She took the soup-pot off the stove, and smiled back.

"You sound very carefree."

"I am. A real piece of luck. Bill and Hine Lancaster are coming to

160

Alpenlinden as a married couple. Leonard will be glad. He knows Bill well. Bill's done shearing here years ago. A splendid worker, and Hine's so good-natured, always willing to lend a hand anywhere. They've evidently been wanting to get away from the farm they are on for some time.

"The farmer is a real muddler, and miserly to boot, though their real reason is that Maraea is nearly four, so next year they'll want to be nearer a school. This other place isn't served by school bus. Hine would have to put her on correspondence lessons. They're coming next week. I did mention the possibility to Leonard and he leapt at the idea.

"After dinner we'll go across to the married couple's house, and see what it's like. Leonard said the other woman was a very poor housekeeper, and had left it in a terrible state, and their accident happened before Joy had a chance to get at it."

The house was set in trees, too, but younger trees than around the old homestead, and the garden was well set out, though weedy. It was a five-roomed bungalow, low-set and attractive.

"Leonard believes in housing his men well, and this is the place where Joy and Len first set up house. Len's father was running the farm then, and when he married Joy, they built this. By the way, Marty, I wrote the Logies' parents last night. They'll get the letter when they arrive in London. They couldn't get a letter before, and it was just as well that they couldn't, for the news of Joy and Len is so much more cheering now. I've told them not to let it shorten their trip to Europe any, they've waited so long for it, and that if they were really needed, I'd let them know."

Marty was appalled at the state of the house inside, though it would be a lovely home when restored. There were inlaid linoleums throughout kitchen and scullery, with a delightful wall-to-wall carpet in the lounge, and charming curtains.

The young couple would bring their own furniture, but there were all conveniences here, a washing-machine, a fridge, electric water heating as well as the wet-back grate in the living-room, which would heat the bath water in winter.

The electric stove was thick with grease, the stainless steel bench heaped with rubbish, and the wallpapers torn and scribbled on.

"If you and I could get it cleaned up, Marty, I could get a firm of decorators out to re-paper and paint it. Haven't time to paint it myself just now. The lambs are coming thick and fast, and Leonard's stud stuff is due to start. It will mean working day and night."

"I could manage most of this myself, Philip. I've got the big house in running order now, and Anne's a tremendous help."

Philip was adamant. "I'll help you with it. You're looking a bit wan. You've worked too hard. You have never been off the place since you came, except to visit hospital. If I hadn't been so busy, I could have left things to Graham, and taken you out for a change, but with two properties it has been hectic. And the Lord only knows when I'll get on with my own building programme again."

His house was obviously unfinished. Philip was building it himself with expert advice when necessary. Marty wondered why, when none of these property holders could lack money. Philip's home had every labor-saving device, but lacked the luxuriousness of Alpenlinden. In time it would be a magnificent home, but his furnishings were very plain, almost utility stuff. Probably Louise had given him up before he had started to furnish his house, and he had lost heart. At times Marty suspected Philip of being cheese-paring. But it didn't matter to her, couldn't . . .

She enjoyed putting the house in order again. Philip took almost a whole day off to help her. They took the twins over with them, and a picnic lunch, and quite enjoyed the change. To Marty the day held a bitter-sweet quality. This was the sort of thing engaged couples did, preparing a house to welcome their living together.

She would be able to tell Mrs. Logie about it when she went in to visit her next. Joy was able to sit up now, and was progressing steadily. Philip was taking Marty in on Friday. She would have liked to have done some shopping in

Ashburton (Rhona said it had quite a good shopping area), but she didn't like to ask Philip to spend the time when he was so frantically busy.

She looked longingly at the Armstrong Siddeley in the garage. The other car was a complete write-off and had gone to the wreckers, but there was a Land Rover and a truck, and this lovely car, sleek and polished.

On a sudden impulse Marty got into the front seat. She examined the dashboard and the gears carefully, started the engine, and backed out into the paddock. Plenty of room here to familiarize herself with a strange car and no harm done.

Marty loved the feel of a wheel under her fingers again . . . that settled it. Tomorrow she would take the twins over to Sanderson's, and continue in to town herself. She would have time then to shop for what the children needed, and some sturdier shoes and a new pair of slacks for herself, but what would Philip say?

She knew he would veto it. She had learned prudence in the matter of farming lore, not attempting anything since her disastrous venture with the cows and ducklings, but in driving Philip could teach her nothing. She picked up a road code booklet from the glove pocket and studied it.

It wasn't like driving on the Continent where you had to accustom yourself to driving on the right side of the road. They used the left here. She scanned through it . . . give way on the right . . . extra caution on the level crossings . . . 30 miles per hour through townships, 50 mile speed limit on the open roads. She'd be all right. But she would not phone Philip — a note on the back door that he could read only after she'd gone, would be better.

All went to schedule. Marty was away at 12:45, and had her shopping done by 2:30, when she arrived at the hospital. She parked the car and got out. Philip appeared, from nowhere seemingly.

"Good afternoon, Philip," she greeted him blithely, albeit a shade defiantly.

"Good afternoon," he said, unmistakable signs of displeasure on his face.

She turned to lock the car doors, her heart behaving most erratically. Philip put out a hand and stopped her.

"Don't lock up yet, I prefer to do my quarrelling in private. Get in." He opened the door for her.

Marty slid in between the wheel and the seat, subduing a dimple. Philip got in at the other side.

She looked up at him saucily. "I can see you are minded to play the heavy hand again," she said, her blue eyes sparkling.

"I could spank you," said Philip between his teeth.

Marty purposely looked surprised, wide-eyed.

"Would the Logies really object to my bringing in the car to do some much-needed shopping for myself and the youngsters, and to visit hospital? I think not."

"That's not the point — you might have killed yourself or smashed up the car."

Marty smoothed her gloves, looking down on them.

"Which would be the more upsetting?" she wondered aloud.

Philip drew in a deep breath. "I think

you know. It was foolhardy, Marty. You aren't used to these heavily-metalled roads. I expected to find you turned over at every corner."

"What an opinion the man has of my driving . . . which is based on ignorance, of course. After all, having driven my father around London . . . London, mark you, for two years, I don't think Ashburton will get me rattled, a little town of — well, what is it? Seven or eight thousand people?"

"Ten thousand. It seems mighty small to you. I know, but you needn't be so upstage about it. And you took a big risk coming in without a licence. You might have got pinched."

"I wasn't born yesterday," said Marty. "I rang the Traffic Department from Alpenlinden. I explained I was more or less marooned, told the transport officer I had driven in London, *and* on the Continent, and he just chuckled, and said: 'Right. You could probably teach me a thing or two. Come right in and I'll give you a New Zealand licence'." She looked up at him, devilment in her eyes. "And, of course, I needn't ask you not to mention this to Mrs. Logie, or Mr. Logie. It would be hardly fair to worry them, would it?"

"You minx!" he said. "It's this round to you, but heaven help you next time you cross me!"

At that moment the door on Philip's side was wrenched open, and the padre looked in. He couldn't help but hear what was said.

He looked amazed. "You two aren't still fighting!"

"These redheads!" sighed Philip, turning the tables. "Well, I hope Joy and Len are improved today."

The padre walked in with them. The Logies were certainly improved. Leonard had been down for an X-ray, and they had wheeled his stretcher into Joy's room.

"We'll leave you here for visiting-time," said the sister.

"I'm getting better for sure," said Joy. "I'm beginning to fret about things at home. I keep wondering how the lambs are getting on, and if any of the fowls have gone broody. Len says it pays to buy seven-weeks-old white Leghorns in September and October. I know it's best if you want winter layers, so we always do, but I think it's lovely to see hens with chicks, so even if they don't pay as well, we get them."

"We've got banties sitting all over the place," Marty told her. "Robin's very good with poultry. He's managing the lot. I'm afraid I don't know much about hens, or ducks — either" — (she caught Philip's eye and hastily averted her own) — "but Anne chops Robin's kindling for him, so both are happy."

Joy looked at Marty fondly. "I'm so glad you've taken to the country life so well. You seem to cope with everything."

Marty flushed. "Oh, I make a few mistakes, Mrs. Logie, but I'm learning."

Joy laughed. "I still make mistakes, Marty, we all do. What I'm really so happy about is that the children have taken to you so well. Rhona says you manage them beautifully, and that they are very happy."

Marty smiled mistily. "Not half as happy as they'll be when you come home."

"I'll be immensely glad of your help then. I won't be able to cope with all the work right away, and if this had happened before you came, we'd have been stuck. Might have been able to get a temporary housekeeper, probably not, and in any case, they don't always get on with the children. You're young enough to put up with their noise and high spirits."

"And young enough to be married within the year," predicted Leonard somewhat gloomily.

Joy looked aghast. "I'd not thought of that. You're much too pretty to last!"

Marty said hastily, to change the subject, "I — I was going to ask you if I could do some sewing. The weather is getting warmer, and the twins seem to have grown out of their last summer's things. I noticed you had some things cut out in the sewing-room. A couple of pairs of denim dungarees, and a lovely yellow checked frock and pantie set for Gaynor, and some dear little brown corduroy trousers for Gregory. I love making tousers."

Joy gazed at her. "Marty . . . you don't mean you can sew, too? Isn't this marvellous? I do sew, but only when I have to, if I can't buy what I want ready-made. In fact, I'd rather drive the tractor than sit at the sewing-machine. Marty, you're a gem. You can bake and you can brew . . . and sew, too . . . and you look like something out of *Vogue*. But I can see what will happen. The moment Marty gets out and about Alpenlinden will just become the happy hunting-ground for all the young bloods of the district. Philip, why didn't you bring someone with the same qualifications, but fair, fat and forty!"

"Blame the padre, not me!" said Philip.

Marty, cheeks flaming, said: "Please stop, you're making me embarrassed. I don't want a retinue."

Philip said, meaning in his tone that only Marty understood: "Oh, there won't be a retinue . . . not if Marty has anything to do with it. Marty is very discriminating, she knows exactly what she wants. You wouldn't play around with a dozen, would you, Marty?"

His tone was light, but Joy looked puzzled and would have pursued it, but evidently Philip remembered that they were to be outwardly friendly for Mrs. Logie's peace of mind, so he said hurriedly: "Marty has another accomplishment, too. She can drive the car."

Marty stiffened, but Leonard said easily: "Oh, that's good. Take the Armstrong Siddeley any time you wish, Marty. Be very handy if you want to bring the older children in for new shoes or anything. Just pick them up after school, and bring them in. Give you a bit of a chance to see around the countryside, too. Take a run out whenever you feel like it. You must be awfully tied in. Only be careful on our heavily shingled roads. You can positively float on shingle, and the car soon gets out of control."

"Thank you, Mr. Logie," said Marty sweetly, "I don't think I'll be able to spare much time for sight-seeing, but it will be handy to be able to come into Ashburton. It's been such a chore for Philip." She flickered a smile in Philip's direction.

# 6

THE Logies didn't get home as soon as hoped. They went by ambulance to Dunedin to the neuro-surgical department there for a check-up. It was rather a strain till a good report for both came through. They had all worried lest the examinations reveal need for serious brain operation for either or for both.

Nevertheless time flew, for the lambing kept them busy. The weather turned stormy as soon as the children started their holidays, with bitter gales sweeping the plains, and cold winds from the mountains, endless rain and hail. The kitchen at Alpenlinden was full of wet, bleating lambs. There weren't enough lamps and boxes for all, and sometimes they had to bath them, rubbing the hot water well in, and drying them in front of the range.

"Hope this won't knock you up," said Philip. "After all, you're not used to this."

"Do I look any the worse for it?" demanded Marty. "Oddly enough, though I admit I'm dead-beat at night, I'm enjoying it. I could have gone to a secretarial job in the city that would have been little different from life in London. This is stimulating." She wouldn't admit that what she found most pleasure in was working with Philip, though they still struck sparks from each other. Even though at times she tried to convince herself she hated him, she was always listening for his steps, his whistle, his voice quietening the dogs.

The pre-fab house for Rhona and Graham came down on a particularly foul day. Nevertheless Rhona was starry-eyed over it, and managed most of the moving-in herself, with help from Marty.

The Lancasters were held up because of small Tiaki going down with measles, so they were still short-handed. Philip spent so much time at Alpenlinden that he took to having lunch and dinner at the homestead.

"It'll be foul luck if this continues till

the stud stuff starts, after such a good lambing season so far," said Philip.

It did. They had mishap after mishap. "You wouldn't read about it," said Graham savagely, looking desperately tired. "Everything that can happen has happened. You'd think there was a hoodoo on the place. Philip is going to feel very badly. It would have happened much the same if Leonard had been here, except that we'd have had much more time to spare for special attention, but Philip feels responsible."

Then, suddenly, the weather cleared. Marty stood the row of indescribable gum-boots out in the sun, scrubbed the back verandah and the kitchen floor, fed the lambs, and got them outside in a wire-netted enclosure.

Philip had been working amongst the stud stuff all morning, some distance from the house, and hadn't bothered with morning tea. He came in, looking pleased, scrubbed-up.

He sat down for lunch. "Much better morning. Wonderful what a bit of sun does. First birth this morning the ewe had twin lambs, perfectly natural birth, bonny lambs. Both rams."

"Are rams better than ewes?" asked Marty, puzzled.

"With stud stuff, yes. Len'll get ten guineas for ewes later on, and thirty for the rams. The next one was good, too, and it continued all morning. I'll go back up after lunch, although I'm not anticipating any trouble."

It was not to be. Graham rang from Ngaio Bend. Philip was needed on his own place.

"If I'm not back by the time young Robin gets home, Marty, get him to take the pony up, and go round those sheep. I'm fairly happy about them, but you never can tell. I'll be back for milking, but I'd be glad if I knew someone had gone up."

At half-past three Marty got a ring from Jocelyn MacNeill at the Manse.

"Miss Reddington, Robin and Anne are here at the Manse, playing. Mum isn't home yet, but we asked Dad before he went out visiting, and he said it would be all right, and they could stay for tea and he'd run them home."

"Yes, it's all right," said Marty. No

use saying any other, for the school bus would be gone by now. She rang to see if she could get hold of Philip, but couldn't raise Ngaio Bend at all. She realized Rhona would probably be away up with the men's afternoon tea. If they were some distance from the house, she would pop the baby's basket in the truck and drive over with it. There were tracks all around the paddocks.

It was no use getting Philip over if the stud sheep were all right, though she was prepared to go over on the bicycle for him if necessary. She'd ride up on the bicycle to see how the ewes were. After all, since she had done maternity she knew enough to decide if any ewe wanted assistance.

The twins were still asleep, they had gone down late today. She had a peep at them, made sure the fire was low, and got out the machine. She pedalled furiously. She really didn't like leaving the children alone for long.

Thank goodness the ground was so flat. There were big shelter belts of macrocarpa in this paddock, and a clump of gums, giant trees, under which most of the ewes were lying. She could ride right up to them. From here none of them appeared to be in trouble. It was a perfect scene, the tall gums, the maternal ewes, the few fleecy lambs, white against the green, and beyond, the breathtaking beauty of the snow-capped mountains.

A huge ewe, still showing signs of the recent birth, was standing up, two tiny lambs beside her. Oh, that would be the one with the twin rams.

There was a slight slope here down to the gums, so the bicycle accelerated its speed. That silly little lamb was bounding right up, its twin following. Marty jammed the back pedal brake on, but not soon enough. The lamb crashed into the front wheel, got its legs tangled up in the spokes, and Marty, the bicycle, and the lamb went down in a heap together.

Marty knew exactly what damage had been done. She had heard the snap of bones as they went down. She was on her feet in a moment, utterly dismayed. The lamb was in a heap, its front legs crumpled grotesquely, bleating piteously.

Marty was aghast, appalled. The ewe

charged up, much agitated. Philip would be beyond words. She felt sick. There was nothing she could do for the lamb. Nothing Philip would be able to do either. But she would have to get him, he would have to put it out of its misery. The tiny thing was so distressed. Just five minutes ago it had been so sweet, like the illustration in the spring number of an English magazine.

If only she knew what was best to do. Should she take the lamb to the house . . . but that would upset the ewe, and hurt the lamb. The bicycle was useless, she must run all the way.

She arrived at the house, took two or three deep breaths, and rang Ngaio Bend. She hoped someone was in by now. She was fortunate there. Philip himself answered the phone. Marty felt courage ooze out of her her legs felt as if they might give way any moment.

She said "Oh, I'm so glad you're in — I — "

Philip said sharply: "What's the matter? I was just leaving here to come over."

He had been ready to come! It was all in vain!

180

Somehow she told him. Philip uttered not a single word of censure or reproach . . . she was right in that . . . this was the ultimate in her blunders . . . he was beyond speech!

He said, tersely: "I'll ride over straight away. I'll not come to the house first, I'll go to the paddock and put it out of its misery. I'll see you on the way back."

That last had an ominous sound. Marty replaced the receiver, heard the twins call out. She went up to them, thankful to have something to do. She went on with the preparations for the dinner, scarcely knowing what she did. She was all the time listening for hoof-beats. They came, stopped.

Marty could see the knife at his belt as he came in the door, his wide shoulders blocking out the sunlight. He leaned up against the bench, looking at her, his face resigned and grim.

Marty backed against the kitchen table, her hands feeling for the edge of it, sure she needed some support. She was directly opposite him. Now the vials of his wrath would be loosed upon her, and

181

she deserved it all this time.

If only she could keep the tears back. She hated to weep, and it always enraged men, anyway. They felt at such a disadvantage, such brutes when women wept.

He took a step towards her, put out a hand.

"Don't look like that, Marty. The skies won't fall because Alpenlinden has one lamb less, even a lamb like that. Leonard Logie won't put that in the scales against all you are doing for his children. Besides, it doesn't only happen to new chums, you know." He grinned reminiscently. "As a matter of fact, I did exactly the same thing once. Lambs are so damned curious they'll trot up to anything that doesn't make a noise. I was only a youngster, and a bit unhappy because it was the year Dad died. I was helping on a farm for the holidays. I got into a frightful row. The farmer clocked me one on the ear."

It was too much for Marty, the sympathetic tone, the sudden lightening of the situation, the stress she had labored under, and the warmth of his hands on her arms. The tears spilled over. Heavens! How humiliating to let Philip Griffiths see her in tears.

She tried to twist and turn away, but he had her fast. His hand came up to her hair in a soothing gesture. Marty crumpled up, buried her face against him and wept. Presently, when her sobs subsided, she found a large handkerchief being pushed into her hand.

"My chest is getting rather dewy," said Philip, laughing.

Marty managed a laugh herself.

"I'm sorry, Philip. I don't usually lose control. I was terrified to meet you, and — and you looked so — "

"I expect I did look fierce. But it wasn't anger against you. If my face was set, it was because, though I do it so often, I just hate killing anything. I can't help it. It never gets any better."

Marty stared up at him, and smiled through her tears.

"Oh, Philip . . . I think that's rather nice."

His eyes glinted with laughter. "You are a little wretch. You do all sorts of things to deflate my ego. You're rather surprised to suddenly find something to admire about me, aren't you?" His tone changed, became more serious. "But the worst of the rough time is over, Marty. The Lancasters arrive tomorrow, and it will be good for you to have another woman within hailing distance. When they get settled, I'll take you out somewhere. All work and no play isn't good for Jill, either."

Marty said, wistfully: "I suppose Hine is very good at the outside work?"

Philip looked down at her, the corner of his mouth lifting in that way that did all sorts of things to Marty.

"Hine would have to learn just as you have done. The hard school . . . experience. Leave the twins with her sometimes, and come up to the lambing paddocks with me for a few mornings. I thought the other day you'd probably be jolly good at it. You took maternity, didn't you? Well, you might be able to give me a few pointers. You'd not be embarrassed, would you?"

"Hardly! I'd love to come. I feel I won't indentify myself with the farming life till I really know things."

Marty was conscious for the rest of the day of a warmth about her heart, a lightness in her spirit. But she must be careful, mustn't let herself reveal how she felt about Philip. There could never be anything more than good comradeship between them. Philip was too eligible, too knowledgeable . . . his wool-clip stood between them. Besides, Rhona had said once: "I don't think he'll ever marry. He worshipped the ground Louise walked on. He's evidently lost heart in finishing his house. No wonder. It must be terrible to plan a place to house the one you love, and to have to occupy it alone." Perhaps Rhona was just measuring Philip's love for Louise against her own for Graham, but there must be truth in it. That was what made him view all women with distrust, ready to believe their motives were mercenary. And for it to have lasted so long meant that the wound had grown deep.

Whenever Marty met Louise she was conscious that this was the type Philip admired . . . cool, poised, exquisite . . . not like Martha Mary, the maid at Alpenlinden, redheaded and impulsive

— forever in scrapes that involved other people . . .

★ ★ ★

The Lancasters were safely installed, and the weather was brilliantly sunny. The daffodils ran riot everywhere, the prunus was a miracle of blossom, fragile and tinted against the morning sky; the almond tree was pink as a bridesmaid, the forsythia showered yellow, and the native kowhai with its laburnum-shaped flowers was attracting the honey-eating native birds.

Hine's mother-in-law came up with her to help her settle, and Marty thoroughly enjoyed the company.

The Friday before the children were due back at school, Philip said: "Any chance of downing tools for the day, and having a picnic? Bill Lancaster can manage here. There's been a record fall of snow at Porter's Pass. How about it!"

Marty was enchanted, her eyes like stars. She had an instant hope that they would go alone . . . that Louise would not come. Nothing was said, Philip merely told her he would help her rustle up some lunch, and got the children organized. While Marty finished the breakfast dishes, they made the beds.

"You'd better wear slacks, Marty. Old ones, and sensible shoes. We'll probably do some climbing. Not far, because of the little ones, but it's rough."

They took the road that led still further west, climbing steadily towards the Rakaia Gorge where the river cut deeply into the hills. It was such a change from the everlasting plains. The turns were hairpin ones and steep, then they swept down to the river which was narrow here, and deep, with a tremendous volume of water.

"Now we are over the border into Canterbury," said Philip. "Away from Mid-Canterbury, and when we get through these hills we will be out on plains again, and strike the West Coast Road."

It was enchanting country, winding about through the foothills, dipping through valleys, sheep everywhere, and trees, many of them English . . . poplars, birches, willows, oaks, sycamores. Marty remarked on it.

"Yes, they must have been homesick for autumn in this evergreen land, the pioneers. Our own bush is evergreen, you know. So they brought autumn with them in tiny seeds and cuttings. That's true colonizing, isn't it? Making a lovely country more lovely still. No, Robin, don't eat any more sweets just now. Put all that packet away, and nothing more till we have lunch. I think we'll have it at Kowhai. That's just beyond Springfield. The Kowahi is a small stream that feeds into the Waimakirri. There's more shade there. It can be unbearably hot in the Pass amongst the mountains."

The came out on to the tar-sealed main west road following the railway at Sheffield.

"Not much like the English Sheffield," said Philip, with a grin for the tiny township.

Ahead of them, at the end of the road it seemed, towered the incredible height of the Alps, dazzling white this morning.

"What a backdrop," exulted Marty.

They turned over the railway line at Springfield, away from the main road, and around to the Kowhai riverbed, sweet with willow, and the hills green with native bush. They stopped where the river purled happily over its shingle bed, and spread out the feast. The air was clear and bracing, butterflies were everywhere, and dragonflies glinted over the water. Away from a bridge, the road wound its way up to the Mount Torlesse homestead, and above it reared Mount Torlesse itself.

"Not a high mountain as they go here, about six thousand five hundred feet, but quite a climb. We go back to the main road and head through the Pass to the other side of Torlesse. They said the snow was down to there, and I think that will be far enough for the youngsters. Besides if we go further through the Pass it's steep, and conditions may be bad. I haven't got chains for the wheels."

He waved a hand. "The South Island scenery is on the grand scale. It's sometimes grim and forbidding, but always magnificent. The North Island is semi-tropical, green and lush, and in the main much more settled. Great dairy country. We must get you up to the North Island some time. Thus far you've only had a glimpse of Wellington."

When they reached the Pass it seemed to Marty the last outpost of civilization. The river threaded through it, and the Pass and the river-flat were just huge expanses of mighty boulders. The snow was right down to the riverflat, carpeting the tussocky hillside in sparkling white, with here and there a patch of dark breaking it where gorse and broom grew.

The children piled out of the car, racing for the snow.

"Wait for us," called Philip. "The twins will have to be helped across the water. I think we'd better put the fizz in the stream to keep it cool."

How odd, with all this snow about, at this time of year, having need to keep things cool. But this was like Switerland, dry snow and brilliant sunshine. It needed only chalets on the mountain-sides and funicular railways going up, and the tinkle of cow-bells.

"When I was a youngster," said Philip, "you could see the ruins of the old hotel there. It was a coaching house. They used to change the horses here."

Marty stared up the road, climbing, climbing, with never a wall or a fence. "You don't mean they took coaches up there?" Her imagination balked at it.

"Oh, yes. How else could you get to the West Coast? I've got some old coaching prints at home, and there are some in Mead's tea-rooms in Rakaia. I'll show you mine. I want to get them framed. The road wasn't good like this, it was narrow and tortuous, and there were the rivers to ford. I believe there was a circus here once, on its way to the coast, and the roaring of the lions upset the horses so much they broke away, about twenty of them. Not a horse to be seen next morning. It was a hive of activity in those days, the Pass."

But the children were impatient. They wanted a snow-fight, and they wanted to climb. The river was shallow here, and they crossed on stepping-stones, Philip carrying the twins over, Gaynor protesting loudly because she wanted to walk over the stones herself.

"I'll have to take my jacket off," said

Marty, peeling it off, and stretching gracefully, and looking very feminine in spite of slacks and shirt.

"You'd better put it on again when we have our snow-fight," said Philip. "Then if it gets too wet you can take it off and put on a cardigan for going home. The children will be all right in their wind-breakers."

Marty was momentarily touched by this thoughtfulness, but dashed a second later when he added: "Can't have our housekeeper going down with 'flu. We'd be worse off than ever, then."

It was glorious fun. The little ones joined in for a while then Philip set them to building a snowman, and he lined Robin and Anne up against himself and Marty.

Each side built a wall of snow and spent a time making their pile of ammunition, then started the battle in real earnest.

The plateau they had built their walls on wasn't large, and Marty and Philip had put theirs too near the edge. They had to step right back to the drop to fire their snow-balls. The fun waxed fast and furious.

Marty stepped back to get a good aim, and at that moment twin shots from the youngsters came towards her. She flung up a gloved hand to protect her face, lost her balance and toppled.

She made a clutch at Philip, who was utterly unprepared for it, and to the delight of both children they disappeared over the edge to land in some really deep snow, five feet below.

Marty landed sprawling, with Philip on top of her. For the moment they were both winded, then he lifted his head from her shoulder, rolled over, and laughed into her face.

The sapphire eyes were close to his, the laughing lips parted two inches from his own. He did what any man would have done in those circumstances — kissed her.

Marty closed her eyes for a brief moment, forced them open instantly, aware immediately that everything within her wanted to respond. She pushed her head back deeper into the snow. There was no mistaking the fury in her eyes. She would not be taunted one moment and kissed the next!

She said, coldly: "I'm afraid I have no taste for casual kisses, Philip Griffiths. Would you please remember that!"

Philip looked at her in a way she didn't much like.

Then he said, quietly: "I'm sorry, Marty. The fault was mine. That was an unforgivable thing to do."

The apology took all the wind out of her sails. She struggled to a sitting position the better to cope with it. She must say sorry too . . . reduce this to an incident soon forgotten . . . at that moment Anne and Robin looked over at them, absolutely convulsed with merriment.

Philip pulled Marty to her feet, dusted her down. Then he scooped up a huge handful of snow and flung it. The children fled, shrieking.

Marty looked up at Philip, her bottom lip caught between her teeth.

"Philip — " she began uncertainly. It was quite evident he didn't want to prolong the discussion, that he was sure she only wanted to argue, not apologize.

"No post-mortems!" he said savagely.

"I hate the things. Let it go, we'll spoil the day for the kids otherwise. They're the ones who matter."

Oh, yes, that was very evident — she didn't matter at all.

Marty was glad when the day was over, the children bathed and bedded, and she could slide into her comfortable bed. But not to sleep. As she turned over still once more, she told herself not to be stupid . . . Philip Griffiths didn't mean a thing to her. Odd then, that she could still feel the pressure of his lips on hers.

★ ★ ★

She saw very little of Philip for the next few days, apart from the times when he had to see her about the farm work. Rhona was feeling very fit again, and had told Marty that she could easily cope with all the meals again now, so Philip no longer took any meals at Alpenlinden.

One morning she answered the phone: a girl at the local exchange spoke, and asked if Mr. Griffiths happened to be at Alpenlinden.

"No," said Marty. "Not this morning.

195

He's at his own place, and I don't think he'll be over because his married couple are away." Rhona and Graham and the baby had gone to Timaru to spend the day with Rhona's mother.

"It's a bit awkward," said the girl. "There's an urgent telegram here, pre-paid. I wanted to read it to him over the phone, and get the answer, and we just can't raise Ngaio Bend at all."

Marty's heart gave a lurch. It wouldn't be anything wrong with the Logies, would it? If anything went wrong now when they were within a few days of coming home it would be — the girl's voice cut across her thoughts.

"It's not bad news, merely farm business, but must be attended to right away."

Marty drew a breath of relief. "I'll go across on my bike and try to find him," she said. "He may be away up the paddocks. I'll make sure I get him, though, and I'll ask him to ring you."

She enjoyed cycling over. It was a glorious morning, with a clean fresh breeze coming down from the gorge. The gates were a perfect nuisance, so many of them. Now if only she could ride, she would be able to jump her mount over them as Philip did. She would like to be able to ride. Perhaps later Mr. Logie would teach her. Robin had said carelessly the other day: "When Mum and Dad are home, and you have more time, Marty, get Philip to teach you to ride."

Marty had said "M'mm" rather vaguely and let it go, for Robin was a very persistent child, but thought to herself: Not if I know it! She could imagine Philip waxing sarcastic at her expense, being impatient and overbearing. At the back of her mind, unacknowledged, was the desire to look as Louise did on a horse, one with every movement, in perfect control . . . and she didn't want Philip to see her awkward, inexperienced and — she must admit it — slightly scared!

She stopped at the farm gate, propped her bicycle against the hedge, and went through into the garden of Ngaio Bend. She glanced into the stableyard as she passed. Oh, Philip must be back, his horse was there, still slightly steaming . . . But he wasn't alone at the house . . . there was another mount there, a dapple grey. Louise! Marty's shoulders drooped a little. She went across to the back door, her steps silent on the turf path.

Just as she raised her hand to knock, Philips' voice from inside came to her with devastating clearness.

"Oh, Louise, Louise!" it said, with a note in it that Marty had never heard. "I loved you with all a boy's idealistic first love . . . "

Marty heard no more, not because there wasn't more, but because she was running away, running silently, swiftly, back towards the gate. If they ever knew she had overhear . . .

She opened the gate without noise, grasped the handle-bars of the cycle — then paused. She couldn't just go away like this. She might miss Philip if she went back to Alpenlinden and tried to raise him on the phone. Oh, if only she had written the message out, she could have poked it under the door. But then he might still have wondered whether she had heard anything.

She'd better go back, and half-way up the path call out for him, as if she thought he was in the stables. She went through the gate again, cupped her hands about her mouth, and called, "Phil — ip? Phil — ip? Are you there?"

By the time she had repeated this a couple of times, she heard the back door opening, and she swung around.

"Oh, there you are . . . I saw your horse and thought you might be around here."

Philip came across to her. Over his shoulder Marty saw Louise appear in the doorway. Looking up at Philip, Marty could see a faint beadiness of perspiration on his brow, a slight look of strain about his mouth.

She said, in a carefully casual tone. "The exchange have been trying to get you all morning. There's a prepaid telegram for you, concerning some stock. Would you ring them right away?"

"Oh, thanks. I've not been back long. I was away up the gully after some sheep. Went up just after breakfast. Are you coming in?"

Marty shook her head. "No, I left something on the stove, it might boil dry."

Louise had sauntered up to them by now. She was showing no signs of emotion, but in the strong sunlight her eyes looked tawny-yellow.

Suddenly Marty shivered, though it was warm in the sun. Something at the back of her mind had just said: —

'Tiger, tiger, burning bright
In the forest of the night . . . '

How odd to think of William Blake's poem now . . . or was it so odd? Louise belonged to the jungle. Why on earth had Philip fallen in love with a woman like her? She thought of what he had just said to Louise . . . he had loved her with a boy's first idealistic love, and he had been a child who had known the slow canker of disillusionment about his mother. Strange that he had fallen for the same money-loving type, but then love was unpredictable. Marty wrenched her thoughts away from that overheard conversation. What was Louise saying?

"Good morning, Martha. How convenient for the exchange to know that if they can't contact Philip, you're always willing to look for him!"

Marty stared. What an odd tone in Louise's voice. Almost as if she resented Marty. But how could that be? Louise wouldn't condescend to be jealous of her, surely? Oh — Marty suddenly understood. She had interrupted a tender scene between the two of them.

She said reasonably: "Well, I suppose in these isolated places we do have to help out with messages at times. I did mutter, 'Another interruption!' I admit." Her tone was purposely light.

They heard a car drive into the yard from the road entrance, and turned. The vet. got out, Morgan Hervington-Blair.

Philip said: "Morgan here again. The fellow seems to spend all his time around Linden Peaks now!"

Marty felt her color rise, and hoped Louise didn't notice.

Philip said as the vet. came towards them, "Hullo, Morgan, want me?"

Morgan shook his head, his handsome face creasing into a smile.

"No, I wanted to see Marty. Hine told me she was over here so I came around by the road, much quicker than opening all those darned gates. Are you finished, Marty? Because, if so, I'll put your bike on the carrier and run you back. I'm after a spot of lunch. You'll give it to me, won't you? I've got a message for you from Mother. She's going to drop in and see you if you're going to be home tomorrow."

Marty could have laughed at the look on Louise's face.

"All right, Morgan, I'll come now. You'll have to take pot-luck, I'm afraid. We're almost out of meat. Bill Lancaster is going to kill this afternoon."

Morgan leaned over the gate and picked up the cycle.

"Well, we'll be on our way. See you another time, Phil, and you too, I suppose, Louise."

Louise said: "You won't, probably, Morgan. I'm flying back to Australia on Tuesday. Tod says he positively can't live without me any longer."

Marty was looking at Philip as she said this, and saw his jaw tighten. She felt indignant with Louise. She certainly believed in turning the knife in the wound.

Morgan put one hand on the bike, and his other cupped Marty's elbow.

"Well, come on, lass. I'm starving."

Marty murmured good-byes and walked off with him. As they drove off, Louise's too-loud voice came to them quite clearly.

"Good gracious," it said. "Wonderful chances for these immigrant girls, aren't there? Bachelors galore around here."

Marty felt her face burn. Morgan waited till they were well down the drive. Then he put out his hand and patted hers.

"Don't take any notice of my catty cousin, Marty. She'll overstep herself one of these days and fall headlong into a real batch of trouble. She's got the manners of a fish wife . . . and the voice too!"

It did Marty good to hear someone being so frank about Louise. She said:

"Your cousin? Is she?"

He nodded. "Her father and my mother were brother and sister. That's where I get the 'Morgan' from. But the less I see of Louise the better. Philip's a fool if he still has any feeling left for her."

The pain Marty was keeping at bay flooded back once more. She lifted her eyes to the mountains — people did, for comfort in moments of stress, but in their rearing heights and chilly grandeur, Marty could find nothing of comfort. They only made her think what a terrific Great Divide they made between the Canterbury plains and the West Coast. There were so few Passes . . .

And between her and Philip there reared impassable barriers with no way through. The humiliating memory of foolish words spoken on the other side of the world, words that had raised an instant barrier of misunderstanding between them — and that other barrier — of his love for Louise.

# 7

THE next day was so busy for Marty she had little time to think about Philip and Louise. There was Morgan's mother to prepare for, and Marty was distinctly nervous at the thought. She didn't want Morgan to become serious about her, and it sounded as if he might be. The Hervington-Blairs lived miles away, and it sounded as if Mamma wanted to look this new English girl over — how on earth did you contrive to convey to a woman that you were not particularly interested in her son? The devil take these bachelors.

Marty was just putting a batch of meringues into the oven and hoping desperately she'd got it cool enough, when she heard a step on the verandah. She didn't need to be told whose it was. Philip's. She turned.

"Bit of news, Marty. Joy and Lennie will be home the day after tomorrow." She'd never seen Philip so delighted before. He added: "They said Joy is well enough to come home today, but she refused to come without Len, and they thought the day or two extra wouldn't hurt."

Marty said: "Well, much and all as I've been longing for them to come home, I'm rather glad it isn't today, with Mrs. Hervington-Blair coming to see me. I didn't like to refuse Morgan, but it seems odd for me to be entertaining. I'd rather she had waited till Mrs. Logie is home."

The mocking drawl was noticeable in his voice.

"I expect Mrs. Hervington-Blair would much rather have you on your own — give her more chance to look you over."

Marty flushed. It was just what she had thought herself, but this was underlining it!

"It could be just a kindly, neighborly call, Philip. Morgan seems to think I must be lonely."

"Oh, he thinks that all right — and tries to offset it quite a lot, doesn't he? But don't worry, Marty, or set out to impress her too much. She'll fall for you in a big way — your English voice, for instance. She's English herself, comes from Suffolk way, too. She married Hervington-Blair after World War I. But she had no idea of the position his people occupied out here. He didn't even tell her he was so wealthy. So in her case it was love."

Marty swallowed. "Why didn't he tell her?" she asked, her voice steady. She mustn't allow Philip's digs to upset her.

He grinned, maddeningly. "He kept quiet on purpose. So Morgan told me once. His father had been chased off his feet over here, and wanted to be quite sure it was love."

Marty said, in a controlled voice. "Is it characteristic of New Zealanders — this attitude?"

"What attitude?"

"A certain wariness towards women. They seem so sure that they are loved for their possessions alone; they seem to doubt their own ability to attract the girls, apart from the size of their wool-cheques. Don't they ever fall in love at first sight — get swept off their feet?"

A silence fell. Marty scraped out the

meringue bowl, put it in the sink, turned the tap on.

Then Philip spoke, and his voice was harsh. "The ones that do get swept off their feet get disillusioned, Marty. And it makes them canny the next time."

She nodded, still cool and unruffled.

"I can understand that. So the next time they are careful to keep their feet? Are sensible and cold-blooded about choosing a wife — as choose one they must, since a homestead needs a woman. Is that any more admirable than marrying with a weather eye on the sheep-market?"

His eyes were hard. "None of it is admirable." He paused, and added: "You've got quite a gift for repartee, haven't you? I can find it in me to be rather sorry for Mrs. Hervington-Blair." He turned to go, paused at the door, and looked over his shoulder to say: "By the way, Morgan is a thoroughly decent chap. I've got a lot of time for him. I wouldn't like him to get hurt." The next moment he was gone.

Marty found her legs were trembling. Morgan's mother was a kindred spirit.

Marty knew that the moment she entered the house. Gaynor rushed to her, as she always did, for Gaynor was always friendly towards folk, but when silent, shy Gregory did too, leaning against her knee and looking up confidingly into her face, Marty suddenly lost her own shyness.

Mrs. Hervington-Blair twinkled. "I told Morgan for goodness' sake not to come over with me, he'd make me unnaturally stiff. So don't feel I'll be weighing you up, Marty. I won't, because I've not come over as Morgan's mother, I've just come over as one Englishwoman to another. I still get a little homesick at times, and when I knew you'd come from Suffolk, I couldn't wait till the Logies got back home. As soon as they are properly well again, we'll have to see that you get out more, meet the people, and see the countryside. I'll come and take you to my sister-in-law's some day, Mrs. Morgan at Wangapeka Homestead. You've met Louise, haven't you? It's her mother. My brother came out here on a visit, and married her. She's a dear, not a bit like Louise!"

Marty burst out laughing. It did her

good. Louise wasn't a bit popular, was she? Except with Philip, and he had loved her.

When Joy and Leonard got home things dropped into a more usual routine, and though both of them had to spend a considerable time resting, Marty found it less tiring than going frequently to hospital to visit them.

For the first day or two Marty labored under a strain, aware that, where at first she had pleased herself what she did and how she did it, now the mistress of the house was home she must walk warily.

She needn't have worried. Joy was frankly delighted with all Marty had done, wondering aloud how she had managed to cope with so much.

At first, after their return, Marty tried to take a back seat in their lives, busying herself with mending or ironing, but Joy soon put a stop to that.

"You work far too hard as it is, Marty. Leonard said so just the other night. Your evenings are your own, just as if you were in a nine-to-five job. For goodness' sake, get a novel, or some of your own knitting, and relax."

To Marty's delight she found the Logies were insatiable readers. A parcel of books from Whitcombe's, Christchurch, arrived every month, there were periodicals galore, and the local library was quite good. Marty felt herself more like a young sister in the house than a mother's help.

She said so, one night, to Joy. Joy looked astonished.

"Couldn't imagine anything different," she said. "Any kind of help in the house is regarded as something just a little less than a miracle in New Zealand. You honestly thought you'd eat in the kitchen, and we'd have ours in the dining-room? Why, we only use the dining-room when we have visitors, and not always even then. The kitchen is the heart of the farm-home. I like this little living-room off it for the evenings, though. I prefer an open fire to sit by."

That evening Leonard was reading his paper by the fire.

Marty said: "Pass me the shovel, would you please, Mr. Logie?"

Leonard passed it. He lowered his paper and looked at her. "Isn't it about time you made it Len and Joy? We never stand on ceremony here, and after all you've done for us, coming into a strange home, and looking after four children, you are entitled to family rights. Besides, to be called 'Mr. Logie' in my own home makes me feel a stranger."

Marty colored with pleasure and embarrassment.

"Oh, I couldn't. It wouldn't seem right. After all, you're — "

"We're what?" he asked with interest as she stopped. "You weren't going to say 'pretty old' were you?"

"No," said Marty indignantly. "I was going to say you were pioneer families. At Home we'd probably say County. If it wasn't for the domestic situation here, neither you nor Mrs. Logie would have to work as hard, I imagine. You'd have a whole staff of servants."

There was a whole-hearted chuckle from Joy.

"Me! County!" she said, put back her head, and laughed. When she sobered up, she added: "I was brought up in an orphanage in Christchurch. I was a real orphan, a foundling. I don't even know who my parents were." She laughed again, and it was evident that it held no sting for her now, secure in Len's love, however much it might have mattered in her childhood. "You'll come to it, Marty. Call us what you wish for now, and when ever you feel you can use Joy and Lennie naturally, please do."

Marty knew a glow at her heart, and a warmth enfolding her, and was conscious of a deep thankfulness that these two people had been restored to health again.

★ ★ ★

Philip had been helping Leonard with some returns one evening, and now they were all seated around the living-room fire.

Joy said, suddenly: "Marty, we're quite well now, thanks to you. It's time we launched you into Linden Peaks Society."

Philip looked up from filling his pipe. "I think Morgan has ideas along that line, too, Joy."

Joy waved that aside. "There's this barn dance coming up — the kitchen

213

evening for the Rutherford girl. Marty would enjoy a barn dance. What about it, Philip?"

Marty's face positively burned. She kept her head down, and stooped to pick up the poker.

"Oh, if I go, Joy, I'll just go along with you and Leonard. It's more fun in a family party."

"I'm not going," said Joy hastily. "Len can't dance at present, and in any case the poor pet gets so bored at dances these days, don't you, Lennie? He just gets into a corner with the men and talks sheep till supper-time unless I simply make him dance with some wallflower. Besides, it means getting a baby-sitter in, and I can't be bothered. But you'll have a marvellous time with Philip, he's a good dancer — oh, how silly of me, you'd know that — I suppose you danced together on board ship."

"Yes," said Marty, her tone as dry as Philip had ever achieved himself, "we danced together." The hot flush had left her cheeks now, so she looked up. She'd have to appear to accept with a good grace, but she would get out of it

214

somehow, later. "It will be informal, I suppose, a sort of flannel dance — ballet length frock would do, would it?"

Joy shook her head. "No, they're rather going to town on this affair. The decorations are to be out of this world, I'm told, and they are getting an orchestra from town. Wear your most glamorous evening gown."

Philip said casually: "Wear your lilac gown, Marty, the one studded with brilliants."

Joy had real surprise in her tones. "Have you got a lilac one, Marty? I've only seen the yellow, and that black filmy one. Redheads are ravishing in black."

Marty took a breath to steady her voice.

"I had a lilac dress on board ship, but — but an accident happened to it."

Philip's eyes met hers squarely. "Pity," he said.

Marty laughed. "Personally I never cared much for it."

The next day Marty made an excuse that she wanted to go over to Ngaio Bend to see Rhona. But arrived there she didn't go to the house, she went across to the

215

implement shed where Philip could be seen working. She plunged into speech, anxious to get it over before Graham joined them — he wasn't far away.

"I just came over," she said, "to tell you not to worry about the barn dance. Morgan is taking me."

Philip laid down a leather punch, and looked at her.

"How nice for Morgan."

Marty dimpled, dropped her lashes, then swept them up, to display twinkling, vividly blue eyes. "And for me," she said demurely.

"I was quite willing to take you when Joy asked," said Philip.

"Oh, yes, quite *willing*," agreed Marty, "but I prefer an *eager* escort, really."

"And preferably one who doesn't know so much about you, I take it," added Philip.

Marty appeared unperturbed. "Exactly," she said. She paused, then made up her mind. "Philip, Joy is terrified I'll find the country too dull, so she's insisting on social life for me. I'm really quite content to stay home, I've not had a real home for years. But to please Joy,

I will take my place in the village."

"Township," corrected Philip.

"Village. She naturally thinks of you as the one to take me. She doesn't realize we — we — " She sought for a tactful phrase.

Philip's voice was ironic. "Don't spare me . . . or yourself. Say it. She doesn't realize we hate the sight of each other. Go on."

Marty was determined not to show any resentment, though she knew that later, in moments alone, that would stab. She continued, "Thank you, that puts it perfectly. Morgan is too far away to escort me to all the doings, so if you're at this barn dance, do bring along all these unattached males New Zealand is supposed to have. Then you'll be spared having me thrust upon you. You see, Joy's not the only one. The padre's wife is a darling in her own right, but a positive menace when it comes to match-making. She has twice asked me over for the evening, and suggested I bring you, and that we can look over the snaps taken on the *Captain Banks*. Thus far I've managed a watertight excuse each time, but I can't do it indefinitely. They'd better both see me interested in other bachelors about here."

"Suits me," said Philip laconically. "I'll see you meet a whole contingent of 'em."

Marty wished him good afternoon, and turned back to where she had left her bicycle. As she mounted it, she looked back at him, over her shoulder.

He was standing exactly as she had left him, looking after her, an unfathomable expression on his face. Marty wasn't sure who had come off better in that encounter . . .

★ ★ ★

Joy had said nothing at all when Marty told her Morgan was taking her to the barn-dance. However, she entered wholeheartedly into the preparations. She offered Marty her short white fur cape, and jewellery, and bought her a pair of the filmiest nylons.

"Just wait till Morgan sees you," she said, clasping her hands together. "He'll be even more besotted . . . Oh, I think

218

I hear him arriving. Marty, pause on the stairs. I'll run down and bring him into the hall . . . now, please do. I'd love him to see you first on the stairway, it's so effective."

Marty gave up protesting, and dallied in the bedroom while Joy went downstairs. She had an idea that Joy's girlhood as an orphan had been devoid of glamor, and she was enjoying it vicariously through Marty.

She paused on the stairs obediently, but with a twinkle in her eye as she heard Joy drawing Morgan into the hall.

But it wasn't Morgan's eyes she met, lifted to hers, but Philip's. Philip, tall and debonair in evening dress — tall and debonair and — and very dear. If only things had been different!

"Isn't our staircase a perfect setting for her?" exclaimed Joy fondly. "Lennie, you come and look, too."

Marty laughed, remained where she was, confused with a lovely confusion, and a foolish, quickly beating heart because, expecting to see Morgan, she had seen Philip.

Marty's frock was a simply cut primrose

taffeta, full as to skirt and tight as to bodice, the hem caught here and there with yellow-centred white daisies. The straps of the gown were formed of tiny daisy chains, and about her throat she wore an old-fashioned locket of black enamel threaded on narrow black velvet.

"You're making me embarrassed," said Marty. "You must remember I'm just Martha Mary, the maid at Alpenlinden."

Philip was looking at her with admiration in his eyes — reluctant admiration, of course. She hoped he wouldn't refer to manbait tonight, she doubted if she could take it. What magnificent shoulders he had; he didn't carry an ounce of superfluous flesh, yet was broad and heavy with it all . . . but what was he doing here?

He might have read her last thought, for he said then:

"So beautiful a damsel really deserves a genuine Prince Charming — Morgan, in point of fact. But I'm afraid, Martha Mary, you'll have to put up with the Liaison Officer instead, even if he is . . . what did you call me once? — blunt and overbearing ... and deliberately unkind!"

Marty caught up her skirts and came down to the foot of the stairs, paused on the last one, which brought her nearer Philip's height, laughed and said: "Did I really call you that once? You must have annoyed me."

Joy and Len looked quite bewildered. Joy rushed into speech.

"Morgan's car has had a breakdown at Methven. He says he'll finally get to the dance, but it will be late, and he rang Philip to ask him to call for you."

"I rather think," said Marty slowly, "that I'll not bother going. It wouldn't be the same without Morgan. What garage did he ring from, Philip? Perhaps I could ring him there, and call the whole thing off."

Philip looked at her coldly. "Oh, no, you won't. You're coming with me." His hand took her wrist in a grip of steel.

Marty drew back as far as she could. "I'm not." Her tone was completely decisive.

"That's what *you* think," said Philip.

He bent, swung his free hand under her knees, took her completely by surprise, lifted her up.

His eyes were dancing. "Open that door quickly, Len . . . into the saddle and off with her . . . young Lochinvar had nothing on me!"

Len, with a bellow of approving laughter, mingled with real mirth from Joy, opened the door, Philip kicked it wider with his foot, said, "Good-night, folks," and kicked it shut, strode across the porch, and over the shingle to the car. He deposited Marty in a flurry of yellow skirts and lacy petticoat frills on the front seat of the station wagon, slammed her door shut, got in the other side, and looked down at her in the light of the bulb in the roof.

"Your own manners leave a lot to be desired," he said.

Marty said nothing.

Philip gave a short laugh. "For once, I actually believe I've left you with nothing to say."

Her eyes flashed. "Oh, haven't I? Ever heard this quotation?

'Oh, it is *excellent*
To have a giant's strength, but it is
   *tyrannous*
To use it as a giant!' "

The grey eyes glinted down at her.
"Adding to your vocabulary of adjectives,
aren't you? Blunt . . . overbearing
. . . unkind . . . now tyrannous! Why
don't you just admit it all adds up to
chagrin because I know exactly why you
emigrated?"
Marty swallowed She mustn't let him
see how this wounded her.
"If you had never heard that conversation, I would still have disliked you
from the moment we meet!" she lied.
"If we are going to this dance, let's go.
Once you've accomplished your stand-in
duty for Morgan, you can abandon me
to the tender mercies of all these surplus
bachelors. I'm now willing to believe
there are as many of them as was
reported. In fact, if you're a sample,
it's a wonder there aren't more."
Philip let in the clutch, and Marty
clasped her hands tightly together to still
their shaking.

Marty was a success at the dance from the very start. She flung herself into enjoying it, simply to drown the memory of all they had said to each other, laughing gaily at anything Philip said as he introduced her. The women were kind to her, telling her how plucky she had been to tackle a new household full of children, right at lambing time. Only one woman struck a jarring note. She said coldly: "Is this your day off?"

Marty simply laughed, and said: "Yes, wasn't it lucky it's the night of the dance?"

She was surprised to see the padre was M.C.

"There's no end to what you get dragged into," Fergus said to her ruefully. "I used to dance a lot when I was young, but it bores me to tears now. I don't know any of these modern steps. You'd better keep a waltz or a foxtrot free for me."

Philip, evidently intent on emphasizing the extraordinary amount of eligible bachelors in Linden Peaks, brought up what seemed like squadrons of men to Marty, and she didn't lack partners all evening. Then he brought up a late-comer.

Hitherto Philip had contented himself with teasing asides to Marty, but this time he said: "Noel West . . . another of Mazengarb's thirty-seven thousand surplus bachelors, and the most eligible of the lot!" He then disappeared, leaving Marty looking up, much dismayed, at Noel, who was very personable, with a man-of-the-world-air about him that many of the others lacked.

"Dear Philip!" she said. "Isn't he outspoken?"

The orchestra struck up again, and Noel whirled Marty on to the floor. He was every bit as good a dancer as Philip. Later they were in a group that included the little woman with the pouter pigeon bosom and the caustic voice who had twitted Marty about being the maid.

She quite skilfully led the conversation around to immigration, and said, with a titter: "They tell me New Zealand House is simply besieged with girls wanting to emigrate these days."

There was a silence. Nobody answered.

"All after our surplus bachelors," she

added. "The men in this district will have to be careful, won't they? You, for instance, Philip, and you, Noel. In fact, you could almost say we've been invaded already."

Marty lost her color. Damn that report.

But this time the silence didn't last. Philip broke it. Marty shivered as she heard him begin to speak. What now?

"But, Mrs. Rivington," he said, his tone holding an undertone of amusement that made the woman's cheeks redden, "You can't imagine anyone as glamorous as Marty having to come thirteen thousand miles in search of a husband, can you?"

There was an appreciative roar of laughter that bore testimony to the dislike most of them had for Mrs. Rivington, and an instant recognition of the absurdity.

Neol laughed, backing Philip up. "I guess they queued up in the Motherland, too . . . Marty, what would you like? A lime-and-soda?"

When Philip came to ask her for the next dance, Marty, remembering his caveman tactics earlier, didn't dare refuse though she had been glad earlier in the evening that partners had been so plentiful.

They danced for a few moments in silence, then Marty lifted her head.

"I don't want to sound like a hypocrite after all that has passed between us on the subject of surplus bachelors, but thank you for rescuing me so neatly from Mrs. Rivington."

Philip's lips twitched. "It goes against the grain to have to thank me, doesn't it, Martha Mary?"

"It does," she said coolly, "but one likes to do the correct thing, after all."

His arm tightened for a moment.

"Then don't do your feelings any violence — it was less from a desire to protect you than to score off Mrs. Rivington. I detest the woman."

Marty's voice sounded weary. "I might have known that it wasn't chivalry." She paused, then added: "But I'm surprised you don't like Mrs. Rivington . . . I would have thought you and she would have had a lot in common."

She looked up and caught a glint of amusement in his eyes, and hated him for it.

"For a minister's daughter," he said, "you hit hard . . . and quite often, below the belt too." Before Marty could say anything to that, he said: "Ah, here's Morgan. He's made it after all."

"What a relief for you."

His voice still held rich amusement. "Never mind, Marty, when you are Mrs. Morgan Hervington-Blair of Blair Hills, you will be able to queen it over us . . . though really, Noel West is an even better catch."

Marty didn't answer, said nothing more till Philip took her across to Morgan.

It was heavenly to ride home in Morgan's comfortable car, to be free of Philip's disturbing and antagonistic presence. Morgan was full of regret that his breakdown had taken up most of the evening.

"Never mind," said Marty sleepily, "I enjoyed it so much more after you arrived. It would have been terrible if you'd not made it at all."

Perhaps it was with some thought of overlaying the memory of all she and Philip had said to each other this night that she allowed Morgan to kiss her good-night.

Odd, then, that she should fall asleep with one hand clasping the other wrist where a faint blue mark showed against the pale skin, where Philip's grip had bruised her.

★ ★ ★

It was because of that kiss, however, that Marty allowed Noel West to take her into Christchurch to the theatre three nights later. She didn't want Morgan to be hurt, and there might be safety in numbers . . . and numbers there certainly were in Linden Peaks.

They went to the Theatre Royal to see the New Zealand Players put on *The Young Elizabeth*. It was a magic evening, with Marty relaxed and happy.

It was after eleven when they came out of the theatre, had supper at a coffee-bar, and there was still a drive of two hours ahead of them.

Marty relaxed as they left the lights of the city behind and headed out over the starlit plains. She loved riding at night,

229

with the low purr of a powerful engine making a rhythmic background to her thoughts. But seemingly Noel wanted to talk.

"I feel we have a lot in common, Marty . . . that we could know a fair measure of comradeship."

Marty, alarmed at a serious note so soon, got in quickly.

"Noel, I feel we could, too . . . but I must be honest. For certain reasons, I — I haven't anything more than comradeship to offer, and I'd like to make that plain. I'm really quite content with life at Alpenlinden. I simply love it. It's a real home, after years in digs. Lennie and Joy seem to think I must get out more, and I love the theatre and an occasional dance . . . but nothing more."

Noel laughed. "That makes it a lot easier for me — for what I have to say. I like the theatre, too, and dancing, only it's that way with me too. I've got nothing more to give any woman."

He fell silent, then continued: "I'd better tell you. I fell in love with someone — once for always. Evidently I'm a one-woman man. She was engaged to someone else, a boy-and-girl affair, drifted into. When we realized how much we cared, we agreed that the only honest thing was for her to break it off. Isobel lived at Lincoln. She left me, to go home, see Christopher, and tell him. We felt that only in this way would happiness come to any of us.

"That was the last time I ever saw her. She rang me that night, told me she was going to marry Chris after all, that she simply couldn't face the fuss and commotion attendant upon a broken betrothal. She was completely adamant. Refused to even see me. I went over, of course, the next day, but she had left by air for Auckland — can't even now imagine why, and her mother said Isobel had told her not to give me her address.

"She married Chris much earlier than they had intended, a quiet wedding, and they left immediately for a trip to England. They have never been back. I was completely bewildered for a while, and I've never shed the sense of loss. I hadn't thought of Isobel as lacking courage. I've told myself over and over again that I am an utter fool, but — I've not ever been able to feel the same about anyone else. I don't want to get married, but I would like a partner. It's a queer sort of proposition, Marty, but . . . how about it?"

Marty sat silently, thinking it through, as the miles slipped by. It would put Philip at a distance, cut out the embarrassment of having Joy and Lennie propose outings with him, and it would be safer than using Morgan . . . and best of all, wouldn't involve either herself or Noel seriously.

She said simply, but with pain in her voice: "I've had a very similar experience, Noel. I — it would suit me very well."

She was immediately conscious of a relief from tension, from misunderstanding. How pleasant to be able to refuse Philip if he should consider it his duty to escort her anywhere, to let Joy and Rachel see she had someone ready — eager to take her out. And there would be honesty between herself and Noel, neither of them asking of the other more than they were prepared to give.

With a shock Marty realized that they

were in the garden of Alpenlinden, drawn up under the big cedar on the front lawn.

Noel helped her out of the car, and took her to the front verandah steps. The verandah was screened with creepers, and the shadows were deep and velvety, but the steps in bright moonlight.

Marty said: "I've got a key, Noel. I'll not ask you in for anything. Joy said I might, but it's so very late and we might disturb the whole household." She was on a step above Noel and turned to him, so that her eyes were on a level with his.

"Thank you for a delightful evening . . . and goodnight." She held out her hand.

Noel looked at her. In the light of the moon that was riding high above the mountains her profile was enchanting, the curve of her mouth young and tender. He laughed.

"I didn't mean quite as cool a friendship as that, you know," and he came up the step, bent his head, and brushed his lips across hers. "And I ought to tell you," he added, slipping his hands down to hers, and holding her a little way from him, and looking down on her, slim and tall in her white frock, "that you look every bit as regal as the Tudor Queen herself!"

She laughed softly. This was balm to a spirit that was really bruised after all her dealings with Philip. She stayed where she was, as if bemused, to watch Noel cross the silvered lawn. He was whistling *Greensleeves* under his breath. Noel switched the lights on, and his car backed then swept silently down the drive, a large, tomato-colored Hudson Rambler.

Marty turned to the door, key in hand.

"Good morning, Marty," said Philip's voice, and he rose up from the garden seat on the verandah.

Marty yelped, and Philip put out a hand to her.

"I'm sorry if I startled you, but I thought you'd get even more of a scare if you suddenly saw a man sitting here."

"I should think so! What on earth are you doing snooping about here at this hour?"

He chuckled, maddeningly. "Well, of course, I couldn't know what a tender little scene I was to witness, but to save Noel's feelings, I kept quiet. I've been playing cards with Len and Joy. I overstayed myself. Finally, Joy tipped me out, but it was such a lovely night, I didn't feel like sleep, so sat here smoking till I felt like walking home. I came the short cut, over the creek and through the front garden."

Marty turned to the door again. Now he would go. She wasn't at all sorry Philip had seen what he did. Had she known he was there, she would have returned Noel's kiss.

His voice said at the back of her: "May I congratulate you?"

"What on?" She kept her back to him.

"On the progress you are making. The little English girl is doing very well — the biggest homestead in the district the finest house — the plushiest car — the most handsome and wealthiest bachelor . . . "

Marty got the key turned. Stepped inside, locked it . . .

Nevertheless, the small encounter had pleased her. Now Philip would leave her alone, and what did it matter to her what he thought of her motives?

Joy was laughing about the amount of telephone calls that had followed the night of the barn-dance, though she noticed that Marty turned down all invitations. Marty would have accepted some had Noel not offered himself as a regular escort . . . not that she longed to go out, but failing Noel it would have been one way of putting a stop to Joy's and Rachel's efforts to partner her off with Philip. So Marty felt more secure.

She hadn't reckoned with Leonard. Philip had been helping at Alpenlinden all day, because some of the work was still beyond Leonard, and in turn Leonard would spare Bill Lancaster to help Philip and Graham.

The men finished earlier than they had thought, and Joy asked Philip to stay for dinner. Just as they finished, Len rose up and took an envelope from behind the clock on the mantelpiece, and threw it on the table in front of Philip.

"There you are, Phil — my birthday

shout for you . . . tickets for tonight for *Macbeth*. Joy went over to Ngaio Bend this afternoon, and got your togs. You can bath here, and take the Armstrong Siddeley. Many happy returns."

Marty was taken unawares. The children raced away to get their presents for Philip, and she managed to join in the birthday wishes that were being exchanged across the table. There was nothing she could do about this. Lennie, dear Lennie, thought he was giving them both a break from the farm routine, and it would be churlish to refuse.

"Leave the dishes, Marty. Anne and I will cope, and you go and get ready. Wear your white frock, I love it," said Joy.

Just as they were ready to go the phone rang. Joy answered it, and called Philip back.

"It's for you . . . Mrs. Morgan."

Mrs. Morgan . . . *Louise's mother*! Marty told herself it didn't mean a thing. Philip was still very friendly with Mrs. Morgan, who was a perfect dear.

But this time it did mean something. She heard Philip say: "Coming on tomorrow's plane, is she? Good heavens, I had a letter from her last week and she didn't even mention the possibility!"

*He'd had a letter from her last week. Then they still wrote to each other.* Marty felt disappointed in Philip. Louise was married to Tod. What was he saying now?

"Yes, I'll drive you in, Mrs. Morgan. I know you don't like driving in traffic. What time does it arrive at Harewood? Right. Yes, it would save time if you drove over here. Yes, I'll drive your car. Louise would look askance at a station-wagon, wouldn't she?" He hung up.

Marty was very quiet on the way in.

"What's the matter, Marty? Something upset you today?"

"No. I'm all right. Didn't sleep well last night, that's all."

"Thought you once told me nothing ever kept you awake?"

"Nothing does," vowed Marty rashly. "I slept . . . but I had a nightmare."

"But you'd soon get over that, wouldn't you? Sure nothing went wrong today? I mean it's not always easy living with the people you work for. If anything goes

238

wrong you can't get away from it."

The unexpected kindness in his tone was almost too much for Marty. If only Philip wouldn't be so disarming at times, it would be easier to convince herself she hated him.

She said: "It certainly wasn't that, Philip — quite the reverse. I ought to be on top of the world. Lennie came in for his afternoon tea when Joy went down with the men's, remember? Lennie had just about had it. When we were having ours, I saw Joy making signs to him. He went to his office and came back with — a cheque!"

Philip nodded. "Your bonus."

"Yes. Did you know I was going to get it?"

"Yes."

"I was completely taken aback, especially when I saw the amount, Philip. It was for fifty pounds!" He smiled at the awe in her tones.

She continued: "Leonard just said casually, 'We always give the men a fifty-pound bonus after harvest. This is for working like a Trojan, and keeping the children so happy when we were in hospital.' I didn't know what to do or to say. I get such a generous wage, plus my keep, and Joy never goes to Christchurch but what she brings me back something. I'm saving money fast. I don't know if I ought to keep the bonus."

Philip looked at her oddly. She realized he was probably thinking it a queer remark from a girl who had openly avowed she wanted to marry money.

His voice was surprised. "Did you have any doubts about keeping it?"

"Yes, of course. I loved looking after the children, and I'm treated just like a young sister in the house. It hardly seems right to take any more."

"You need have no qualms whatever. Take it and enjoy it." It was a pity that he had to add: "After all, you may need it for a trousseau soon."

Marty loved Shakespeare, but she did wish tonight that it hadn't been one of the tragedies. She was more in the mood for something like *Twelfth Night* — something with a happy ending. *Macbeth* was history, bloody and cruel, and unforgettable.

Not that she could help being caught

up into it. In some of the scenes she found that as usual she was holding her breath. She even forgot that tomorrow Philip was meeting Louise.

But after her nightmare of last night *Macbeth* was just too much for her. This was the day of the year that she kept tryst with the past, and old sorrows and old griefs threatened to overwhelm her . . . "Old, unhappy far-off things."

She said, as they came out of the theatre: "Philip, I'd rather have supper when we get home than go anywhere now. It always takes me a little time to come back to the present day after an experience like that, and it's too sudden a transformation to go to a modern coffee-bar."

So they walked silently to the car and began the drive home. Just past Dean's Avenue in Riccarton Road there was a small, exclusive gown shop, brilliantly lighted. Marty gave it no more than a glance, but Philip braked hard.

Marty glanced quickly around, fearing an imminent crash, for Philip was a good driver and never drove on his brakes.

She looked up at him inquiringly.

"What are you stopping for?"

He drew into the curb, got out, went around to her door, opened it for her, and indicated the frock shop.

"Oh!" said Marty.

They walked up to the window.

"It's exactly like the frock you threw out of the port-hole, isn't it?" asked Philip.

Marty started to agree, realized what he'd said, and changed it to: "*What* did you say?"

"You heard!"

Their eyes met, his hard, compelling, challenging her to dare deny it.

"You knew?"

"I knew. I was too disturbed to go back to the dance that night. I stayed by the rail, smoking, looking down. Presently I was startled to see something flung out of the port-hole. It was rolled up, but the breeze took it, and it opened up, the brilliants caught the starlight for a moment, and as it settled on top of the waves, I saw it was your frock. I was very ashamed of myself."

Marty looked away quickly. When Philip spoke like this she was only too

242

ready to forget all the other bitter and hurtful things he had said to her, and she mustn't let him see how much it mattered to her.

She said, as carelessly as she could achieve: "Oh, it's all history now. I was . . . rather het-up that night. It's of no importance now."

"It is — to me. It's reproached me ever since. Coming around the corner tonight, and seeing this, I thought — I thought — "

"You thought?"

"I thought you might allow me to give this to you, it looks about your size."

They turned back to the frock. It was even more exquisite than the unfortunate one Marty had jettisoned. It was more grey than lilac, with lilac underskirts, a filmy material with a delicate design of cobwebs traced upon it.

The webs were outlined with tiny sequins to stimulate dewdrops. It was perfect, it was inspired . . . and it would cost the earth.

"*Would* you allow me, Marty?"

She looked up at him and hardened her heart.

"You want to give it to me so that the thought of it no longer reproaches you, don't you? It's not a warm-hearted gesture at all. You people seem to think everything can be squared up with a cheque-book, even Lennie. I loved looking after the children for them. I didn't know them then, but I could see the room Joy had prepared for me, and I loved her for it. I'd have done it without pay at all . . . and then, tonight, Lennie gave me that cheque, and it just cancelled out everything I'd done."

Philip was silent. Then he sighed and spoke. "Nothing more to be said, is there? . . . As far as the frock is concerned — but about the bonus, don't let Len know you feel like that, will you? Len likes to give, just as you do. You gave service — he's got an abundance of money, and likes to share it. I don't think any cheque he could offer you would equal the peace of mind the Logies knew after they had met you and realized how happy the kids were with you."

In silence they came to Rakaia. They turned up Elizabeth Avenue, heading west between ghostly trees of late cherry blossom, and ahead of them, looking incredibly near in the moonlight that was almost as bright as day, was the backdrop of the Alps, in all their splendor. Tree shadows, sable against the silver thread of the road, fell across them.

Marty didn't want to fumble for her handkerchief to wipe away the tears she couldn't stop from welling into her eyes. She let them run unheeding down her face on to the white crepe frock.

On the left was a rutted drive leading into dense trees, a little-used back entrance into some old homestead. Philip slowed down, turned into, stopped the car under the trees.

Marty came to herself, and turned to him, startled.

"Philip — I — it's late." She put out a hand in some agitation.

He took it gently — for Philip. "Don't be afraid — I'm not parking for any ulterior motives — it's not my line. You've not been yourself tonight. I saw a tear fall just now. The moonlight caught it. What is it?

" . . . It's not just the fact we didn't agree about the dress, is it? We've had worse quarrels than this and you've not cried. What is it, Marty?"

She wouldn't want him to think she wept because they had quarrelled, anyway. She looked up at him, something defenceless and childish in the exquisite oval of her face in the moonlight.

"It's nothing I can talk about. I never have. I'll — I'll just mop up thoroughly, and cheer up. I'm sorry to have been such a poor companion."

"Marty!" His arm was warm about her shoulders. This was the best side of Philip, the true side. The side that had made him such an excellent Liaison Officer . . . when his cynicism fell away from him, and he became as he would have been before Louise had embittered him.

"Look up at me," he said. She looked up. "There are few things that won't bear talking about. Are you sure it isn't something you could exorcise by talking? You've got nobody of your own here. Couldn't you tell me?"

She considered it.

Philip continued: "Remember in the play tonight, Malcolm saying to poor

246

tortured Macduff: 'Give sorrow words
. . . the grief that does not speak, whispers
the o'er-fraught heart and bids it break.'
Give your sorrows words, Marty, I'm a
poor substitute for anyone of your own
kind, but — "

Marty said, slowly: "Tonight is the
anniversary of the night the bomb fell
on the Vicarage. I had the nightmare
about it last night. I dread it. It's always
the same. I come back to consciousness
with the smell of dust in my nostrils and
throat, and black darkness, just as black
when I open my eyes. In my dream I
always open them, and darkness presses
on my eyeballs, I can feel it. And it's so
quiet. The quietness, the awful stillness
that meant Dorothy and Peter and Rob
were — gone.

"I've tried shutting it away in my
mind, trying to lock the door of memory
on it . . . I couldn't talk it out to
Daddy and Mother, ever. It brought
back the loss of the three children to
them too much. I was all they had left,
so they were terribly concerned about
me. Concerned lest it leave a mark on
me. I overheard them talking about it

once. They didn't know I was there. They said: 'It's wonderful how she's got over it,' and Daddy said: 'Thank God for the resilience of youth'." She shuddered violently.

She felt Philip draw her close. Odd, wasn't it? This was Philip, and there had been hard words between them, yet it was to him she had confessed this.

"I don't profess to be a psychologist, Marty, but now you have told someone about it, you may not have any more nightmares. Bottling it up isn't good, but in any case if you feel like this again, or if you want to talk about Dorothy and Peter and Rob, you'll come to me, won't you, and I'll try to help."

Marty suddenly knew two things. That she could go to Philip with this, if with nothing else, and that he would help. He despised her for what he thought were her motives in emigrating, and he had a cynical twist about women, but the innate kindliness in his nature that was revealed in all his dealings with the very young and the very old, would pity the ten-year-old Marty who had known such shock.

She looked up at him and moved away. "Thank you, Philip." Her voice no longer had that brittle quality. He took his arm away and backed the car.

They had supper at Alpenlinden in an intimacy they had never before known. Joy had banked the fire in the living-room for them, there were sandwiches in the fridge, her note said, asparagus rolls and savories, and coffee in the percolator.

They talked of the play, of the way Rhona's health had improved since she and Graham had had a home of their own, of Philip's adventures with housekeeping for himself.

"I sometimes feel a bit guilty about suggesting that, because though it has made such a difference to Rhona, it has been harder on you. I know she gives you your midday dinner, but you haven't got the comfort. Are you going to try to get a housekeeper?"

Philip looked across at her. "Thinking of applying?"

He looked at her lazily, his long legs stretched to the fire.

"A farmer is at a great disadvantage without a wife. Perhaps I'll advertise for one . . . 'Wanted a wife, strong, capable, good cook, able to milk, garden, sew, preferably attractive'!"

Marty said, laughter in her eyes: "When I listed the qualities I wanted in a husband, you said: 'and what about love?' Dare I ask you that? I don't see why not — what's sauce for the goose . . . "

Philip was lighting his pipe. He looked at her over the flame of the match. "Yes, you can ask me the same question. I'll answer it the way you answered me . . . *I've tried love!*"

Marty picked up the poker, stirred up the fire. She found she was trembling.

Philip continued, lightly: "We seem to be in the same mind about marriage, Marty. Perhaps we ought to join forces. Neither of us would have an illusion about our motives in marrying, would we? And it would be a convenience all round."

Marty managed to laugh. She must treat this moment as lightly as he, and he must never know that speaking of marriage stabbed at the hidden dream in her heart. She met his eyes. The grey eyes looking into hers glinted with amusement.

"Another point," he said, "worth considering . . . there might be a cessation of nightmares . . . there would always be somebody beside you!"

The hot color flooded Marty's cheeks. He laughed.

"You're easily shocked, Marty."

She kept silent. Much better to let him think her blush due to prudishness than to have him guess how her pulses had leapt at the thought.

He dropped the bantering tone. "By the way, we're not so busy now. I thought I might teach you to ride. Everyone in this part of the country ought to be able to — you can take a message so much quicker." (She supposed this last remark was to make her understand that it was merely as a matter of convenience for the Logies, and not as a desire for her further company!) "We'll try you on old Randy first, the children's pony. They all learned on her. How about coming over tomorrow to my place? Or will Joy need you? She said to me the other day it was time I taught you."

Marty swallowed. "I'm afraid I can't come. As a matter of fact Noel has promised to teach me. We're going to start lessons next week."

Philip got up. "Good. That's fine. You couldn't get a better tutor."

Strange to feel that in an instant the closeness that had sprung up between them tonight had suddenly gone. Perhaps it had never existed, was merely wishful thinking on her part. Joy had suggested the lessons, Philip would do anything for Joy . . . and he was evidently relieved that Noel was going to teach her. So don't think he's warming towards you, Marty, you're so apt to look for softening of his attitude . . .

Philip said he must be going, paused, and added: "I can find it in me to be sorry for Morgan . . . he was quite in the running till Noel appeared on the horizon, wasn't he?"

Marty's chin came up. "What makes you think Morgan is *out* of the running? I'm going to his sister's coming-of-age ball at Blair Hills this month."

Philip whistled. "My word! And I'm told it's to be almost exclusively a family affair . . . has to be, because they want it in the homestead, and the Hervington-Blairs are related to half the county, anyway. Well, I don't blame you; just as well not to burn your boats. After all, Noel West is one of our wiliest bachelors, he's lasted longer than any of us . . . "

Marty was inwardly proud of the way she kept a rein on her temper these days — she certainly had plenty of practice. Philip lifted a quizzical eyebrow, as if surprised she had nothing to retort, and said: "Then I'll be seeing you at Blair Hills."

Marty said quickly: "Didn't you say only family?"

"I said 'almost exclusively family.' But then, after all, I was once expected to marry into the clan . . . didn't you know Mrs. Hervington-Blair still persists in thinking of me as a nephew! Besides, Louise will be there, and will want me to escort her!"

His last words fell into a stillness of spirit that seemed to engulf Marty. So . . . whenever Louise beckoned, Philip would come running . . .

"Philip," she said, "I thought you

would have been above playing around with another man's wife. Thought you would have respected the marriage bond. You sat in judgment on me because I — what was it you said once? — 'had an eye to the main chance in marriage' . . . but at least I would have played fair. And if I married for money as Louise did, I'd have kept my part of the bargain."

The words had said themselves out of the despair that had washed over her, with a forlorn hope that candid speaking might yet save Philip from himself, but she was appalled at the effect they had on him.

She had seen him angry so often, stirred either to hot speech, or to biting sarcasm, but she had never before seen him white to the lips, beyond words.

He turned, reached for the door, shut it with a finality that was to Marty symbolic of all that lay between them. From now on nothing would bridge the gulf. Philip would never forgive her.

# 8

PERHAPS it was just as well that they were exceptionally busy the next couple of weeks. Work could at least fill the days, Marty thought forlornly, even if you couldn't stem back your longings and regrets when at last you found yourself alone in your room.

"Marty, do you have to work quite so hard?" Joy demanded one day. "You don't seem to be relaxing at all. I know it's a busy time, but it's almost always busy on farms, if not with one thing, then with another, and you're positively looking for work. At a time like this I don't worry too much about the spit and polish . . . And you're looking thinner in the face — are you homesick?"

"No. I'm not homesick." In that, at least, Marty was completely sincere. She had realized, long since, that it was people and not places that mattered, and while at times fleeting nostalgia swept her for England's green and ordered fields, for gentle hills and neat, mellow villages, she was aware that had things only been different between them, home for her would always now be where Philip was.

Joy wasn't convinced, and decided that shopping, of the exciting feminine kind, might work a change and put the sparkle in Marty's eyes.

"You must do us proud at the Hervington-Blairs' dance, Marty. It's to be in the old-time style, back in the early days when the old homesteads had parties, and they rode in from far and near, from Surrey hills and Alford forest, through the mountain passes and over the plains, and made a houseparty of it."

"Oh, I shan't be staying," said Marty, alarmed, knowing that more than a few hours in Louise's company would be more than she could bear. "Morgan said would I at least stay the one night . . . they plan to dance till dawn, have an old-time breakfast in the big barn, then all turn in till lunch time, but I told him I'd have to get back."

"You could stay, Marty. You've never had a night away from the place since you came." Joy paused, then added mischievously, "but of course riding home with Morgan in the dawn might appeal more to your romantic sense."

Marty laughed. "Not with Morgan, Joy."

Joy looked at her shrewdly. "I believe you're quite sincere about that. Morgan's just a friend to you, isn't he?"

Marty nodded.

"I'm glad you're like that, Marty. Most girls would have their heads turned when the son of a family of that sort is so obviously smitten. But not you. You're not impressed by any of the young bloods around here, are you? And certainly they pursue you. Lennie says he's never had so many offers of help on the farm."

A faint smile touched Marty's lips. "You make me sound rather snooty, Joy. They impress me all right. They're grand companions, and wonderful workers, and they are so sincere and natural. But they don't . . . don't — "

Joy finished it for her, watching Marty with a little smile playing about her lips: "But they don't touch your heart?"

Marty went on scalding out the milk-cans, stooping over them.

"My heart's been well immunized against such things," she said quietly.

"We've not seen much of Philip this last week or two, have we? In fact hardly once since that night of his birthday."

Marty stooped swiftly over the can again, but not before Joy had seen the tide of revealing color sweep up from her throat over her entire face. Oh, so that was it ... and something had gone wrong. Joy bent down, picked up a bucket, said: "Well, I must get back to the house. Come on up and have a cup of tea when you're finished, Marty." Joy was very thoughtful going back to the house.

Perhaps Joy got more pleasure out of her shopping expedition than Marty did, though Marty managed to respond satisfactorily enough to please Joy, who flung herself into it heart and soul.

The result took Morgan's breath away, when he called for her. Marty looked about eighteen, tall and girlish in filmy white, with a fichu swathed across her creamy shoulders and caught low at her breast with a nosegay of yellow rosebuds. It clipped in tightly at her waist, then flowed out in tiers of flounces to the floor, and a trail of the yellow rosebuds clung to the skirt. Lennie had been in on it too, and had presented her with a cameo necklace and earrings. Marty had been enchanted, and touched to tears.

"You spoil me, both of you," she had said, wiping the tears away. Lennie had grinned. "We think of you as our little sister," he said.

Marty had smiled mistily. These dear, dear people. She hoped she would never do anything to hurt them.

"All right, Lennie . . . as long as I don't appear to take all."

Morgan looked down on her as they drove off under the stars.

"What a night," he said, his eyes warm. "What a night, what a dress, what a woman!" His hand touched hers.

Marty lifted her face towards him, her eyes clear and candid.

"But that's all it is, Morgan; just starshine and fine feathers!" There was warning in her tone. Morgan sighed.

When they reached the Blair Hill

homestead it was like fairyland. The lovely garden beneath the shadow of Blair Peak was threaded with colored lights like fireflies. Chinese lanterns gleamed from the wistaria-wreathed verandahs and shone from the rosy mass of a great hawthorn tree. The old house, built in the colonial yester-year style, was ablaze with lights.

Marty was welcomed warmly by Morgan's mother and swept upstairs with the other girls, laughing and chattering. She presented her gift to Stephanie, who was charmed with it . . . a Dresden china shepherdess, and then Marty came downstairs again, just as Louise made her entrance, with her mother and Philip behind her.

Marty knew a ridiculous wave of gladness because Mrs. Morgan had evidently driven over with Louise and Philip.

Louise was breathtaking in a frock that must have cost far more than any other frock in the room. It breathed Paris. It had a high plain neckline that didn't mean a thing since the bodice was swathed to reveal every curve, a bodice of a soft silver material that was shadow-patterned in large leopard spots, and a skirt that clung seductively, then swirled out above the knees to the floor, a plain black satin skirt. She wore fascinating, barbaric bangles about her wrists, and enormous earrings to match. Her gaze was sultry. Then she moved under the lights and Marty saw that centred in each shadow-spot were green brilliants that gleamed balefully from the silver folds.

Philip's eyes met Marty's defiantly. Marty turned to look up at Morgan beside her, smiled slightly, and moved away with him. After all, she need have very little to do with either Louise or Philip this night.

She was wrong. Before long they were all grouped together. Louise was smoking a cigarette in a long amber cigarette-holder. Her eyes narrowed as they fell upon Marty.

"But how sweet, Martha," she said, a hint of rich amusement in her tones. "So young, so innocent . . . how clever of you. Fresh as an English daisy. Just right to appeal to my aunt."

Marty lifted up sapphire eyes that were as demure as her gown.

"Oh, well," she said, "we all have our day, of course. No doubt you can still remember *your* debutante days."

There was a shout of delighted laughter. Morgan's was loudest of all.

"It's no good, my dear Louise," he said. "You've met your match in Marty. She hasn't got red hair for nothing!"

Philip saved the situation. He put a hand on Louise's arm. He was laughing too. "Come on, jungle-woman, we're wasting this music." He whirled her away. But Marty felt she had made an enemy. Better far to have ignored that jibe, and simply turned away. Why couldn't she keep a guard on her tongue!

The big ballroom was crowded. Marty realized in very truth that the Hervington-Blairs must be related to half the county if this was a family party. She didn't lack partners, so it didn't matter that Philip didn't ask her for a single dance. He was making the most of his time with Louise. Marty supposed it was mingled pain and pleasure for him.

She wished, oh how she wished,

she might have fallen in love with Morgan Hervington-Blair. His family was delightful, completely free from snobbery, and evidently liked her.

She found herself dancing with Stephen Hervington-Blair, Morgan's father. He was a marvellous dancer, and she told him so. He smiled, "And my heart is light tonight. Nothing like a light heart for keeping the spring in your step, Marty."

She smiled up at him, he smiled back at her paternally, she looked over his shoulder, and caught Philip's eye, Philip, who was dancing with Louise, but watching her with a sardonic look. He thinks I'm making the most of my opportunities with a future father-in-law. Her step faltered for a moment. Morgan's father drew her a little closer, and they were caught into the rhythm of the music again.

She said: "You mean your heart is light because this is Stephanie's twenty-first, and all your family is here? It must be a wonderful occasion . . . a sort of fulfilment."

"It's more than that, Marty. It's

a thanksgiving that my daughter can dance."

Marty looked up at him inquiringly.

"Didn't Morgan ever tell you? Stephanie had polio at fifteen. She lay on her back for two years. Stephanie . . . who loved to ride and swim and ski and skate . . . but with careful nursing and endless massage and the most expert advice, here she is today with only the slightest of limps to betray the fact that anything was wrong"

Marty's eyes were like stars looking into his. The music ended. Morgan came up.

"You can stop looking at my father like that," he said, "and try it on me."

Stephen Hervington-Blair's face creased into a smile. "Take her out into the garden, lad," he said. "That's a better place than a crowded ballroom — or so I always found."

Marty allowed herself to be led outside into the scented garden. Morgan draped a stole about her shoulders, but the air was mild and warm. Above the dark dreaming hills a moon was riding high, drenching the garden with silver lights and deepening the shadows to black velvet. Into a patch of shadow by the big hawthorn Morgan drew her. He bent his head towards her. Marty put out a hand. Things were going too fast for her, both with Morgan, and with the calm acceptance of his family . . . she would have to say —

At that moment another voice cut in. It was meant for a whisper, but the person it belonged to had a carrying quality in her voice.

It said: "Philip . . . Philip?" and there was entreaty in it.

Morgan and Marty turned, silently, swiftly.

Through the boughs of the blossom-laden hawthorn they caught a glimpse of a silver gown and the emerald gleam of brilliants.

Marty grasped Morgan's hand, drew him silently away. They paused for a moment on the veranda, looked at each other.

Marty said slowly: "Let's stay in the ballroom, Morgan. That sort of thing rather puts one off secluded spots in the garden."

He pulled a face. "That doesn't

improve your impressions of my cousin, does it?"

His cousin . . . Louise . . . as if that mattered. What did matter was that Philip, for all his strictures upon her own conduct, was a cheap philanderer. Marty's thoughts were bleak.

The rest of the night passed like a dream for Marty. She moved mechanically through it all, even the one dance Philip asked her for, purely for form's sake, she knew.

There was a faint radiance in the sky over Blair Peak when at last the ball came to an end. The orchestra stopped, and Stephen Hervington-Blair held up his hand for silence.

"I know it's customary to sing Auld Lang Syne," he said, "but this for us is so much more than a formal dance to celebrate our daughter's coming-of-age. It's a thanksgiving that she can walk. I would like you all to sing the Doxology, please."

There was a moment of complete hush. Then Stephen Hervington-Blair himself moved to the grand piano, sat down at it.

Stephanie and Morgan moved to their mother, each took one of her hands. It was entirely unrehearsed, completely moving.

Marty thought she would remember it for ever . . . the doors of the ballroom open on to the garden where now the dawn wind rustled faintly, the sky paling over the Alps, Stephen's hand moving over the keys of the piano and the huge gathering singing:

"Praise God from whom all blessings
    flow,
Praise Him all creatures here below,
Praise Him above ye heavenly host,
Praise Father, Son, and Holy Ghost."

Stephen came from the piano, took his daughter's hand.

"Now, breakfast in the barn," he said.

What a breakfast it was . . . bacon, eggs, delicious lamb chops, tomatoes, steaming cups of coffee and tea, mounds of toast. Marty wondered what the caterers would charge for all this.

Then it was all over and the party beginning to break up. Those who lived near at hand were preparing to go to their cars, but most of the young ones, eager to prolong the fun and unusual flavor of the party, were going to divest themselves of their glad rags and doss down on palliasses on the floors of the bedrooms and shearing-quarters.

"Of all the devilish luck. A horse has been injured. One of the best of the racing stud at Middle Forks. I've got to go. But Philip's going your way. He'll take you home."

Marty was aghast. "Morgan! I've not got to go all those miles in Louise's company, have I?"

Morgan scowled. "I'd be better pleased if you did have to. She's staying here — Philip Griffiths will have you all to himself, blast him!"

Marty laughed. "Morgan, you needn't worry. Philip and I are just about as compatible as Louise and I."

Morgan's brow cleared.

Marty said: "I'll slip up to the bedroom and get changed."

She was down in a few moments, carrying her case, her evening make-up wiped off, and a day-time one substituted, clad in a yellow polo-necked sweater and grey slacks.

Philip, his jaw set, took her case, put it in the back of the station wagon, drove off.

As they got clear of the homestead gates, five of them, across the paddocks, he said, glancing at her:

"So you decided not to waste your glamorous set-up of last night on me?"

Marty lifted her chin. "I wouldn't have worn my evening frock home if, as I would have preferred, I had gone with Morgan. I didn't borrow these slacks — I brought them with me. It looks dissipated to career across country in the early morning in frills and flounces." She paused, then added: "And by the way, Philip Griffiths, this frock wasn't of my choosing. I knew it was too young for me . . . too girlish and appealing . . . I'm much more mature than this, believe me. But Joy loved it, and wanted to buy it for me so much, I just couldn't refuse her."

Philip's tone was mild, reasonable. "I wasn't aware that *I* criticized your frock, Marty."

She flashed back: "Louise did. It comes to the same thing."

That was identifying the two of them with a vengeance, but she didn't care. She heard Philip draw in his breath between his teeth.

He said: "If you don't mind, Marty, we won't discuss Louise."

No . . . he wouldn't discuss Louise . . . it was nothing to do with her, Marty, what Philip Griffiths did with his life, was it? That was what he was telling her, in effect.

Marty relapsed into silence.

The dawn raced across the plains, turning every dewdrop to sparkling crystal. There were gossamer webs, miracles of construction, glinting silver from solid green macrocarpa hedges, birds singing, streams rushing down from the hills, fleecy lambs gambolling beside their staid mothers, rose and gold and mother-of-pearl clouds above the mountains whose snows were stained with the colors of the rainbow.

Something of the peace and loveliness of it all seeped into Marty's disquieted heart.

After some miles Philip looked down on her.

"Tired?" His tone was curt, lacking tenderness.

"No. But there is only small talk to fill in with, and small talk seems very trivial in surroundings like this . . . compared with the big fellows there! I almost resent the magnitude of this scenery. It dwarfs me, makes me feel insignificant . . . puny."

He nodded.

"And yet," she said, "If ever I had some trouble — something that was looming too large in my life, getting out of all proportion, and causing me heart-ache and bitterness, I should saddle Fran and make for the mountains."

"Fran?"

"My mare. The one Noel has given me. Short for Francesca."

She saw his hands tighten on the wheel.

"I thought you didn't accept presents from men," he said. "Aren't you rather inconsistent?"

"You mean the matter of the lilac dress," stated Marty coolly. "As to the horse . . . I couldn't refuse that — the way it was offered. I'm only allergic to gifts when they are offered in repayment of a debt."

"And what does Morgan feel about your accepting a mount from Noel West?"

"I might remind you," said Marty, "that anything that happens between myself and Noel and Morgan is no more your business than what happens between you and Louise is mine."

There were ten miles to go, ten miles that were covered in absolute silence.

Philip was seen less and less at the homestead these days, for with the Lancasters well into the work, and Len's single man back from his three months' military training, he wasn't needed so much, though Marty knew there were times when he and Graham did do some work on Alpenlinden. Nevertheless, Philip appeared to avoid all invitations there for meals, merely returning to his lonely house when work was done.

But one night he stayed for dinner, mainly because Joy had ridden up to the paddocks where he'd been helping

Leonard with some fencing on the boundaries of the two farms, and Philip hadn't been able to say no to her.

It had given Marty the usual mixture of pain and pleasure to see him come in, freshly scrubbed-up, and take his place with them. She had been very silent all through the meal, grateful for the children's chatter and their usual diversions.

It had been a very hot, late November day, and now they were resting on the terrace that looked over to the mountains. Over the ranges, which were rapidly losing their snow and thereby swelling the river, was the nor-west arch.

Philip was lying back in a cane chair, on the other side of the terrace, lighting his pipe. Joy was pouring ice-cold drinks, a delectable mixture of pineapple juice, iced water and ginger ale, so the children were in great evidence, quarrelling over the size of their glasses and offering more cracked ice to anyone who wanted it.

"Well, Marty," said Philip, addressing her directly for the first time, "are you a crack rider by now?"

Before she could reply she had to

swallow, and by that time it was too late. Gaynor had decided to reply for her.

"Oh, Noel says she doesn't need any more lessons. He said she was a Briton. Why did he say that, Mummy? Of course she's a Briton, she comes from Britain!"

Robin said scornfully: "He means she was good to stick at the lessons. You get pretty sore, you know."

Gaynor said very clearly: "Oh, I knew he thought she was good. He said: 'Good girl, Marty!' and kissed her, right on the end of her nose!"

Joy gave her darling daughter a reproachful look, and when she showed signs of enlarging upon the subject, hurriedly picked up a box of snapshots she had been looking through and said: "Like to look at these, Gaynor?"

Gaynor was pleased. As a rule they wouldn't let her get at the photos just because she had once, when she was very, very little, torn some up. She sat down on the tiles and began looking.

They all began talking then, at once. Marty said something about how heavenly cool it was, now; Philip waved with his pipe at the sky, and said, "Another nor-wester tomorrow." Lennie said to Joy, "Your hawthorns are past their best now," and Joy said, "Would anyone like another drink?"

Everyone waited for everyone else to answer these remarks, singly or collectively, and in the pause Gaynor held up a photo and said:

"Oh, here's that tiger-lady!"

"What tiger-lady?" asked Gregory with interest. "Do you mean one what's in a circus, Gay? Let me see."

She shook her head. "Oh, not a circus lady, Greg. I mean the lady who was here from 'stralia. Daddy called her the tiger-lady. Why did you, Daddy? Why didn't you like her?"

Leonard made a sort of strangled sound.

"You know, Daddy," pursued Gaynor, in helpful innocence, "you said just the other day you didn't know how Mrs. Morgan came to have a daughter like that."

Leonard got to his feet. "Time the twins were in bed," he said, in a tone that for once brooked no argument. "Come on, Joy. Time for their baths."

Gaynor looked up at him. "What are you so cross about, Daddy? I don't like her either even if she is pretty. She told us we were horrible brats."

"So you are!" said Leonard, and yanked his daughter out of the room.

Marty tried not to catch Philip's eye but somehow couldn't avoid it. His look was unfathomable. He jerked his head in Gaynor's wake.

"Every inch a woman, isn't she? Even at not-quite-four! Women are inevitably jealous of other beautiful women."

Marty was saved a reply by Anne.

Anne, who adored Philip, looked straight at him, and said calmly, "Gregory can't stand Louise either!"

Philip got up, said laughingly, "*I* can't stand this . . . the whole family seem bent on dropping bricks tonight. I think I'll go."

Despite his laughter Marty felt the gulf was wider than ever between them. His first loyalty would always be towards Louise.

# 9

THEN quite quickly, too quickly, it was almost Christmas, and every one at Linden Peaks seemed determined to show Marty that although the temperature might soar, the skies become brassy, and the roses in the gardens shout defiance that this could be December (as the Archbishop of Canterbury had once said), that here, in Maoriland, the same customs still prevailed.

So the puddings and cakes were baked, shortbread and mince-pies, hams baked, Marty doing them the Suffolk way with a sweet, crisp crust on the outside. Up went the decorations, larch, spruce, fir, with imitation holly and mistletoe.

There were endless Christmas parties to mark the breakup of all the organizations, Church, Institute, School. There would be a six-weeks break from school for the youngsters.

A succession of thunderstorms set in

which badly delayed haymaking and shearing.

"I'll go stark staring mad," declared Joy, "if we get word again that the shearers can't start. I don't mind filling tins for the cuppas, that stuff keeps, but cooking all this meat and beetroot ready for the next day, then having to try to eat it up ourselves, makes me wild! Just look, Marty . . . eighteen pounds of steak! And, perversely, it makes me feel like nothing more solid than a lightly-boiled egg!"

But, finally, mercifully, it was done, the shopping was finished, and on Christmas Day they began to talk about their holidays.

"There's one thing," said Leonard, "with all this rain, harvest won't rush in on us like last year. Did us out of our usual holiday at the Sounds. Let's get away on New Year's Eve, Joy. You'll love the Marlborough Sounds, Marty."

She blinked. "But won't I have to stay home to keep the house right? I think you and Joy should be on your own."

They brushed that aside. "It won't be half the fun if you don't come. We've got

278

a cottage of our own there, in a gem of a bay all to ourselves, and a launch and a dinghy."

Robin got in, "And Philip's got a wizard of a speedboat. Boy, can she travel!"

"Does Philip go too?" Marty didn't know if she felt glad or sorry.

"Yes. He built himself a one-roomed *whare* just above the cottage, almost in the bush. He always comes with us, Marty," said Leonard. "Philip is one of the family, you know. He practically grew up with Joy."

Marty hadn't known that. She supposed it meant that Philip had been in this district most of his life, for Joy had been brought up in a Christchurch orphanage, and had come out to Alpenlinden at holiday times. All the folk in Fergus's parish seemed interested in the Presbyterian homes for orphans and old folks, and the collector came once a year. He stayed at Alpenlinden as often as at the Manse, and visited the farms for donations. Ever so many of the farm-folk took children at Christmas to give them a holiday in the country.

Leonard's mother had always done that, years ago, and Joy had spent many holidays there, finally coming to Alpenlinden in the position Marty occupied now. Which was why Joy was so considerate towards her, she supposed.

Joy had said: "Lennie's mother was so sweet to me. I was very fortunate, I've never thought of her as a mother-in-law, but rather as the mother I never knew. I'll be glad when they get back from this trip abroad. I do miss them. They have retired in Christchurch."

★ ★ ★

It was New Year's Eve, early in the morning. The cars had been packed the night before. Philip's station waggon was a boon, it held so much gear.

Marty was apprehensive; right at the last she realized that they had planned for her to ride with Philip, and Robin and Anne. She said to Joy, desperately: "Don't you want me with you, to help look after the twins?"

Joy had shaken her head. "No, they go to sleep half-way there, and there'll

280

be more room to tuck them down if you go with Philip. Besides he'll not want the children's unadulterated company. He'll be glad of adult conversation."

They left at seven, going over the Gorge Bridge into Canterbury proper, and headed into North Canterbury. They stopped at Cheviot, a little village with an English air, surrounded by rolling hills and leafy hedges. Then on through country that was as different from the plains as might be.

It was a beautiful coastline, with a vast variety of scenery great bluffs dropping down to tumbling breakers, sheltered bays, mountain passes, and green valleys, magnificently clothed in native bush, and whenever they stopped for the children to stretch their legs, there was a chorus of birdsong.

They came to Picton in the cool of the evening, right at the northernmost tip of the South Island. They came over the hill and dipped down to the foreshore, with the Memorial Gates framing the incredible beauty of the Sounds.

They stayed for just a moment feasting their eyes on it all, then went on to

281

the boat harbor, for it was going to be dark, it had taken time to travel the hundreds of miles they had come. Marty could have stayed and taken it all in . . . it was a sub-tropical town, climbing its hillsides, and before them small craft rocked on the wash of a returning pleasureboat. At one wharf, the *Rangitira*, one of the inter-island ferry steamers, was unloading cars for folk from the North Island disembarking for a tour of the South Island.

Soon they were in the boat, and speeding out on the cool waters, heading across the harbor. On the other side as they came near were little cottages cut into the hillsides, some completely surrounded by bush, looking as if some day the bush would reclaim its own and cover them.

They drifted into their own jetty on the golden sand, and Philip sprang out and secured the launch. The children were out and up the steps in a trice. They were loaded with luggage, even the twins, and they clamblered up some natural rock steps to the veranda of the little pine-wood cottage.

Marty had imagined, since the Logies had so much money, that their beach-house might be a luxury one. Not so. It looked as if it had grown among the bush. Rickety wooden steps led up to a wide, glassed-in veranda furnished with a motley collection of chairs and forms.

"We eat out here mostly, because of the view," said Joy, dropping her bundles on a big, scratched table. Inside was a kitchen-living-room, with a bedroom off it and two sunporches. Marty was to sleep in one porch, with the girls.

The beds were made up very quickly, because the twins were dead-beat, and had bowls of cornflakes, glasses of milk, and were tucked down, flushed and sweet.

"Let's have a jolly good meal ourselves," said Joy. "After nothing but sandwiches and cakes on the way I'm starving. How about a mixed grill?"

So presently they sat down to bacon and egg, sausage and tomato.

"Did ever anything taste as good?" demanded Joy. "I'm dying to show Marty around, and to explore the garden, but it's too dark and I'm too sleepy. We'll leave it all till tomorrow. I'll wash up, Lennie can dry, and perhaps you'd take some linen, Marty, and go up to Philip's sleep-out and make up his bed?"

The sleep-out was up the hill and built out on to a platform. It was one large room with a couple of bunks at one end. It was very simply furnished, some native matting on the floor, a print of the landing of Captain Cook in the Sounds, some native kit-bags hanging on a nail, ideal for bringing fish home, Philip said, a couple of chairs, a bookcase.

By the time Marty had made up the bed, it was pitch-black outside, so she was glad of Philip's arm as they slithered down the rocky hillside. That was the only reason she felt glad she told herself fiercely. She drew away from him the moment they reached more level ground.

Yet somehow she slept better than she had done for weeks. They were here, in the playground of the South Island, would be living in close contact for the next two or three weeks, and Louise . . . Louise was safely back in Australia with her husband . . .

Marty was enchanted with the Sounds. They were all thrilled that she was, since, they admitted, the Sounds were practically an obsession with them.

"I try to induce my family to see more of New Zealand," Leonard complained, "but they're just besotted with the place. Still, I do admit it's hard to beat."

There was a minimum of work to be done at the cottage; they simply made the beds, tidied up, swept the sand out of the door, and spent the rest of the day outdoors except for siesta-time.

There was an unacknowledged truce between Philip and Marty. Probably it was because they owed it to Joy and Len not to quarrel in this happy holiday-time, perhaps because they never had disagreed in front of the children ... perhaps because there was less cause for hostility here. Noel and Morgan and Louise were all absent, and there were no mistakes here to be made through ignorance of New Zealand farming conditions. Marty thought wistfully that she didn't dare to hope that it was because Philip was forgetting all that lay between them, hot, unconsidered speech and hasty judgments.

Yes, this was a time of respite . . . long, lazy halcyon days.

There came the day when, instead of a launch with a party of holiday-makers cruising past, one proceeded in to Konini Bay and tied up.

Len was at the porch window. "What a cheek! Wonder if they want water, or something. I'll soon get rid of this crowd. But I'd better let them come up."

Marty watched as a rather tubby little man, balding helped a girl ashore. As she straightened up on the rock steps, Marty gave a gasp of dismay, so did Leonard. The girl had smooth, dark hair, neat and shining, parted in the middle and caught back into a knot. Her movements were graceful and sensuous, her ease of movement accentuated by the sunfrock she wore, with a wide, white skirt, and a top that was patterned in striking black and gold stripes. About the slender column of her throat was a necklace of some odd native ware, and there were bracelets to match on her arms.

Louise!

286

Marty thrust back her hair with an impatient gesture. She had been romping around the floor with Gregory on her back, and she felt anything but well-groomed. Even her knees were dirty. As Leonard and Marty watched, the girl sprang lissomely up the steps, and at the moment she gained the path, Philip came round the corner of the house.

He stopped dead. Marty saw his face tighten. Was that for self-control, or what?

Louise lifted sultry eyes to his. Odd that her eyes were like that and the rest of her so cool, so poised . . .

As Marty watched Louise held out beautiful hands to Philip, who perforce, had to take them, even while he was probably acutely conscious of the little tubby man in the background.

"Where did *you* spring from, Louise?" asked Philip.

She waved a hand. "From the next bay. The guest house. We've got a party there." She gestured towards the launch. "They are all there. Some are tourists from Australia. Friends of Tod's. Mother told me you were all up here."

287

Leonard had reached the door, greeted Louise with a marked lack of enthusiasm, then he and Philip turned to Tod, puffing a little in the rear. Philip shook Tod's hand quite heartily.

Joy emerged with a sleepy-looking Gaynor under her arm, and proceeded to garb her daughter in a brief sun-suit.

She cocked an ear. "Someone here?" she asked Marty.

"Louise!" said Marty.

Joy had only time to wipe the look of horror from her face before they all came in.

Gaynor sat up, looking alert, sleepiness gone.

"Is that the lady Daddy said — " She got no further, for her mother had clapped a firm hand over her mouth, and under cover of the greetings said: "Now be quiet! One word about that, and see what you'll get!"

Louise was all sweetness and charm. "We just couldn't resist calling in. Ages since we saw you. So glad you are all here."

By *all* she would mean Philip, of course.

"May I bring the crowd up? We brought refreshments, of course, wouldn't expect you to provide for all so unexpectedly. We were in Picton this morning, and knew we'd be calling, so we looked in at the Post Office and collected your mail. Tod will bring it up."

Under cover Joy said to Marty, "Take Gaynor out to Anne, will you, and tell her to keep an eye on her? The little wretch keeps muttering: 'Mummy, you don't like red finger-nails, do you?' I'll be a nervous wreck if I have to keep on creating diversions."

Marty went through the sun-room, and on the way back took the opportunity to comb her hair, apply some lipstick, and scrub furiously at her knees with a face-cloth put to dry on the window-sill.

She came back to see Louise handing out mail to Philip and Joy and Lennie. Then Louise turned and said: "Quite a bunch for you, Martha." She paused, added teasingly: "They must be love-letters. They seem all from the one person. I scent romance. I might have suspected they were from my dear cousin,

Morgan, but my aunt told me that was all washed up. Still, they're from Linden Peaks . . . do tell me? Who is it? I love romance!"

There was a little silence. No doubt Louise was used to carrying off bad behaviour like this.

Then Philip raised a devastating eyebrow.

"Do you love romance, Louise? I rather thought you were more interested in money-bags!"

After one quick glance to make sure Tod hadn't come up from another trip to the launch, Louise recovered herself.

She said: "Oh, fie! Naughty, naughty! Sour grapes, darling."

Philip scooped up the letters and handed them to Marty.

"Forgive us the vulgar interest in your affairs, Marty. Go to your room, and read them in privacy, my dear."

Marty did as she was told. There was too much tension, better to be away from it. As she went she heard Louise laugh. It sounded as if it had real amusement in it.

"Philip, my dear, haven't you improved?

You used not to be nearly so good at repartee!"

Marty sat on her bed, the unopened letters on her lap. She would read them tonight. Philip had come to her rescue. He had spoken harshly to Louise. What did it mean? Could it mean . . . but oh no, useless to dream that perhaps this holiday had drawn Philip and herself together. It simply meant that Tod was here, and Philip was being cautious.

There was the sound of more laughter on the rock steps, and a host of folk coming into the porch. They had brought refreshments, yes, Joy remarked to Marty as the two of them made sandwiches, but mostly the liquid kind. "What an invasion!" she said, with disgust. "I haven't got one thing in common with these people."

"Never mind," said Marty, "perhaps they won't stay long."

Joy said gloomily: "Tod and Louise are back in Christchurch to settle, she tells me. They are going to live on Cashmere." She turned to Marty. "Do protect Philip from that predatory female."

Marty said coolly: "Do you really think

291

he'd need protection? I thought he did pretty well."

Joy was sober as she replied, "He needs protecting more than we dream of. If only he could maintain the attitude he adopted today."

Marty looked at her swiftly. What did Joy mean? That Philip's heart was still involved? That he saw through Louise but was still irresistibly attracted? There were women like that . . .

It was late when the crowd left, and the children were tired and disgruntled because they had had so little notice taken of them.

"Poor mites," said Joy, "they love the holidays because Lennie and I have so much more time for them. We haven't at home to the same extent because there is so much to do."

Marty leaned against the wall, and looked at Joy with love in her eyes. "Joy, you're about the most perfect mother one could meet. The atmosphere of your home is wonderful. I'll always remember your first night home after the accident. You were so weary, and I knew the journey home had exhausted you, yet you had all the children curled up on your bed talking ninety to the dozen, and you wouldn't send them away because you knew that was what they wanted, the assurance that their mother was home, and all was right with their little world."

"This is lovely, pet," said Joy. "Do go on, you're doing wonderful things for my inferiority complex. Believe me, after a few hours with Louise Morgan — I mean Walberry — this is a refreshing change. That girl looked at Robin and said: Really! Isn't that child like the Logies! then added: of course we wouldn't know whether he resembled the Watsons or not. I was Watson before I was married, Marty.

"I looked her straight in the eye, and said: well, hardly, seeing the matron at the orphanage got my name out of the telephone directory. Not that it set Louise back. She's a law unto herself. Later on, as one of her friends had ground a queen-cake into the hearthrug, I picked up a banister brush and shovel and, unobtrusively I thought, swept it up.

"Dear Louise said, laughing: 'Poor Joy,

still the little Orphant Annie touch, I see!'"

Lennie looked across. "What did she mean?"

Joy made an expressive gesture with her hands. "Didn't you ever hear that rhyme, Lennie? . . .

'Little Orphant Annie's come to our house to stay,
To wash the cups and saucers up and brush the crumbs away.'

"Louise has never let me forget the fact that Mrs. Logie took me from the orphanage to work for her. Or the fact that she would have liked Lennie herself. She tried hard enough. Yes, Lennie darling, I know I'm being catty, but that girl brings out the worst in me, all the most feline. She once said to me: 'Well, you did pretty well for yourself, didn't you, darling?' as if I was a jolly fortune-hunter!"

"Instead of which," said Lennie, "she even fled to the Chatham Islands to get away from me."

Marty sat up. "Oh, Lennie, do tell

294

me? It sounds interesting. Where are the Chathams?"

Joy started to speak, but Lennie waved her down. "*I'll* tell it. I'm the only one who can do it justice. You'll play down your nobility, darling.

"The Chathams are away out from Lyttelton, Marty, very remote and primitive, though improved of late." He lit a cigarette. "I lost my heart to Joy when she was twelve and I was fifteen, when first she came to stay at Alpenlinden. There was never anyone else for me. Then when she was old enough to leave the orphanage, she came to us. I was away a good deal just then. Dad insisted on my going to Varsity, and then having a course at Lincoln College, and I went with a Young Farmers' Conference to Australia and the Argentine.

"When I came back I fell in love with her all over again, but she would have nothing to do with me. Thought I ought to marry someone from one of the old pioneer families too. Like Louise, for instance . . . perfect example of breeding and the old school tie."

"I never did want you to marry

Louise!" broke in Joy indignantly.

Lennie blew a couple of smoke-rings, watched them curl and dissolve.

"This is my story, funny-face," he reminded her, "and I'll tell it my own way. She would even have thrown me to a jackal like Louise, just in order that no one would ever be able to say she married me for my money. Absolutely mad. I knew darned well she loved me. Never doubted it. Finally, in an excess of altruism, Joy ran away. We hadn't a clue where.

"I engaged a detective and he finally traced her as booking a passage on the cargo boat for the Chathams. I nearly went mad. There was no air-freight service to the Chathams then, and a ship only once about every three months. Finally, Mother thought I was going into a decline" (Marty and Joy began to giggle) "and what do you think she did then? — Mother, I mean? Ran away too! Left Dad and me stranded right in the middle of harvest . . . well, all right, Joy . . . at the end of the harvest, but it makes a much better story to say the middle. I wish you wouldn't keep interrupting me, it puts me off.

"Now where was I? Oh, yes. She rang us from Lyttleton and said now it was too late for us to stop her, she would tell us what she was doing, and she didn't care if it seemed interfering, because she wouldn't for worlds leave the handling of this to me because I would only botch it as I had botched it from start to finish, so I could leave it in her hands and all would be well!

"By this time I was just about dancing with frustration at the end of the wire, and told Mother if she didn't come to the point and tell me what she was up to I'd be a gibbering idiot. She did. She calmly announced she had chartered a small ship for the Chathams, and would be sailing in half an hour! Well, it did the trick, Mother convinced Joy of her folly, though I believe it took some time. In fact, at one time I believe Mother threatened to shanghai Joy on board" (there was a protesting outcry from Joy which Lennie ignored) "then blest if Mother didn't decide that while she was there she'd have a good look around the Islands. Mother used to write articles for the *Dairy Exporter*, and thought this was too good a chance to miss. She had to pay wages for the seamen of the chartered ship all the time she stopped there, and wharfage dues and heaven knows what else, until in the end Joy felt she had better give in, or else, to pay for all this, Alpenlinden would be mortgaged up to the hilt.

"So back they came, Mother gave us the most slap-up wedding you ever saw, plus the cottage, and we — more or less — lived happily ever after."

Marty said, shining-eyed, "Oh, how I'd love to meet your mother."

"You will," said Lennie. "And woe betide you if you haven't got your love-life in order before she arrives back. She's a worse matchmaker than Rachel MacNeill."

Just then Philip came in. He had been fixing himself a cupboard in his sleep-out. He looked keenly at Marty.

"What are you looking so starry-eyed about?" he asked.

"Lennie's just been telling me his love-story." She sighed happily. "What a perfectly lovely ending."

Philip jeered, but laughingly. "Thought you hadn't any time for love, Marty," he said. Marty's face flamed, and she was grateful for the lamplight and its shadows.

As Philip brushed past her he said: "Maybe the Sounds are having an effect on you . . . a softening effect." He patted her hand as he passed. Their eyes met.

Marty told herself that it was only the lamplight that had brought that softer look to his eyes, or else . . . or else Philip had the same ideas as Joy, that he needed protection from Louise. That would be it. There was nothing else to account for it. He had realized that with Tod on the scene he could not play fast and loose with Louise. He was going to use Marty as a smoke-screen.

That this was exactly what Philip thought became increasingly evident in the days that followed. Louise's crowd took possession of Konini Bay coming up over the track sometimes, though not often, for as Lennie said (quite openly and in front of Philip) they were more loungs lizards and hikers, and preferred the launch.

It was so difficult to be putting-off, Joy complained helplessly to Marty. They arrived with bulging hampers of food and crates of drink. They vowed Konini was a heavenly place, what blissful solitude.

"I ask you," said Lennie to Marty, "solitude! It's what we had once, but now the blasted bay is invaded with upwards of a dozen people all day . . . and what people!"

"It's Louise's doing," vowed Joy, endeavouring to get the twins down for their rest while wild shrieks sounded from up the hill. "I know her. Tod is fine as a husband, as a provider, but Philip has the looks, and she wants the crowd to be impressed with the sort of escort she can dig up, husband notwithstanding. Heaven knows what she has said to the crowd about the reason she and Philip parted. She may even have hinted at parental opposition or something. Thank goodness you're here, Marty, it has done Louise good to see that Philip hasn't exactly pined away."

"You mean, don't you, that Philip is paying me marked attentions to annoy Louise."

Joy hesitated. "Well — yes — I mean — " she broke off, and looked quickly at Marty. She was relieved when Marty laughed. Marty was proud of that laugh. It was quite an achievement, for Joy's careless words had stabbed. If it was evident to Joy too, then that *must* be the reason for Philip's changed attitude towards her. She had told herself that that was the reason, but under it all she had hoped desperately . . .

But it was quite evident that Philip was using Marty for his own purposes. Joy had the idea that this just served Louise right, but Marty knew it for an endeavour, an abortive endeavour, to prove to himself that Louise no longer mattered, and perhaps — and Marty hated the thought of it — to prove to Tod that the affair was finished.

Marty liked Tod, she felt instinctively drawn to him. She was sure he wasn't altogether happy with this crowd, and sure also that in spite of the way Louise treated him, patronizingly and cruelly, he loved her.

She found herself partnered off time and again with Tod, and in short intervals they managed to have quite a number of odd conversations — odd because they weren't in the least the type of topics you would expect to discuss with a near-millionaire.

Joy and Lennie were able to excuse themselves quite often from the lunch parties and fishing excursions on account of the children, and Marty even suspected them of bribing the youngsters to say they preferred to stay at the bay.

"It's most noticeable," said Joy, with a regrettable lack of charity, "that although Louise wears the most glamorous bathing suits imaginable — daring too — she hardly ever gets wet. She only lounges about in studied and provocative attitudes. I suppose her make-up won't stand it. Not like Marty here who emerges looking like a wet, red-haired mermaid."

Marty laughed. "I'm afraid you see me through rosecoloured spectacles, Joy. Philip said I looked like Rusty when he's been in the water-race."

The night they went to see the glow-worms, Marty offered to look after the children so that Joy and Lennie could join the party.

"Never in your life," said Joy hastily. "I'm all for a quiet night at home knowing that crowd won't pile in here for drinks and snacks at some unearthly hour."

"Besides," said Philip, coming in, "I need some moral support."

Yes, that was all she was to him, moral support. If only it meant that, and more too . . . if it meant that he had taken her cruelly candid words about other men's wives to heart, she would assist him right royally. If only he would come out into the open with it, she would enter in wholeheartedly!

They went by launch, across the Sounds, and up a faintly defined track through dense bush, to wind upwards to the crest of a hill where there was an excellent look-out across the waterways.

Marty would have enjoyed it had she been in different company and walked in silence, one with the purple dusk, but the climb was just a continuation of the wise-cracking and rather cheap jokes that passed for conversation.

At the top, Philip said to Marty: "It's idiotic bringing a crowd like this to see glow-worms, because glow-worms don't like noise. They put out their lights. We'll only get glimpses now and then."

As soon as it was dark enough they came down again towards the bay, keeping close together and now and then flashing a torch to see the way was clear of tree-roots or holes. Presently, under the overhanging banks they saw the first few will-o'-the-wispish lights, in an unearthly green, lighting the way. They all wanted to examine them closely, using torches to do so, and of course, discouraged by all this candle-power, most of the lights flicked off. Marty noted that Louise seemed to need much aid from Philip to reach up to the banks, and then pretended to be revolted by the tiny, transparent worms slung in their webs.

She also noticed that Tod's eyes were on them during all this, so the roughness of his tone was probably for Tod's benefit. They came to colony after colony, but still the noise continued, and the displays were disappointing.

Suddenly Marty found her hand taken. She freed it instantly with a shiver of distaste. A voice in her ear said, "It's all right, it's only me." *Only Philip*! The voice went on: "We're just coming to a fork in the track, it bears left. Let them go straight on, and turn with me, but don't let the others see."

Marty knew she should have pulled her hand away, refused to go, but curiosity . . . and something else, the foolish hunger for Philip's nearness, made her go. The ruse was successful. Philip took her arm, and helped her uphill. It was terrifically steep and stony.

"Where are we going?"

"To the most perfect grotto of glow-worms you'll ever see."

"Why didn't you bring the others? They'll think it mean?"

"I couldn't care less. If I'd brought the others there'd have been none to see. It's not far."

They stepped off the path, if path it could be called, into a tiny clearing, half-circled by rocks, that overhung the banks. There, set like miniature stars in a private heaven, were clustered hundreds of glow-worms, each casting its other-worldly radiance.

For a few brief seconds, Marty lost all her suspicions of Philip, and they stood spell-bound, fingers linked. Finally, without speaking, they moved down the hill.

The moon was high above them, and up from the fernsweet valley a morepork hooted as the little owl went ahunting. There was a large outcropping of rock here, rounded and smooth with the rains of thousands of years, perhaps millions.

"Let's sit down and have a cigarette. Then we'll catch up with the others, or they'll be sending out a search-party," said Philip.

He took off his jacket and spread it on the rock for them. Marty gazed up dreamily at the moon as he smoked. She wondered how much the old moon could see over the limitless inlets and waterways . . . how wonderful to have a moon's-eye view . . . she turned, to find Philip regarding her closely.

She stood up abruptly. This nearness was too much for her. Every pulse was clamoring for his arms about her, for all tension to be eased . . . there was danger ahead . . .

"Let's get going," she said. "I've appreciated seeing the glow-worm grotto, but we can't sit here dreaming for ever. I can't imagine why you wanted to bring *me*, anyway!"

His eyes glinted, he took a step nearer her. "Can't you? Believe me, I had my reasons."

Marty took a step backwards, her hands behind her back, because everything in her wanted to hold out her hands to him.

"I'm not interested in your reasons," she said. "I want to go back to the others."

It was distinctly annoying to have Philip laugh at her. "It's not the time or the place to go into them, is it? — with a crowd like that waiting."

Marty was puzzled. It was all very unsatisfactory.

Just then the sound of voices, coming nearer, floated up to them. Philip put a hand under her elbow, helped her down the last few yards, and they regained the track.

Philip was quite unperturbed when some reproached him.

"I remembered there was a really good grotto of glow-worms just up here. Wasn't even sure I could still find 'em. So we explored, and found them. In the dark all these forks look alike, you know. Didn't want to take you on a wild-goose chase. But we found it. Anyone want to go up?"

He added. "It's very steep, but rewarding. Don't think I'll go up again." He and Marty sat down on a bank. Tod and Louise came to sit beside them.

Louise said petulantly: "I had been relying on you to light the way, Phil. You know this track, we don't."

Philip replied, "Tod had a torch. You couldn't possibly go wrong if you kept near him."

Tod laughed. Marty wondered if that was what Philip had said it for ... to reassure Tod. But whatever Philip meant he was playing some game of his own ... either putting Louise at a distance, or using Marty as this smokescreen so that Tod shouldn't guess that anything still existed between himself and ... Tod's wife.

The mad whirl went on, moonlight

picnics, and launch excursions, and once a barbecue, with huge fires lighting up the dark beach, and everyone grilling sausages and bacon and potatoes, and cooking freshly-caught fish on the hot stones. It had a beauty all its own, a lurid, barbaric beauty.

"But a very synthetic beauty," said Philip, seating himself beside her on the sand, as she made the remark.

"Why synthetic?"

"Because this sort of thing was meant to be all simplicity, and for people who love building bonfires, and living the natural life. Look at that one over there . . . that Zena something or other, simply wallowing in gin, and eating her fish out of a paper napkin wreathed with rosebuds!"

Marty giggled. "But do be fair, Philip, the fish is hot."

"Well, she should eat it out of a bit of newspaper or a couple of *taupata* leaves or something. I've never seen anything so affected in all my life. When this mob is gone we'll have a family barbecue of our own. The children can be the main figures then, and we'll sit here, all of us, in the quiet of the night, and listen to the waves lapping by the shore, and lie and look up at the stars."

It moved Marty profoundly. It did sound as if, at last, seeing Louise in the crowd she liked to move with had sickened Philip. Perhaps ... he put his arm around her shoulders, lightly, good-comradely fashion, and smiled at her. She felt as if they were in a world of their own, united in their distaste for a cheap crowd.

It didn't last long; suddenly Louise was with them. Oh, that explained it. Philip had seen her coming and had made the gesture. Come back to earth, Marty my girl! said her reason to her heart.

Louise said, "Oh, there you are, Phil, you're my partner in a treasure-hunt. Tod wants to take Marty."

There was nothing else for it, since Tod was there with Louise, and Marty wouldn't for anything hurt the little bewildered man, trying to keep up with a crowd far too young for him. As they flitted in and out of the bushes, dark figures against the blaze of the barbecue pits, Marty felt as if it was something out of a technicolor film, something as pagan as a sacrificial fire.

She felt sick of it all and turned to Tod. "I'm headachey, Tod. Let's find a nice cool rock apart from it all where we can just sit, and you can smoke if you want to."

They climbed the hill and found their rock, set against a thicket of scrub, and sat on it, dangling their legs in carefree fashion.

"No, I'll not smoke, thanks," said Tod. "Pity to give away our whereabouts when we've just found ourselves a spot of peace." He looked down on the scene below. His voice sounded weary. "This could go on for hours yet. They're just warming up."

Marty was hardly aware that she had spoken till the words were out: "Then why put up with it?"

There was a silence. Marty bit her lip. She put out a hand to Tod's arm. "Tod, I'm sorry. I shouldn't have said that. I — "

He patted her hand. "Don't apologize, Marty. It was sincere . . . something I don't get much of . . . sincerity or candor.

I'd like your advice on something. You're a woman — perhaps you understand Louise better than I do, being a man. What — "

Marty broke in. "Tod — are you sure you want to tell me?"

"Yes. Very sure. In spite of your age, Marty, there's something very wise about you. A maturity. Besides, I must speak to someone. What am I going to do about Louise? She's restless, unsatisfied. I knew when she married me she didn't love me. I thought that because I could provide her with the things that matter so much to her, she *would* be happy.

"How wrong I was. I'm not happy either. I can't stand this sort of life. I want to settle down. I want to spend a few evenings beside my own fireside. I want children."

Marty wanted to run away. If she did, she would fail Tod in his need. If she stayed, she would somehow feel disloyal to Philip.

She said, slowly, "Tod, do you still love Louise?"

The way he answered "Do I?" convinced her.

Her voice was soft. "Then that's the answer. Your love has got to be powerful enough to compel her to return it. It's very odd for a man in your position, but you haven't any confidence in yourself. Despite all your abilities, you've a fair-sized inferiority complex."

Tod said with bitterness, "The business world is the only one I've succeeded in. And that was only because I was determined to be successful in at least one thing — to count for something."

Marty said crisply, "Why shouldn't you succeed in other things?"

He was quick to answer that. "My looks. I've always been very short, snub-nosed, went bald very young."

Marty said: "You've got a blind spot about that, haven't you? We all have about something. You ought to know, with your experience of the world, that looks may be part of a personality, but not the main part. The most fascinating man I ever dealt with in business circles was completely bald. We were all decidedly romantic, and we all fell for him in a big way. Your trouble is you will measure yourself against Philip.

"That's natural, perhaps, because Louise was once engaged to him. You think he's got everything . . . don't you? Magnificent shoulders, a powerful jaw-line, attractive, clean-cut features . . . the real picture of a bronzed colonial — but there's got to be more to a man than that. In any case you've more than he has — *you've* got Louise!

"But because Philip has the looks of a Greek god, you think she must have married just for your money. I don't believe it. She probably married you, whether she knows it or not, for those very qualities that brought you to the top of the business world . . . grit, determination, integrity.

"But with Louise, you're inclined to play these things down, too anxious to please her, to please her friends. Too much the lap-dog, eager for a pat. You ought to be firm, even a little hard, you ought to put your foot down. She's only spoilt, Tod. Her mother said that to me not long ago. They indulged her too much, and you carried on. Try caveman stuff, modern fashion. Make her anxious to please you."

314

"I believe you're right," said Tod, weariness dropping from him. He stood up, Marty with him.

Tod said, "Just one thing, Marty, one thing I can't fight. Do you think she still cares for Philip?"

Should Marty answer that or not? She drew a deep breath, then plunged. "I very much doubt if she ever did. I think it was nothing more than surface attraction, and didn't last. I know Louise has been very provocative, very tantalizing, but if I were you, I should ask why. You said she is restless, unsatisfied. Mightn't it be her way of trying to provoke you into . . . well, into action? Mightn't she, too, wonder why *you* married *her*? She might . . . she just might think you married her because you need a beautiful hostess, poised, well-groomed."

Tod looked startled. "That's something I never thought of. You could be right. It gives me something to work on. Bless you, Marty." He looked down on the scene below. "I'll just go round this crowd up." He reached out, took her two hands in his, brushed her lips lightly with his own, and was gone.

Marty stayed where she was, feeling suddenly weak. She brushed a hand across her eyes. There was something so defenceless, yet so gallant about the little man. It was rather a strain when someone asked you to give an opinion on such things.

There was a rustle in the bushes behind her. She turned quickly, ready to run. There were men in the party with whom she would rather not be alone, and their treasure-hunt might have brought them up here.

Then she felt rooted to the spot, and couldn't run, no matter how much she wanted to. It was Philip! He stood looking down on her, hands on his hips, his expression inscrutable. Marty couldn't hide the dismay that rushed over her. Bad enough at any time to be caught talking about someone's affairs, but this . . . this . . . she and Tod had discussed Louise's feelings, past, present, future . . . Louise whom Philip, however foolishly, loved. A wave of real nausea came over Marty. All in that desperate minute she tried to recall what she had said.

She said accusingly, "You! Here! How long have you been here?"

There was a sarcastic drawl in his voice that flicked her on the raw. "Right from the time Tod first opened his heart to you. You ought to be on the Marriage Guidance Council, Marty!"

Marty rallied. "So the proverbial fate of the eavesdropper overtook you!"

"Yes. They are supposed to hear no good of themselves. In trying to save Tod from his inferiority complex you've probably given me one . . . but you've no compunction about throwing me to the wolves, have you, Marty? And in any case, you may know so much about psychology that you can still counteract any harm you may have done to my ego . . . eh?"

Marty resolved to keep attacking, it was the only way.

"What were you skulking up here for, anyway? You should have come out!"

"I'd found the treasure," said Philip with disgust, "and I was disposing of it. Didn't want to be caught, and thought a spoil-sport, so when I heard voices, kept quiet. When I realized what you were talking about, decided to lie doggo — didn't want to embarrass Tod."

"But you don't worry about embarrassing me?"

Philip made a sudden savage movement towards her. Marty, alarmed, drew back.

"What did you mean," she asked breathlessly, "when you said you were disposing of the treasure?"

The question halted Philip. "It was another crate of liquor, and that crowd has had more than enough already, and is getting quarrelsome. Len's ropeable now. You've never seen Len in a real temper? No? Well, like most placid people, he loses it properly and we all dive for cover. It's time the fires were damped down and the crowd off to the guest-house.

"We'll not have any post-mortems on your conversation with Tod, Marty . . . there are all the ingredients for a first-class row in it, and there'd be nothing gained. Joy's gone up with the children. You go up too."

Marty took a track round the hill. Philip would never forgive her this meddling . . .

★ ★ ★

The crowd turned up next day, late. Due to hangovers, Lennie vowed. But in the middle of the afternoon they were heard coming. Philip and Marty, outwardly good friends for the Logies' sake, were diving. The launch drew in, the crowd piled off, and in an instant the peace of Konini Bay was shattered.

The afternoon grew hotter and hotter. They sunbathed, took a plunge in the water, frolicked, sunbathed again. Louise appeared in yet another swim-suit, patterned in the leopardskin spots she was so crazy on at the moment. She certainly knew what suited her personality. The law of the jungle, thought Marty, was the only one she would obey. Marty got up and ran down to the jetty to dive again.

Philip was standing on the edge, looking down into the water, and whistling aimlessly. Tod was standing right beside Marty. She had been conscious all afternoon of tension. Tension between Tod and Louise. Had Tod said anything to Louise? If he had, it had only had the effect of making her more

319

provocative than ever. She was foolish. The little man wouldn't stand much more.

Philip was still whistling. Louise sauntered up, slipped her arm casually through his, and said: "Thank you, darling. I recognize my signature tune . . . you still have it on the brain, I notice."

Recognition of the tune clicked in Marty's mind . . . a jingling tune, years old but often revived.

"Every little breeze seems to whisper
  Louise,
Birds in the trees keep on singing
  Louise,
Each little sigh tells me that I . . .
Adore you, Louise!"

Philip looked blank. "Oh, was that what I was whistling? Had no idea."

Louise laughed. "Then I'm still in your subconscious . . . an even nicer compliment."

Tod stepped up behind them. Marty knew a moment of alarm. It was nothing to what Louise had said and done hitherto, but she knew it only took a slight pressure to trigger things off sometimes.

Louise hadn't lowered her voice. In fact she had said it with deliberate clearness. This was to provoke Tod. It did.

With one movement he hooked Louise's elbow so that her arm slipped out of Philip's, and with his other hand smote her flat in the back.

"About time you got that glamorous bathing-suit wet, Louise, instead of standing around here looking purely ornamental!"

Louise, whose every movement was studied and elegantly graceful, went over the edge in a wide, clumsy fashion, legs spread out, hands clutching wildly at the air. Down into the green water she plunged, to rise to the surface the next moment, gasping, furious.

Philip reacted quickly: he laughed, turned, seized Marty. "That's right, Tod, treat 'em all rough. Into the drink with you, too, Marty." He went over the side a second after her.

Tod, who was, surprisingly, a beautiful diver, followed like a flash, surfaced as quickly as Marty and Philip. He shook the water from his eyes, laughed, and said to Louise:

"Look out, my lass, you're in for another ducking!"

He dived at her feet and pulled her under. Marty gave a squeal as Philip came at her. The crowd on the jetty howled with laughter.

There was only one thing to do to save the situation, and Louise did it. Marty couldn't help but admire her for it. She laughed with them all, as if this was a piece of horseplay she had enjoyed as much as any of them. She turned like a flash, caught Tod off his guard, and ducked him.

Philip caught Marty's hand, turned her away from the Bay towards the open Sounds. They swam out with strong, effortless strokes.

"Thanks for playing up," he said. "You understood it was just a bit of face-saving, didn't you?"

Yes, Marty understood very well, but for whose sake? A chivalrous gesture towards Louise? Or as one man to another to save Tod's face?

Besides, Marty was still nervous. She

had an idea that later on, Philip would seek her out and have a reckoning with her. It was quite evident she had started something, and Philip wouldn't tolerate interference with his affairs. She was wrong: it wasn't Philip who sought her out, but Louise. It was quite dark and they were farewelling the crowd. Louise must have been keeping an eye on Marty's whereabouts. She drew her behind a spreading koromiko, keeping a long, cool hand on Marty's wrist. In the light of the moon Marty could see her eyes, intent, cruel.

Her voice was hostile. "You've been very clever, haven't you? But you've lost. You've been carried away by these attentions Philip has given you, you little fool! Didn't you realize we planned them all, to throw dust in Tod's eyes! How Philip and I have laughed at the naive way you took it all!"

She waited for Marty to speak, so that she might wound her again. Marty said nothing. Goaded by her silence, Louise said: "Well, aren't you going to say anything?"

Marty said evenly, fine scorn in her

voice: "Is there anything to say? Good night, Louise."

For one frustrated moment, Marty thought Louise was going to strike her. Then she turned and went down the path to the jetty.

Marty stayed where she was. No one could see her, and for a little while, at any rate, she could find refuge here. Marty dropped down on to the ground, put her face on her arms. She mustn't weep, there must be no tell-tale marks about her eyes for anyone to notice, as they tidied up.

She could have forgiven Philip for using her as a smoke-screen to keep Louise away, but not for planning it with Louise "to throw dust in Tod's eyes." Besides, there had always been the little hope through it all that the tenderness might have meant something. Now, even that was gone . . .

★ ★ ★

After breakfast next morning Joy said firmly, as she cleared the dishes: "Now, I'm going to cut sandwiches as soon as the mail-boat arrives with fresh bread, and we'll take the launch and go away up the Sounds towards Tory Channel. We'll find some lovely unoccupied beach or island to picnic on — have a day to ourselves. I can't stand any more of this crowd, even if Mrs. Morgan is one of my best friends."

Lennie looked up from the window-seat where he was untangling a fishing-line of Robin's.

"Yes, we will do that, but they won't be coming, anyway."

Joy sounded astonished. "How do you know?"

"I told them not to. Told Tod and Louise."

Philip stopped filling his pipe and looked at Lennie. Marty stopped the tap running and looked at him too.

"I told Tod and Louise that we'd come up here for a quiet holiday, and I was sick to death of a bunch like that let loose in our private bay, drinking and swearing in front of the children." His tone was matter-of-fact.

Joy swallowed. "You said just that. Like that?"

"Yes. Why not? It's our holiday."

Joy began to giggle. "Lennie . . . you're so simple and direct. Here I've been planning all sorts of ways to get rid of them. Even toyed with the idea of saying we'd been called home, then sneaking back. And all you have done is to tell them we didn't want them." She bestowed a rapturous kiss upon him. "But tell me — what did Louise say?"

Lennie looked at them across the tangle of line.

"Tod did the saying for both of them. He said: 'My God, and I don't wonder. I'm completely browned-off myself. I'm only the mug who pays for their everlasting drinks.' Then he turned to Louise and said: 'I'll have an urgent business call back to Christchurch tomorrow.' You and he must think alike, Joy. And he added: 'But we'll go to Nelson instead and take the plane from the North Island and spend the rest of our holiday at Rotorua or Lake Taupo or something — on our own.' Tod has suddenly wakened up."

Marty avoided Philip's glance. Then Lennie answered the question which Joy had asked earlier, and which still hung in the air: "And Louise said meekly: 'Very well, Tod.'"

Philip got up abruptly and went outside. "I'll put some more petrol in the tank," he said, over his shoulder.

From the window by the sink Marty watched him go down. Philip had taken Joy's and Lennie's criticism of Louise very well. Her eyes hardened. But all the time, he and Louise had been laughing behind her back, at the way she, Marty, had been taken in. Someday she would let Philip know it hadn't deceived her at all — if she could do it without giving away her real feelings.

And now, of course, all the little attentions would stop.

Lennie said, "Run down to the launch with all this fishing-gear, will you, Marty?"

As she stepped aboard the launch which was rocking on a full tide, Philip put out an arm to steady her. She was perfectly skilled at coming aboard by this time, but accepted the help without a hint of the tumult his touch caused her.

The mail-boat came in at that moment, laden with provisions and mail. When they had waved good-bye to the friendly pilot and the few passengers, they sorted the letters.

"What a pile," commented Philip. "I'd better look through it in case there's any mistake like last time, and they left us some for the guest-house."

He leafed through it. Then he shrugged. "But this time it's nearly all for you, Marty."

She colored as she took the letters. This was ridiculous. Noel had written every day. It was beginning to make her feel uneasy. She didn't want to hurt Noel, but —

She looked up and met Philip's gaze.

"All from Noel, aren't they?" he probed unpardonably.

"Yes."

"I gather from what Louise said, and from the absence of letters from Morgan, that that affair is finished?"

"Yes." She couldn't trust herself to say more.

"Then it's definitely Noel?"

Marty turned her back to him, the

letters clutched tightly in her hands. She gazed out over the beauty of the Sounds, unseeingly. What should she say? The memory of Louise's and Philip's duplicity washed over her . . .

Philip's hand were hard on her shoulders, gripping them till his fingers bit into her flesh.

"Tell me," he demanded. "Is it Noel?"

"Yes, it's Noel," she said defiantly, "but we aren't announcing anything yet."

He released her so suddenly she almost fell. He turned and left the launch.

Marty was glad when they were back at Alpenlinden once more.

# 10

THEY came back to find the plains scorched and brown, with the wheat heavy in the ear, and the barley and oats and grass seed ready for harvest.

Work seemed never ending, there was no time for re-pining. Even Noel could spend little time at Alpenlinden and there were no evening jaunts to Christchurch. The great headers went lumbering through the paddocks, there were sacks of wheat everywhere, and the men got incredibly dusty, coming in to wash before their huge meals, with eyes rimmed black with grime and sweat.

Marty felt she worked flat out from the time she heard the first rooster crowing, till, with the supper dishes washed and the huge breakfast table set, they went to bed.

Despite all, there was no muddle, there was a rhythm about it all, when, if Marty hadn't carried an ache at her heart, life could have been near perfect . . . this was life as it was meant to be lived . . . reaping and sowing, one with the cycle of the seasons.

Moments such as when Joy, bundling the twins in their Huckleberry Finns into the Land Rover, said: "We'll all have dinner in the paddocks today, Marty."

The paddock was an eighty-acre one, the furthest away of all Alpenlinden's paddocks. You had to cross the Peaks Road to get to it, and it wound back almost to where the foothills rose from the yellow plain. There were some mighty blue-gums at one end, in a cluster, and some green willows edging the shallow stream that ran out of the gully in the hills. Here was shade, and actually a patch of green.

Joy spread rugs, and assembled the dinner. She found a deeper spot in the shady stream and stood a cream can in it to keep cool. Then she called the men. This was magic, thought Marty, cool in a green linen smock, and her hair tied back with a green ribbon. At least it would have been magic if there had been any friendliness in Philip's glance as their eyes met, but since the return from the Sounds, never a kindred word had bridged what lay between them.

The wind, for once, was north-east, so blew coolly about their temples, and the sound of the creek in its pebbly bed, with a tui singing its magical song in a gum tree, added its own sweetness to the hour. What could a London office offer in comparison with this?

By night-time the north-easter was blowing strongly, and they were listening-in anxiously to the weather reports for Canterbury . . . changing tomorrow afternoon, with showers near the Alps in late afternoon, and in the evening nearer the coast. Further outlook — unsettled.

Lennie groaned. "Wouldn't it! Another forty-eight hours and we'd be finished. I was afraid of this when the wind went around to the nor'east. We often get three days of rain then. Not like the sou'west. That's colder and more blustery, but it gets over."

Later, it was decided that Philip, Graham and Lennie's single man would use the lights and work all night on the header, finishing about five. Then Lennie and Bill and the padre would take over. The padre often played the extra man on the header when his duties allowed him. He loved it.

"After a wash and a meal we'll feel like giants refreshed," said Philip, stretching wearily. "Bags I the shower in the wash-house."

Marty said to Lennie at supper-time when he and Joy, exhausted, were relaxing in big chairs: "Did I hear you say you were going to take a meal up at one a.m.?"

"I tried to insist on it, Marty. It makes all the difference to fatigue if you get a proper meal, but Philip said flasks and sandwiches would do."

Marty said: "Do let me take them up a meal. I'd love to say in my letters home that I was serving bacon-and-egg pies to the harvesters in the wee sma's. Honestly, it would be worth a night's sleep."

Lennie looked at her and laughed. "What it is to be young and romantic. Personally, I'd rather have my sleep," while Joy, more practically, said: "But we haven't any bacon-and-egg pies."

Marty sprang up. "No, I know. I'll make them now."

They left her to it. She didn't feel in the least tired. Fresh tea would be better than flask tea, so she made an immense teapot full, and sat it in a wool-lined nest they used on such occasions and swathed it in an old blanket.

What a night. Above the distant ranges a moon was riding high, a harvest moon, paled now from its first orange glow, shining down on a field of late barley, turning it to an ashen white. The shadows were velvet, the leaves on the orchard trees glinting silver.

The gates were rather a nuisance, but Lennie was gradually replacing them with cattle-stops. Marty closed the last one, with a sigh of relief, and began driving up the rutted track of the vast paddock.

The men couldn't hear her for the noise of the machinery whirring through the grain. She came to the blue-gums and stopped. She lifted her head, listened. Why, the men were singing, harmonising beautifully, the sound just rising above the engine. They were completely unselfconscious, unaware that anyone was within hearing. But — but what were they singing? Across the ripe wheat it came to her . . .

"This happy breed of men, this little world,
This precious stone set in the silver sea,
Which serves it in the office of a wall,
Or as a moat defensive to a house,
Against the envy of less happier lands;
This blessed plot, this earth, this realm,
This England."

The sound of men's voices, singing as they reaped past midnight in order that the grain might be gathered in, were paying tribute to an England thirteen thousand miles away.

The whirring of the machinery cut off, and three figures leapt down and came towards her. They had seen the Rover as they turned. She had her reward then, in their appreciation of the meal. They did full justice to it. To Marty there was a hurting pleasure in cutting wedges of pie for Philip, putting slices of lemon in his tea, even though she never met his eyes.

When they had finished, and had a smoke, Philip said: "Right, you chaps go and start her up. I'll pack the crocks for Marty."

Just common politeness, Marty told herself. In silence they packed them in the Rover. Marty got in, sat at the wheel.

Philip leaned on the door. "To think I once doubted your driving powers! The little English girl has certainly turned out pioneer quality, hasn't she? This track, bumpy with roots, takes some negotiating."

The sudden kindness in his tone was almost the undoing of Marty. She looked about her. What a night . . . the sort of night for Shakespeare . . . "How sweet the moonlight sleeps upon this bank." The words said themselves over in her heart. She felt close to Philip in spirit, not only in physical presence. After weeks of estrangement it was sweet.

She lifted her face to his, her eyes large

and luminous in the moonlight.

Philip drew back a little. He gave a short laugh.

"Too bad, isn't it, that it's not Noel you're playing ministering angel to!"

Marty put her thumb down on the self-starter, the engine whirred into life. The savage pressure of her foot sent the clutch flat to the floor-boards. She slammed the gears in, backed. Going home she saw nothing of the star-sequined, sable-shadowed beauty of the night.

★ ★ ★

February slipped into March, and the bottling and jam-making was over, and, as Joy said, they could come up for air.

Noel rang Marty and asked if she would like to go to the ballet one night. He added: "I'll take you to dinner first, at the Clarendon. Celebrate this grim time of toil ending."

Marty had a new frock for it, bought out of Lennie's bonus for her part in the harvest. It was palest apricot, and the design, embossed on a filmy background in chiffon velvet, was in a deeper tone

337

that flattered the lights in the red-gold hair.

Joy had made Marty dress early and come downstairs to show them. Marty was laughing, pirouetting on her velvet sandals.

"This is the craziest household," she was saying, laughter in her voice, and deep effection for them in her eyes. "Who would think I was the maid? I'm only Cinderella, you know, the real me, these days, is in slacks and gum-boots, taking swill to the pigs!"

From somewhere, a "voice off" that sounded like Gaynor's, said: "Do come 'n' look. She's just like a fairy princess."

That would be Noel; he must have come to the verandah. The French windows were pushed open. Philip!

Joy said gaily: "Come in, Philip. Don't you wish you were escorting Marty to the ballet?"

She didn't expect an answer, it wasn't meant for a question, but Philip said: "Oh, a lesser mortal like myself can't compete with Noel West."

Marty gathered up her shining skirts, said: "Well, I must get my wrap," and fled upstairs, and didn't come down till she was sure Noel was there. She came down to find him waiting at the stairs, tall, debonair, a warmth in his eyes that unfroze her heart a little.

She merely put her head around the drawing-room door, said, "Night, night, folks. See you in the morning."

It was quite a relief to be with Noel. No barbed thrusts. Marty realized that harvest . . . or something . . . had tired her.

Going home they lapsed into a comfortable silence as the miles sped by. That was the only thing about living so far out; when you went to anything in the city, it was woefully late when you got home. Hardly worth it. She would sooner have stayed home.

As the thought leapt into her mind she realized one thing: *she'd sooner have stayed home because Philip was at Alpenlinden!* Philip, who had used her shamefully, in a shabby plot with Louise! Philip, who had imputed to her all sorts of motives. Philip whom she still loved in spite of everything. Oh, Marty, Marty, have you no pride?

Noel stopped under a huge Wellingtonia that kept ward over the drive entrance to Alpenlinden. Marty roused herself and looked up inquiringly.

He said, answering the look: "I've something to say before we say good night."

She waited.

He added, slowly, "I've not pretended with you, ever, have I, Marty? I told you from the start I only wanted friendship."

She nodded, puzzled.

"I've changed, Marty. I've found your friendship very sweet, but it doesn't satisfy any longer. I want more than that. I want my home to be really a home. I want a wife, children, someone to carry on. I want you. I think perhaps we could make more of a go of it like this . . . friendship deepening into something more . . . than if we had been swept off our feet at the first. Will you . . . ?"

Marty looked up at him, her eyes sorrowful.

"Noel, I couldn't. I don't think marriage was meant to be like that . . . approached cold-bloodedly. I don't particularly believe in love at first sight either, so I don't mean I only believe in physical attraction. It would have to be more than friendship, though. It would have to be a — a sort of recognition. There's got to be something irresistible about it, something compelling . . . " She stopped.

Noel said patiently: "But, Marty, isn't that an idealistic way of looking at it? A fairy-tale sort of love? The kind that doesn't really exist outside the pages for a happy-ending novel."

Marty moistened her lips. "Noel, I'm not meaning to be cruel, but we must talk this out . . . is there really anything commonsense about love? Was there, when you fell in love with Isobel?"

"Look how that turned out!" said Noel harshly.

"But would you want to go into marriage without something of what you felt then? Noel, my father and mother loved madly, truly, constant all their lives to each other. I wouldn't set up home unless I could do the same." She grinned. "It's the moonlight, and the ballet, and this dress. You'll be glad in the morning that I said no." When she spoke again her voice was matter-of-fact.

"Probably this isn't fair to you, going about together. Shall we call a halt?"

For the first time he showed real emotion. Anger looked out of his eyes.

"No. The days are too empty."

Marty reached for his hand, held it to her cheek for an instant, comfortingly.

"Noel, that means you still care for Isobel."

He said, still with anger, "I was trying to put her out of my life."

Marty's tone was gentle, understanding. "If ever you really fall in love again you won't have to try."

She leaned forward, switched on the ignition for him.

"Let's go on."

* * *

Marty had been in town shopping for a new autumn suit. Noel had taken her in, and was to meet her at the Bridge of Remembrance. He did.

"I'm afraid we can't leave town yet, Marty. We'll have an hour or two to fill in. I've got to pick something up at the

342

Loan and Mercantile Company. Won't be ready till five. Where would you like to go? Thought I might run you up the hills for a cup of tea at the Sign of the Takahe, or would you like to go out to Harewood to see the planes come in?"

Marty was ever afterwards to be glad she had plumped for the airport.

They were told a plane from Australia would be down soon, so they went into the glassed-in cafeteria overlooking the airstrip. They had finished their tea before the loudspeaker announced that the plane was due to land.

They stood on the ramp, watching. Someone Noel knew came up and spoke just as the passengers were disembarking. By the time the friend moved off the passengers were re-emerging from Customs.

Suddenly Marty heard Noel give an exclamation, instantly suppressed. Marty looked up at him, and then followed the intense direction of his gaze.

A woman was coming towards them. She had dark chestnut hair and a sweet, yet sad, face. She was perfectly dressed with a decided Continental air, but her features wore a curious dream-like expression. It was arresting. Almost as if she moved in her sleep.

She was only a few paces from Noel when she saw him. The effect was startling. A sudden awakening. She stopped. The fur fell from her shoulder, the bag from her hand, and they dropped unheeded at her feet. Noel was at her side in a moment, catching her out-held hands.

It didn't need Noel's incredulous "Isobel!" to tell Marty who it was. There were tears running down Isobel's face, silently, as the expensive fur lay unheeded in the dust. She was looking up into Noel's face unbelievingly, hungrily. Their hands were still gripped together.

A few people, stepping around them, looked curious. Marty felt a dismay creep over her. Here was a pretty coil. Isobel was married to her Christopher. Had she left him? Would she disturb Noel's life again?

"Noel," she said urgently, "don't you think you had better seek the privacy of your car? Please! I'll wait in the lounge, take as long as you like."

Noel had a bemused look. He pulled himself together.

"Yes. Come on, Isobel. Is anyone meeting you?"

She shook her head. "No one knows I'm coming."

Marty thought it sounded like a flight. From what? From Christopher? She stooped, picked up the bag, the fur, hung them on Isobel's arm. She turned away. They must have time to get this straightened out. They would soon come to themselves and see things in their right perspective.

A quarter of an hour later Noel came in.

He said: "Look, come out on the ramp. More private."

Marty had a sense of pity in her heart. Oh, better far if Isobel had never come back. What a mess. Had Isobel felt, as Noel had said, that she couldn't face the fuss of a broken engagement? And now, knowing the folly of a loveless marriage, had broken Christopher's heart, too? But Noel didn't look in need of pity, he looked as Marty had never known him, less wordly-wise, less weary.

"Marty," he said, taking her hand. "This is unbelievable. More than I can take in. It will take time, I'll try to explain coherently. When Isobel left me that night to go back to Lincoln, she called in at the local doctor's to pick up a prescription for her mother.

"The doctor told her he had wanted to see her, anyway. Christopher had been attending him, unknown to Isobel, and certain tests had been taken. The results had arrived that day. Christopher was suffering from some obscure and incurable disease. It was only a matter of time. The doctor wanted Isobel to be there when he told him.

"Isobel knew that when Christopher heard, he would release her from the engagement. She persuaded the doctor not to tell Christopher, that she would herself — after they were married. She dared not tell me, lest I act precipitately. She speeded up the wedding, and left, as had been planned, for England.

"It wasn't till six months later, when Christopher became really ill, that he knew he could not get better, and he never knew she had known beforehand.

She gave him a happy year, the last six months in Switzerland. He died just a year ago. He never knew she loved me, but he told her he had no wish for her to go lonely through life. She'd had no word of me since leaving New Zealand. She knew she might come back to find me married, or so disillusioned there would be no bridging the gap."

Marty found her lashes were wet. She looked up at him, her eyes shining. "Noel, I can't even begin to tell you how glad I am. It's beyond belief." She dimpled. "It's certainly as well I turned you down the other night, isn't it?"

Noel reddened. "Marty . . . "

She shook an admonitory finger at him. "Now don't try to be tactful, my dear. You're beyond diplomacy at the moment, and no wonder! But I couldn't resist saying 'I told you so'."

"Well, come and meet Isobel. She says she'll be eternally grateful to you for deciding on the airport. She had come back with such mixed fears, and to have them all resolved the moment she stepped on to New Zealand soil was the most wonderful thing that has ever happened to her."

Marty found her eyes wet again as she talked to Isobel. Perhaps those tears did more to bring the two of them together than any length of acquaintance could have done.

"Now," said Noel, "we'll get back to town, and I'll pick up this stuff, and we'll take you to Lincoln, Isobel, on the way home."

Marty shook her head. "If you think I'm going to make a third all the way home, you're mistaken. You'll want to see Isobel's mother, too, Noel, and stay awhile." She looked at her watch. "The Methven bus will have left town now, but we could pick it up on Riccarton Road, if you step on it, and don't argue."

By the time they reached the bus stop, they had decided that nothing should be said in Linden Peaks till after Noel and Isobel were married, which would be almost right away.

"It will be very quiet, Marty, but I should like you to be there. We'll have it in the Lincoln Anglican Church, it's very lovely, with just you, and Mother, and Nan, and a friend for Noel."

Marty caught the bus by seconds. She wouldn't have five miles to walk, because after the bus left the township it came nearer the farm, but there would be a good two miles.

The bus pulled up at the cross-roads, and as Marty got down she found Philip there, to pick up a parcel from town. Nothing unusual in that, of course, but — well, he *would* be there today! His astonishment at seeing her equalled her dismay.

"Good heavens! Joy told me you were in town with Noel. Did his car break down?"

"No. But he quite suddenly remembered he had to go to Lincoln, so I got him to put me on the bus. I didn't want to be late home."

Philip looked amazed. "But Joy wouldn't have minded. In fact, you could have rung her from Christchurch. You do do some idiotic things. Don't know what Noel was thinking of. Two miles home, on these roads, on those heels, would be an endurance test."

Marty said hastily, "I insisted on it. He was going to — to see some friends."

"Well, it's odd . . . to take a girl out and leave her to find her own way home!"

Marty said, desperately, "Does it matter? I mean it's between Noel and me."

Philip looked at her, set his mouth. "You mean — it's nothing to do with me! I'm to mind my own business. Have you quarrelled?"

Marty looked up at him. "We haven't quarrelled, Philip. Actually Noel would be very hard to quarrel with, not like — "

"Go on, say it! Don't spare me!"

"Well — I'll let you have it . . . it would take a saint not to quarrel with you, Philip Griffiths, and — "

"And you're certainly no saint. They don't have red-headed ones, Marty. Hop in, and I'll take you home, you nuisance!"

# 11

MARTY was most surprised, a few days later, when Philip walked in after dinner one night, and said: "Mrs. Morgan rang me and wants us to go over to Wangapeka tonight. I've dodged this invitation several times, but couldn't rake up an excuse this time, so how about it? We could ride."

"That's a flattering way of asking a woman out," said Marty candidly, "but I'll come, because Mrs. Morgan has asked me several times, too, and I'm not keen on going alone."

"Why?" His glare was keen.

"I'd rather not say," said Marty, and there was finality in her tones. The last time she had gone to Wangapeka Homestead Mrs. Morgan had talked incessantly of Louise. She was worried about her girl, vowed Louise wasn't at all happy, though even so, she had gathered Mrs. Morgan was more worried on Tod's account. With Philip there, surely Mrs.

Morgan would keep off the subject.

Mrs. Morgan was busy in her drawing-room with her collection of stamps. She was very keen. Philip was very much at home in the Morgan house. No wonder, thought Marty unhappily, when he had almost been the son-in-law. He sat down in a leather chair, one leg over the arm of it.

Mrs. Morgan said: "Louise is home. She'll be down presently. I'm a bit worried. She's very restless."

Philip said nothing. Marty said nothing.

Mrs. Morgan dropped some stamps into a saucer of water, picked up her tweezers.

"She's got some ridiculous idea into her head that Tod has tired of her. Louise isn't used to that sort of thing. She's genuinely worried for once. Came away to see if he might miss her. I don't know how to advise her."

They heard Louise descending the stairs.

She was as lovely as ever, Marty thought. She was wearing a dark red frock that set off the matt-white skin and dark eyes, but with her hair cut short and set into waves she looked decidedly less hard.

Greetings over, Philip said: "How about a game of cards?" Marty was glad, much less chance of tension or of saying the wrong thing.

They were still at it when they heard the dogs barking.

"Just the men coming back, I think," said Mrs. Morgan. "Both my men were at a committee meeting at the Hall."

The next moment they heard someone at the french windows on the verandah.

Philip got up and went towards them, but before he got there, the heavy velvet curtains parted and Tod stepped through, but a Tod almost unrecognizable.

He usually looked ruddy and genial, but now there wasn't a particle of color in his face. Even his lips were bloodless.

Louise stood up quickly, throwing down her cards.

"Tod! What's happened? Have you had an accident?"

He swayed a little on his feet. Laughed and looked across at his wife. "Not that sort of accident, my dea . . . no . . . I'm through. Failed in business.

I'm a pauper . . . think of that, Louise; you're married to a pauper, a man without a penny." He laughed again, a queer, mirthless laugh. "In fact, that's an understatement. I'll be going through the bankruptcy court."

Louise stared, unable to take it in.

"Yes, look like that," jeered the little man. "You've looked on me as a fathomless bank, haven't you? Always plenty more where that came from. But you needn't worry . . . *you* won't be poor. Your marriage settlements will take care of that. They were well tied up . . . and divorce is easy."

Louise said slowly: "You're very sure I will get out, aren't you?"

Tod looked at her uncomprehendingly.

Louise said bitterly: "It's a great compliment, isn't it? To expect me to desert you? And everyone else will think the same. I suppose I deserve it. But I'm damned if I will! Tod! Listen! Do you mean everything's got to go?"

He nodded. "Yes. The house, the cars, the furniture . . . everything."

She said crisply: "And the money in my name? How about that? Is it enough to save you from the bankruptcy court?"

For the first time Tod looked at her as if he was capable of taking in what she was saying.

He swayed again.

Philip said, "I'll get you a drink, Tod. Hang on, man."

He added, as he crossed to the sideboard, "Then Marty and I will go . . . this is between the two of you."

As he gave Tod the drink Louise said, "Don't go yet, Philip, we may need you. And Marty is a nurse." She made Tod sit down.

"Have you had any dinner, Tod?"

He shook his head.

"Go and cut him some sandwiches, Mother." She sat down, close to Tod.

"You needn't face the bankruptcy court, Tod. That money in my name is yours . . . *ours*." A little smile touched her lips. "You can start again — *we* can start again. Let everything go. We'll rent a furnished flat. We may salvage something anyway. I can get myself a job. Eustace Keller approached me the other day to see if I would do some photographic modelling for him. So that's that."

Tod had got his color back. He lifted his head and looked at his wife. There was that in his eyes that . . . Philip got up, looked at Louise. "You don't need us any longer. Come on, Marty."

At the french windows Philip paused, looked round. Tod was on his feet and walking unsteadily towards Louise. Mrs. Morgan was going out of the other door.

"Good-night," said Philip softly, "and good luck."

Marty and Philip cantered slowly home, over velvet turf, passing trees silhouetted against strong moonlight. An autumn dew was silvering the cobwebs in the hedges.

At the stables Philip lifted Marty down. Not that he needed to, but Philip was always punctilious in such things. He looked down on her, still holding her, standing close against the warmth of the mare.

Marty was at a loss for words. The situation needed commenting on, because, ignored, it could lie between them. But it would be so easy to say the wrong thing . . . Philip had once loved

Louise, and twice he had seen her go to Tod.

She said, trying to lighten it, "I seem to have a positive genius for being present at other folks' happy endings. It's most embarrassing."

He looked down on her curiously. "What do you mean? What other happy ending?"

Marty realized she had almost given away the secret she had been asked to keep. Noel and Isobel would be married in three days' time. Never do to give it way now, and even if she swore Philip to secrecy, he might taunt her with having let the district's most eligible bachelor slip through her fingers. So she didn't answer, didn't look up.

Philip said: "Do you mean Bernard? Is that still a sore spot? Poor little Marty!" He bent and put his cheek against hers. Marty pulled away. "No, I don't mean Bernard," she flung at him, her voice quivering, "and I don't want your sympathy either, Philip Griffiths. There's nothing so dead as yesterday!"

She fled into the house, leaving him to stable her mare.

# 12

THREE days later, and mid-afternoon, Marty decided to make herself a cup of tea. She was all by herself in the homestead. She was ready for it. It had been quite a day. Noel and Isobel had been married at eleven and now were speeding towards Noel's cottage at Diamond Harbor for their honeymoon.

Marty was glad the wedding was over, and would soon be known. She had permission to tell Len and Joy tonight. Marty had asked Joy for the morning off, saying she was going to town with Noel at nine, and would be back to cook the evening meal. Joy wasn't at all curious, for farmers often went in early to the city, and Marty had met Noel at the road-gate so no one should see him dressed for his wedding. Nan had been with him.

Marty had her tea and started the dinner. She had floured the steak and was peeling carrots when the phone rang.

It gave a long, urgent ring, something the local exchange did if it was an urgent toll call. It wasn't toll, but still urgent.

There had been a bad accident at one of the homesteads near the Gorge. A tractor had overturned. They had got the young lad out, but he had lost a lot of blood, and though they were getting the ambulance out from Ashburton, would Marty come and see if, as a nurse, she could help. The doctor's wife was trying to locate the doctor.

Marty said she would, and hung up. She wasted no time, but it was the very deuce. Lennie had one car, Joy the other, the truck was having a valve re-ground, and the men had the Land Rover. She would have to ride the mare.

Better, anyway, perhaps, because Mrs. Morrison had said the injured lad was some distance from the farmhouse, and over rough country. The ambulance would have to take a stretcher.

Marty ripped off her skirt, donned jodhpurs, took a first-aid kit from the cupboard, stuffed it into a bag and ran for the stables.

It was nearly seven, and twilight when

she came wearily home, walking Fran, because the mare had certainly been ridden hard on the way up.

As she came into the stableyard Joy appeared at the back door, anxiety, then relief, written all over her. Marty tied Fran up at the rail; she would get Robin to rub her down.

Joy took in Marty's dusty and grass-stained knees, and the stains of blood on her white shirt-blouse.

"Marty! You've been thrown! Just what we thought! Where have you been? We've been nearly out of our minds!" Joy's tone was sharp.

Marty said: "There was an accident at Morrison's. Up the Gorge. Tractor turned over. Inflicted terrible gashes. I couldn't wait, even to write a note. I did manage to — help. It needed tourniquets. They had got some on, but not expertly. I — "

Joy said gently: "I'm sorry, Marty, if I sounded cross. You see, we thought . . . I thought . . . "

Marty looked at her curiously. "You thought — what?"

Joy said hastily. "Oh, never mind that

now. Perhaps you don't know. Let it wait. Come on in and have a hot bath, I'll make you some tea." She led the way in.

"We nearly went mad when we got home and saw the steak snatched out of the oven, and the pan of milk and seameal taken off, and the carrots only half done. *And your mare gone.* No one has had any dinner. We'd not heard about the accident, and the mail-man, when questioned, told Philip that from the Gorge Road he had seen you going hell-for-leather up the paddocks, not even stopping to open the gates.

"Philip and Lennie and Bill are up the Gorge now, trying to get news of you."

Marty stopped, horrified. "Oh, heavens, and I cut back through the paddocks, and they'll miss Morrison's that way. Whatever made them think I'd go riding at this time of night with the dinner still to be cooked?"

Joy said: "Well, you see, it was Philip. He heard . . . " Joy came to a sudden stop and looked confused.

"Go on, Joy, what did Philip hear?"

Joy evidently felt past explanations.

"Look, Marty, let Philip tell you himself. I don't feel equal to it. In fact, things have been hectic." Joy's eyes suddenly filled with tears. "I've been picturing you thrown, perhaps your foot caught in the stirrup, being dragged . . . "

Marty put her arms round her. "Oh, Joy, I'm terribly sorry. If only I'd taken time to leave a note, but they said they thought he had an artery severed, and every moment might count. I thought I'd better get there like lightning. I did, too, over fences I wouldn't have put Fran at ordinarily."

Joy mopped her eyes. "No. It's all right. It's not your fault. I'd have done the same. Look, Marty, have your bath, and I'll see if I can get anyone up the Gorge to stop the men on the road." She turned away, then looked back to say: "And Philip can deal with you himself."

Marty thought it sounded ominous as she turned the taps on. But she had a watertight excuse . . . and why Philip and not Lennie? She shook inwardly. Philip had a genius for putting her in the wrong. He didn't suffer fools gladly.

362

There would be bound to be some way *he* would have let folk know!

She wanted to appear cool when she did meet him, and mistress of the situation, and she felt suffocatingly hot, so she donned a white suit, shaped in at the waist, and white sandals. She went downstairs, the blood-stained blouse and jodhpurs dangling from one hand.

Just as she reached the foot of the stairs, she heard men's voices, and Joy's, reassuring them she was home.

She heard Philip say: "Where is she? Is she all right? What . . . " and realized he was coming into the hall.

He stopped, the door handle still under his hand, as he saw her. He looked at her searchingly, his eyes dropped to the garments, saw the tell-tale stains.

He took a quick stride towards her, pushed open the drawingroom door, and gestured to her to go in. She went in, back towards him, then turned to face him.

He wasn't angry. She had never seen a look quite like that on his face before — for her.

He came across to her, took her hands.

"Marty," he said, "Marty, my dear, don't look like that. You mustn't take it like this."

She gazed up into his face uncomprehendingly.

"But . . . I'm not upset . . . I don't go to pieces so easily."

He looked down on her with infinite compassion . . . at least that was what she thought it was, and respect too. But what was he being sympathetic about?

He said, his hands still holding hers, "You're brave, my dear, you've got what it takes. But for it to happen to you twice!"

Marty blinked. Twice! But what?

"Philip," she said firmly, "I don't know what you're talking about. *What's happened twice?*"

"First Bernard . . . then Noel. I realized that morning in the launch that this was happening to you, that you were falling in love with Noel. Then we heard this afternoon that Noel had been married today to a girl at Lincoln. A widow, I believe. Marty — "

She started to laugh. Philip took it for hysterics.

She gasped: "But I knew — I knew all along. I was there. I was Isobel's bridesmaid . . . what?" But Philip wasn't listening. He took her shoulders.

"Marty, you don't have to pretend to me. But don't let this make you more cynical about men. You see, I thought at first you were only attracted to Noel because . . . because — "

Marty finished it for him, icily. "Because he was the district's most eligible bachelor! And now you think I'm either in love with Noel and brokenhearted, or else just plain chagrined that someone else has got in. It's a rare compliment.

"Let me tell you something once and for all, Philip Griffiths, what I said in New Zealand House was merely an idle comment on a ridiculous report. I was there merely to read New Zealand papers and to find out more information about the country I was going to. I had my application in, you idiot, for more than eighteen months before that, and my passage booked for six. But tell me — I'm all at sea . . . what in the world has all this to do with me not being home when Joy got in tonight?"

Philip shook her. "Listen, and I'll tell you. You're trying to cloak things with anger. You said once, the night I brought you home after the Blairs' ball, that if ever you were in trouble, you'd saddle Fran and make for the mountains. So when I heard you were heading towards the Gorge today I knew why!"

Marty twisted from his hold, took a step back and faced him. His eyes dropped again to the blood-stained clothes.

"I don't care if you are as wild as blazes, Marty, you are still in the one piece. Did Fran throw you? Where?"

Marty made a gesture of hopelessness.

"If only you would listen! You seem to think you're the Lord Omnipotent . . . and reach the wrong conclusion every time." She threw the clothes into the hearth.

"Let me tick things off . . . item one, this is not *my* blood! I came home today after a delightful wedding, the smallest and happiest I've ever been to. I had a cup of tea, and started the dinner. I got an urgent ring from Morrison's. A young lad had got into trouble with a tractor over-turning. Artery cut. It was going to be some time before the doctor got there, or the ambulance." Marty paused, she had lost track of her items long ago. Then she rushed on: "I seized the first-aid kit and took Fran because there was no other way of getting there." She held up a hand. "No. Let me finish.

"I knew all about Noel's Isobel the first night I went out with him. I can't tell you all about it, because it was told to me in confidence, but she was the only woman he had ever really loved, and he made that clear. We agreed to be partners — he was lonely, and I . . . I wanted to be free of Joy and Len throwing me at your head. And . . . *mark this well, Philip* . . . in spite of this, Noel did ask me to marry him about a month ago."

Philip's voice held sheer surprise. "Why didn't you accept? Surely Noel has all the qualifications?"

Marty said, between her teeth: "You still can't realize the fact that that was all just built up out of your own mind? Well, Noel did have all the qualifications for a husband . . . save one . . . I didn't love him."

She wasn't prepared for the sudden change in Philip. He crossed the hearth-rug, took her hands again.

"Then, Marty, if you find you do believe in love after all, love me! In spite of all our quarrelling, I've sometimes thought . . . admit you love me!"

Marty froze. *Admit she loved him?*

She said, in a tone Philip had never heard her use before:

"I wouldn't marry you if you were the last man on earth. I'd want the man I loved to have trust in me. You can't have love without believing. You've always been ready to believe the worst of me, and now your colossal vanity leads you to think I might love *you*. Ye gods! Even today you were ready to believe I would leave my work with no explanation to the people who have been so good to me, to ride off my supposed feelings about Noel getting married.

"You've taunted me from beginning to end about looking for wealth in the man I might marry. I don't want to marry anyone . . . and to think I'd marry

368

*you* — I wouldn't want to marry a man who made love in a moonlit garden to another man's wife while he was in Australia . . . who deliberately paid me attentions to throw dust in that husband's eyes . . . Oh, don't look at me like that, Louise told me you had plotted just that together . . . Philip, go! And don't ever speak to me again."

Philip's hand dropped to his sides. He reached the french windows in three strides, wrenched them open, and disappeared into the twilight.

Marty dropped to the couch, completely worn out with emotion . . . the joy of the wedding, the gruelling ride, the vigil by the injured boy, the scene with Philip. She didn't hear the door open, didn't know anyone was there till she felt Joy's hand on her hair and her voice saying: "Marty, what is it, dear, tell me?"

Finally, when she had sobbed it out, Marty sat up, rubbed her hand childishly over her eyes, and said:

"It's Philip."

"What did he do?"

"Asked me to marry him." All Marty's defences were down.

"Then why don't you? You love him, don't you?"

Marty covered her eyes. "Yes. But how can I marry him? He believes I came here to look for a surplus bachelor, a wealthy one. He's the last person I could marry. I tried to convince him about that just now. But no rich sheep-farmers for me with their fabulous wool cheques . . . if he'd been a wage-earner in the city, on the basic wage, I'd not have hesitated."

Joy, simply astounded by this piece of news, collapsed into a deep chair and gave way to irresistible mirth.

Marty, deeply indignant, uncovered her eyes and looked up.

Joy, between gasps of laughter, said, "Marty! You duffer! Philip a wealthy sheep-farmer! Really! Have you any idea what it costs to stock a place these days? Have you any idea what sort of mortgage Ngaio Bend carries? Of all the things! What other false ideas have you been harboring? Then you blame poor old Philip for getting things wrong about you. I could knock both your heads together."

She sobered up, came across to the

couch, took Marty's hand in hers. "Marty, would you listen to me without interrupting? I think it's time I told you a little about Philip. You knew about his mother running out on his father?"

Marty nodded.

"And his father taking him home on a business trip that was destined to give the father promotion on his return? Of course, you know the father never reached his home again. There was very little left. The mother had left a mountain of debts. Philip had to be put in the same orphanage I was in, but I was leaving soon.

"He left school at fifteen, and had a far from easy time. Worked on various farms. It's lonely for a young lad, living in a one-room *whare*, coming in to the farmhouse only for meals. Then I came across him again, and my father-in-law-to-be offered him a job at Alpenlinden. Wages were good by then, and Philip saved consistently. The land next to us was subdivided, and he took it. He had very little capital, Mr. Logie wanted to finance him, loan without interest, but Philip was too independent, except to allow him to stand bond for him. He's still struggling against frightful odds.

"He became engaged to Louise, a romantic boy's first love. When she realized the struggle it was going to be, she gave him up. I'm sure, though, that he would have seen through her himself had they been engaged longer, and made the break himself. In fact, at Picton, after Lennie got rid of them, Philip said to me, 'What an escape I had.' Besides, he'd met you then. But do you wonder, Marty, after first his mother, then Louise, that he was doubtful about the motives women marry for? He may have huge flocks of sheep — they aren't paid for. His wool cheque is spent before he gets it. He got that pre-fab house for his married couple, and because of that, he can't yet finish his own house. Do you wonder he struggled against loving you?

"Yes, despite all that, he sent me a radio-telegram from Panama recommending you to me . . . it wasn't the padre, as you have always thought. Philip just couldn't let you go out of his life, Marty! And in spite of these financial odds, he spent twenty-five guineas on a dress for the girl he loves, hoping that some day she might accept it from him. A lilac dress, Marty, made of cobwebs and dew. He got me to buy it for him . . . do you doubt now, Marty, that he loves you?

"*I* nearly spoiled *my* life, Marty, because I couldn't bear Lennie to play King Cophetua to my beggar-maid, but that situation doesn't exist between you and Philip. If you marry him you'll have to watch every penny for a few years."

Marty said falteringly: "But — but you see, he'd been having a trip round Britain and the Continent, so I thought — "

"He did that on a travelling scholarship he won. Farming research. He was even glad of the Liaison Officer's salary coming home. Ngaio Bend won't be all Philip's for years."

She finished, sat back, looked at Marty.

Marty got up, weariness falling from her like a cloak, young, eager, shining-eyed.

"I'll go to him now," she said. "I'll run all the way . . . and, Joy, say a prayer for me, won't you . . . that I can make him understand?"

Before Joy could answer, a voice came from beyond the curtains over the french windows.

"You won't need to run all the way, darling . . . or at least only to here. I came back. Did you really think I would take no for an answer once I realized you didn't love Noel . . . once I cooled off? And I've got to tell you — you too, Joy . . . that I never did make love to Louise after she was married. I know it's more honorable for a man not to tell, but I'm not letting any more misunderstandings flourish. Louise made the overtures. I — oh, I hate saying this . . . I had to repulse her . . . I'll explain it all later, privately, Marty.

"And, Marty, I'll grovel if you like, I mean about ever thinking you were out here to find a wealthy, surplus bachelor. I must have been mad that day in New Zealand House, but I'd made so many calls that morning, and in every one some stupid girl asked me were there really bachelors growing on every tree. I foresaw all the fuss and false ideas that were going to arise.

"Joy, you've made a wonderful job of

374

doing my proposing for me, much better than I did it myself, but . . . I'm giving you fair warning . . . we can dispense with your presence right here and now. And when we've come down to earth again, later, we'll come to see you and Len."

There was a pause, during which Marty was dimly aware that Joy chuckled, opened the door into the hall, and vanished.

Philip's voice came to her through the curtains, like a "Voice off."

"I'm finishing the explanation from here, Marty, because, when you come to me, you aren't going to be able to talk for quite a while. I think I loved you from the start, Martha Mary, but we were always at cross purposes, weren't we? But you've got to know and believe me that I never discussed you with Louise. When we went on holiday and got to the Sounds, I thought all enmity was disappearing . . . then Louise and her crowd came and complicated things. And you said, that morning in the launch, that it was going to be Noel.

"I never dreamed that you'd think

I was on a par with all these other sheep-farmers, so I kept taunting you, hoping you would retract the first words I ever heard you utter. The going isn't going to be easy at Ngaio Bend, Marty, but together we'll make out. You'll never know what I went through today when you were off on Fran . . . unheeding, uncaring, and rabbit-holes everywhere . . . "

His voice changed. "I say, I can't stand this much longer. I've done with explaining. I'm here, Marty, waiting . . . "

She crossed the room, parted the curtains, looked up at him. Philip looked into her eyes, drew her out into the enchanted, moon-bewitched shadows of the scented garden.

She looked up at him, perfect trust in her eyes at last . . . and now, after stormy scenes, she would hear words of love from him.

She saw the corner of his mouth lift in the way it had.

"You red-headed fiend!" he said, as his lips came down on hers.

# NO ROSES IN JUNE
# THROUGH ALL THE YEARS

*Other titles in the*
*Ulverscroft Large Print Series:*

## TO FIGHT THE WILD
### Rod Ansell and Rachel Percy

Lost in uncharted Australian bush, Rod Ansell survived by hunting and trapping wild animals, improvising shelter and using all the bushman's skills he knew.

## COROMANDEL
### Pat Barr

India in the 1830s is a hot, uncomfortable place, where the East India Company still rules. Amelia and her new husband find themselves caught up in the animosities which seethe between the old order and the new.

## THE SMALL PARTY
### Lillian Beckwith

A frightening journey to safety begins for Ruth and her small party as their island is caught up in the dangers of armed insurrection.

## CLOUD OVER MALVERTON
### Nancy Buckingham

Dulcie soon realises that something is seriously wrong at Malverton, and when violence strikes she is horrified to find herself under suspicion of murder.

## AFTER THOUGHTS
### Max Bygraves

The Cockney entertainer tells stories of his East End childhood, of his RAF days, and his post-war showbusiness successes and friendships with fellow comedians.

## MOONLIGHT
## AND MARCH ROSES
### D. Y. Cameron

Lynn's search to trace a missing girl takes her to Spain, where she meets Clive Hendon. While untangling the situation, she untangles her emotions and decides on her own future.

## NURSE ALICE IN LOVE
### Theresa Charles

Accepting the post of nurse to little Fernie Sherrod, Alice Everton could not guess at the romance, suspense and danger which lay ahead at the Sherrod's isolated estate.

## POIROT INVESTIGATES
### Agatha Christie

Two things bind these eleven stories together — the brilliance and uncanny skill of the diminutive Belgian detective, and the stupidity of his Watson-like partner, Captain Hastings.

## LET LOOSE THE TIGERS
### Josephine Cox

Queenie promised to find the long-lost son of the frail, elderly murderess, Hannah Jason. But her enquiries threatened to unlock the cage where crucial secrets had long been held captive.

## THE TWILIGHT MAN
### Frank Gruber

Jim Rand lives alone in the California desert awaiting death. Into his hermit existence comes a teenage girl who blows both his past and his brief future wide open.

## DOG IN THE DARK
### Gerald Hammond

Jim Cunningham breeds and trains gun dogs, and his antagonism towards the devotees of show spaniels earns him many enemies. So when one of them is found murdered, the police are on his doorstep within hours.

## THE RED KNIGHT
### Geoffrey Moxon

When he finds himself a pawn on the chessboard of international espionage with his family in constant danger, Guy Trent becomes embroiled in moves and countermoves which may mean life or death for Western scientists.

## TIGER TIGER
### Frank Ryan

A young man involved in drugs is found murdered. This is the first event which will draw Detective Inspector Sandy Woodings into a whirlpool of murder and deceit.

## CAROLINE MINUSCULE
### Andrew Taylor

Caroline Minuscule, a medieval script, is the first clue to the whereabouts of a cache of diamonds. The search becomes a deadly kind of fairy story in which several murders have an other-worldly quality.

## LONG CHAIN OF DEATH
### Sarah Wolf

During the Second World War four American teenagers from the same town join the Army together. Forty-two years later, the son of one of the soldiers realises that someone is systematically wiping out the families of the four men.

## THE LISTERDALE MYSTERY
### Agatha Christie

Twelve short stories ranging from the light-hearted to the macabre, diverse mysteries ingeniously and plausibly contrived and convincingly unravelled.

## TO BE LOVED
### Lynne Collins

Andrew married the woman he had always loved despite the knowledge that Sarah married him for reasons of her own. So much heartache could have been avoided if only he had known how vital it was to be loved.

## ACCUSED NURSE
### Jane Converse

Paula found herself accused of a crime which could cost her her job, her nurse's reputation, and even the man she loved, unless the truth came to light.

## A GREAT DELIVERANCE
### Elizabeth George

Into the web of old houses and secrets of Keldale Valley comes Scotland Yard Inspector Thomas Lynley and his assistant to solve a particularly savage murder.

## 'E' IS FOR EVIDENCE
### Sue Grafton

Kinsey Millhone was bogged down on a warehouse fire claim. It came as something of a shock when she was accused of being on the take. She'd been set up. Now she had a new client — herself.

## A FAMILY OUTING IN AFRICA
### Charles Hampton and Janie Hampton

A tale of a young family's journey through Central Africa by bus, train, river boat, lorry, wooden bicycle and foot.

## THE PLEASURES OF AGE
### Robert Morley

The author, British stage and screen star, now eighty, is enjoying the pleasures of age. He has drawn on his experiences to write this witty, entertaining and informative book.


## THE VINEGAR SEED
### Maureen Peters

The first book in a trilogy which follows the exploits of two sisters who leave Ireland in 1861 to seek their fortune in England.


## A VERY PAROCHIAL MURDER
### John Wainwright

A mugging in the genteel seaside town turned to murder when the victim died. Then the body of a young tearaway is washed ashore and Detective Inspector Lyle is determined that a second killing will not go unpunished.

# DEATH ON A HOT SUMMER NIGHT
## Anne Infante

Micky Douglas is either accident-prone or someone is trying to kill him. He finds himself caught in a desperate race to save his ex-wife and others from a ruthless gang.

# HOLD DOWN A SHADOW
## Geoffrey Jenkins

Maluti Rider, with the help of four of the world's most wanted men, is determined to destroy the Katse Dam and release a killer flood.

# THAT NICE MISS SMITH
## Nigel Morland

A reconstruction and reassessment of the trial in 1857 of Madeleine Smith, who was acquitted by a verdict of Not Proven of poisoning her lover, Emile L'Angelier.

## SEASONS OF MY LIFE
### Hannah Hauxwell
### and Barry Cockcroft

The story of Hannah Hauxwell's struggle to survive on a desolate farm in the Yorkshire Dales with little money, no electricity and no running water.

## TAKING OVER
### Shirley Lowe and Angela Ince

A witty insight into what happens when women take over in the boardroom and their husbands take over chores, children and chickenpox.

## AFTER MIDNIGHT STORIES,
### The Fourth Book Of

A collection of sixteen of the best of today's ghost stories, all different in style and approach but all combining to give the reader that special midnight shiver.

## DEATH TRAIN
### Robert Byrne

The tale of a freight train out of control and leaking a paralytic nerve gas that turns America's West into a scene of chemical catastrophe in which whole towns are rendered helpless.

## THE ADVENTURE OF THE CHRISTMAS PUDDING
### Agatha Christie

In the introduction to this short story collection the author wrote "This book of Christmas fare may be described as 'The Chef's Selection'. I am the Chef!"

## RETURN TO BALANDRA
### Grace Driver

Returning to her Caribbean island home, Suzanne looks forward to being with her parents again, but most of all she longs to see Wim van Branden, a coffee planter she has known all her life.

## SKINWALKERS
### Tony Hillerman

The peace of the land between the sacred mountains is shattered by three murders. Is a 'skinwalker', one who has rejected the harmony of the Navajo way, the murderer?

## A PARTICULAR PLACE
### Mary Hocking

How is Michael Hoath, newly arrived vicar of St. Hilary's, to meet the demands of his flock and his strained marriage? Further complications follow when he falls hopelessly in love with a married parishioner.

## A MATTER OF MISCHIEF
### Evelyn Hood

A saga of the weaving folk in 18th century Scotland. Physician Gavin Knox was desperately seeking a cure for the pox that ravaged the slums of Glasgow and Paisley, but his adored wife, Margaret, stood in the way.

## DEAD SPIT
### Janet Edmonds

Government vet Linus Rintoul attempts to solve a mystery which plunges him into the esoteric world of pedigree dogs, murder and terrorism, and Crufts Dog Show proves to be far more exciting than he had bargained for . . .

## A BARROW IN THE BROADWAY
### Pamela Evans

Adopted by the Gordillo family, Rosie Goodson watched their business grow from a street barrow to a chain of supermarkets. But passion, bitterness and her unhappy marriage aliented her from them.

## THE GOLD AND THE DROSS
### Eleanor Farnes

Lorna found it hard to make ends meet for herself and her mother and then by chance she met two men — one a famous author and one a rich banker. But could she really expect to be happy with either man?

## THE SONG OF THE PINES
### Christina Green

Taken to a Greek island as substitute for David Nicholas's secretary, Annie quickly falls prey to the island's charms and to the charms of both Marcus, the Greek, and David himself.

## GOODBYE DOCTOR GARLAND
### Marjorie Harte

The story of a woman doctor who gave too much to her profession and almost lost her personal happiness.

## DIGBY
### Pamela Hill

Welcomed at courts throughout Europe, Kenelm Digby was the particular favourite of the Queen of France, who wanted him to be her lover, but the beautiful Venetia was the mainspring of his life.